MURDER AT BULL RUN

ED TESSLER

Acknowledgements

First, I want to thank my wife Bonnie, without whose help and support this book would never have been written. Also I appreciate the valued input of my sons Danny and Nathan.

I also want to thank the Baseball Hall of Fame and the Brooklyn Historical Society for the materials they provided to me.

My friend Debra Groisser turned this book into a book, Larry Gemmell provided incredibly helpful comments, and Barbara Ismail gave many helpful pointers on writing.

Many others read early drafts of the book and provided useful suggestions. So additional thanks to Laura Philips, Geoffrey Wright, Tony Ross-Trevor and others.

Contents

PROLOGUE

November 20, 1861

I was resting in my tent, thinking about how far I'd come in the eight months since joining the Union army. I signed up with the 14th Brooklyn at the beginning of the war, a seventeen-year-old immigrant boy from Williamsburg. I learned how to shoot a musket and how to march and drill. I became part of the Company B base ball team. I fought in a major battle, I probably killed some rebs, and oh yeah, I solved a murder no one other than the murderer even knew had been committed.

This is how it all happened.

CHAPTER ONE

April 15, 1861

In April 1861, the Confederates fired on Fort Sumter and President Lincoln called for 75,000 volunteers for a three-month term to put down the rebellion. I knew I was going to enlist immediately after Lincoln's plea. I had to get into the army and join the fight before it was over.

Being a soldier who fought in a war was about the grandest thing I could think of. I pictured myself leading the charge, being the first to the enemy's line, and grabbing their regimental colors. In my mind, there was no blood or smoke, only beautiful women giving me tokens of their affection after the battle. I knew we were fighting to save the Union and that appealed to me, a little. But what we were fighting for paled compared to the romance of it all.

I had seen the 14th Brooklyn drill, and I envied those lucky men wearing their handsome uniforms. I didn't need any time to decide that that was going to be my regiment.

"Mama, I have something important to tell you!"

"Mein Gott! What has happened? Are you sick? Did you lose your job?"

"No, Mama, it's nothing like that. The president has asked for 75,000 volunteers to fight against the rebellion, and I'm joining up."

"You mean you're becoming a soldier?" "That's right, Mama. I'm going to war."

"Ach, mein baby," my mother cried. "You can't do that! You'll get killed! One child only I have. There's plenty young men who want to fight this war. They don't need you. If the South wants to make their own rules, let them. Why should you care?"

"Mama, I'm not a baby, and I know you don't feel that way. You love this country as much as I do. When Papa had to leave Germany, this country took us in. And I know you believe the Union should stick together.

That's the way this country was made and that's the way it should stay. You just don't want your only child fighting for it. Nobody does. I understand that. I'll be careful."

"Careful?" my mother yelled. "You think maybe I'm stupid? A soldier follows orders. If you're ordered to do something dangerous, you do it. If you don't do it, that's even more dangerous because the big men in the army will punish you so bad you'll wish you had been killed. So don't talk to me about being careful."

"All right, Mama, then let's just say I have to do it." My mother had started crying the first time the word 'soldier' was used. By now the tears were flowing freely. That's the moment my father picked to arrive home. When he came in and saw my

3

mother bawling, his eyes opened wide. He stopped in his tracks and looked at me in alarm. "What's the matter here?"

"I just told Mama that I'm joining the army."

My mother's tears hadn't changed my mind. Now I braced for another difficult conversation with my father.

"Papa," I repeated stubbornly, "I'm going to sign up for the army." He surprised me.

"I knew it," he replied. My father started stroking his chin, which he always did when he was thinking really hard about something. "When I was your age, I also wanted more than anything to be a soldier, but my papa, he wouldn't allow it. I don't want you to go, but I won't forbid it. We come from a long line of scholars. I broke that line when I became a lawyer in Germany, over my father's objections. I know you believe in this country. It has been good to us. We work hard, but we are free. I supported the revolution in Germany, but I didn't fight. Others fighting for me; this I regret. And I had to flee the country, anyway." My father had obviously thought about this, and was prepared for my decision. I should have realized that my papa would be a step ahead of me. How can you not respect such a brilliant man?

My father concluded, "What you feel you have to do, you should do." I could hear my mother's sobs in the background. "After you've gotten the fighting out of your system, then you'll see what you want to do. You have a fine mind, my son. Much better than mine. I pray you survive the war so you'll be able to use that brain."

4

My father's almost blessing made me feel worse than my mother's crying. I promised them both I would send money home, because I knew that without my wages, things would be rough for them. I went to bed just as determined to join up as I had been before I spoke to my parents.

The next day I got up, washed, dressed, packed some clothes and, without even bothering to eat breakfast, headed over to the armory on Henry and Cranberry Streets, where the 14th Brooklyn was recruiting soldiers. There was a large number of men waiting to volunteer. I worried that the ranks would be full before they got to me. A man in a sergeant's uniform walked down the line, asking who was ready to sign up and report for duty today. I could see that most of the men hadn't bothered to pack anything, so they must have been counting on going home after enlisting.

I caught the sergeant's attention and told him I was ready. He motioned me over to a separate table. I picked up my sack containing some clean clothes, a shirt, underwear and one pair of socks, and followed him.

Another man in uniform told me he needed some information for the roll or register of the regiment. I gave him my height, age and occupation, then signed where he told me to. As soon as I was done signing the roll, I was directed to another area of the armory for my physical. The surgeon had me strip so he could examine me. He had me bend over, kick, and jump while he thumped my chest and back. While he was doing that, he asked me some questions to see if I was insane or an imbecile. He checked my teeth, then he held up a couple of fingers. He asked me how many he was holding up, and I said two. I guess that was the test to make sure I could see. Then he checked my hearing by whispering, "Can you hear me?" I responded yes and passed my hearing test.

I must have passed the physical because the surgeon sent me to another part of the armory to sign yet another form. In this one, I swore that I wanted to serve in the 14th Brooklyn for ninety days. I gave the uniformed man sitting behind the table my name to fill in on the form. After the soldier filled in my name, he gave me the document to sign.

That's when I noticed the surgeon had already signed the paper, certifying that I was "free from all bodily defects and mental infirmities" that could prevent me from performing my duties as a soldier. He must have signed it before my name was even on the form.

The soldier behind the table told me to stay put while he found an officer to administer the oath. He returned with another soldier in a couple of minutes. The officer was pleasant enough but didn't even tell me his name. He just said, "Raise your right hand and repeat after me." I then promised to "bear true allegiance to the United States of America" and serve it "against all their enemies" and "obey the orders" of the President and of the officers appointed over me.

Both men congratulated me and told me I was mustered into Company B of the 14th Brooklyn Regiment. "That was it?" I wondered. "I'm in the army now?" In the span of an hour, I went from Brooklyn boy to soldier. I didn't feel any different.

This was not the way I imagined it would happen. There was no band or ceremony. Maybe that would come later.

The sergeant told me that I would be staying in the armory overnight, and then, with a number of other new recruits, go to Fort Greene Park where the 14th Brooklyn was camped. When I got there, I was to report to Captain Mallory, who was in charge of Company B. He would tell me what to do.

My night in the armory was exciting but uneventful, if that makes sense. I was issued a blanket for sleeping, which was all I needed. A number of boys were in the same position as me: new recruits. We spent hours talking about how great it was to be in the army, and what we were going to do to the rebs. We all agreed that the war would end quickly and that we were going to make that happen. We were served a hot supper which consisted of a piece of meat, a chunk of bread, and some potatoes. It wasn't Mama's cooking, but it was enough.

The next day we marched over to Fort Greene Park. "March" is probably the wrong word since we didn't know what we were doing. We walked there briskly. From the armory on Henry and Cranberry Streets, we headed down Henry Street to Clark Street, then to Tillary Street to Jay Street, and finally to Myrtle Avenue, which led us right to Fort Greene Park.

On each of these streets, I saw beautiful multi-storied homes of wood, brick, or brownstone. These were nice well-to-do areas where people kept their houses in fine condition. I also passed stores where I could look in the windows to see what I would like to have –from clothes to watches to books – but couldn't afford.

We weren't wearing uniforms, so strangers on the street would come up to us and ask what we were doing. When we said that we had just joined the 14th Brooklyn and that we were marching to camp, those same people started slapping us on the back and congratulating us. Pretty girls gave us flowers. I didn't know what to do with the flowers, but it felt wonderful to get them. We were heroes before we were even soldiers. I may not have gotten the celebration when I first signed up, but this was my band and ceremony.

When we arrived at Fort Greene Park, I got separated from my group, so I asked somebody where to find Captain Mallory's tent. I walked in the direction I was told, looking for the captain's tent. There were rows and rows of tents of different shapes and sizes. Most of them looked like Indian teepees that I'd seen in books. Others were larger with sloped roofs and short walls, looking a bit more luxurious than the teepees. I guessed those were for the officers.

Boys in and out of uniform were standing around or sitting on logs throughout the camp. Some were writing, others were playing cards or checkers, but most were just talking. I overheard a couple of them discussing what they were going to do to the rebels when we caught them. Since neither of the boys were in uniform, I assumed they must be new recruits like me.

"Those I don't shoot, I'm gonna stab with my bayonet," one of them said. "You'll have to get in line behind me," the other replied. "You can have all that's left over."

I couldn't hear anything else, but I was impressed by their confidence. I wondered if the enemy were saying the same thing about what they would do to us. If so, someone was going to be wrong.

After a while, I realized that I had no idea where I was going. I could smell food cooking and coffee brewing. The smell seemed to come from one of those larger tents, but this one had no sides. It was the kitchen, and it looked like the folks working there were boiling everything, and I guessed that was their favorite way of preparing meals. I saw someone in uniform sitting on a log reading a book, so I went over to him to ask where to find Captain Mallory's tent. Since he was in soldier's attire, I figured that he'd been in camp for a while, and would know his way around.

"Excuse me, can you help me out?" I asked.

"Sure," he replied. He closed the book and gave me his full attention. "Are you one of the new recruits?"

"Yes, I am. My name is Jack Muller."

"I'm Michael Gorman. Pleased to meet you." We shook hands, which seemed like the right thing to do.

"Sorry to interrupt your reading, but I was wondering if you could tell me how I could get to Captain Mallory's tent?"

"Of course. I was just reading this book on military tactics, which can wait. I'm not getting much out of it." Michael sighed. "The author is a Prussian officer, and the translation is not very good. If the translator didn't know the correct English for some German phrase, he just didn't translate it. That makes for difficult reading."

"Maybe I can help. I can read German. Let me see the phrases that are giving you a problem." I sat down on the log and joined Michael. We spent about twenty minutes while I translated the phrases from German to English. "Anything else?" I asked.

"No, that's all of them for now. Thanks so much for your help. You're a real lifesaver. I don't know what I would have done without you. Now I know who to go to if I get stuck on the language again."

"Anytime, glad to help."

"Let me show you around camp, and then take you to George's - or rather Captain Mallory's - tent. It's the least I can do for you after all your help."

We walked around camp while Michael pointed things out and described them to me. "A camp is like a little city," Michael said. "You see those teepee-looking tents? Actually they're called Sibley tents. Soldiers live in them. " "Why are they called that?"

Michael shrugged. "I don't really know, but I figure they must have been invented by some man named Sibley, who liked the look of the Indian teepees. They're pretty roomy inside, and can hold four or five men real comfortably, or up to a dozen men uncomfortably. Right now we're trying to build up our strength, so the Sibley's aren't fully occupied. The problem with the tents is that they're really hard to take down and move. You need wagons to relocate those long poles that hold them up. And with all the other things that an army has to transport, you don't want big posts taking up wagon space."

"What about those tents over there?" I pointed to a group of tents that look like the letter 'A' with the ends cut off.

"They are called wall tents. The angles at the bottom are replaced with straight up and down sides. That size is for commissioned officers. Those walls at the bottom around the tent make them more comfortable because you can stand up easier in them. Commissioned officers don't have to share their tents." Michael talked like a teacher speaking to children. It was perfect for me since I didn't know anything, and there was so much to learn about camp life.

Michael was still talking. "That real big structure over there is the hospital tent. I hope you don't ever have to see that one up close, but if you go on sick call that's where they put you. There's another big one with open sides that you can't see from here. That's the cooking tent where the regiment's meals are prepared. There are other smaller tents with side walls for administrative duties like processing enlistments and doing the paperwork that goes with running an army.

"I'm sure you've noticed a lot of the boys just kind of lolling around. There's a lot of down-time in the army and the soldiers use it in different ways. I was reading because I already finished writing a letter to my wife. But you can see for yourself that some of the boys are writing, and others are playing games or just bragging about what great soldiers they are. Truth is, most of them have never been in a fight.

"It will help you find your way around if you know that each company has its own area with its own flag. So to find Captain Mallory, you would look for the Company B flag and go to the tent next to the flag. That's where you'll find his staff who could tell you whether the captain can see you.

"See," he said, pointing, "There's the flag for Company B, and I see Lieutenant Uffendill outside."

"Hey, Isaiah," Michael said. "Let me introduce you to Jack Muller. He's one of the new recruits. Jack, this is Isaiah Uffendill, or rather Lieutenant Uffendill, who is the adjutant for Captain Mallory. Isaiah, Jack was instructed to report to George for duty."

I was surprised at the informality between a soldier and an officer, but Lieutenant Uffendill didn't seem to think anything of it.

"Nice to meet you, Private Muller," he said. "Captain Mallory is busy right now. Come back in a while, and the captain will be able to see you."

"That works out well," Michael said. "I can keep showing Jack around, and we can talk some more. See 'ya, Isaiah," Michael said with a salute that looked more like a wave. We walked off together.

I couldn't stop myself from asking, "Michael, are we allowed to be so familiar with the officers?"

"Actually, you're right. I should keep to the formalities more, now that we're adding new recruits. I don't want to set a bad example that will affect regimental discipline. Isaiah and I go back a long ways and the regiment was more casual before the war. You see, officers in the volunteer army are elected by the soldiers. So generally, there's kind of an informality between them because the officers need the soldiers' vote. But I have to be more careful. Thanks for making me aware of it, Jack."

I was surprised at the way Michael accepted my question as criticism, and then accepted the criticism without being defensive. Since he was an old timer in the regiment, I was flattered that he listened to me at all, let alone admitting that I was somehow right. Michael impressed me.

As we walked around some more, Michael asked me about myself. Surprisingly, he seemed really interested in my answers.

"There's probably not a lot to tell," I began. "I'm seventeen, and I've lived in Williamsburg for almost twelve years since my parents came over from Germany."

"You don't talk like a German," Michael interrupted.

"I was young when I came here and anyway my father is very insistent that now that we're in America I shouldn't speak like a foreigner. My Papa was an attorney back in Europe, and he ran into some political trouble, so we had to leave. He can't practice law in this country so he's a laborer here in the Navy Yard. He always wanted me to follow in his footsteps. He thinks that an American lawyer shouldn't speak like a German, just like a German lawyer shouldn't have an American accent."

"What's an American accent?" Michael asked, smiling. I laughed because I knew what he meant. Americans think that the way they speak is the right way. So there is no American accent.

"Anyway," I continued, "ever since I could read, my father made me read aloud books like Shakespeare and the Bible to correct my English, and teach me not to speak like an outsider. My father didn't even want me to talk like my friends because he said they didn't use proper English. Funny, I think his speech has improved because of all his work with me."

"Is that why you want to be an attorney; because your father wants you to be one?"

"I guess that was it initially. From the time we got to this country that was all my father said, but I started to have second thoughts. You know, why should he be deciding something like that for me? Then I realized that just because my Papa wanted it doesn't mean I shouldn't. I work with him in the Brooklyn Navy Yard and that life isn't easy. We couldn't afford a lawyer if we needed one. Lots of people are in the same position, or worse. As an attorney I can help them. My father did that in Germany. We were not rich, but we lived comfortably. That's what I want to do."

"Is your dad bitter about being a laborer in this country when he was a lawyer in Germany?" Michael asked.

"Not at all," I replied. "He says he's grateful to this country for giving him a job, and for the hope that his son will do better."

"It sounds like your dad was pretty successful in Germany. Why did he leave? What do you mean when you said he ran into 'political trouble'?"

"He did all right," I spoke slowly as I recalled our life in Germany. "Papa doesn't talk about it much, but I heard enough to know his leaving had to do with the unsuccessful revolution against the Emperor in Austria. He wasn't one of the ones fighting in the streets but he supported the liberal views of the revolutionaries. After the revolt failed, folks started turning in people. Those people then turned in others. One day, my father found out he was named as being a part of the revolt. So we left Germany fast."

"It seems to me you should be really proud of your dad. He's made a new life for himself in a new country, and he's looking toward the future -- you. Do you have any brothers or sisters?"

"No," I answered. "I'm an only child. That's one of the reasons I haven't tried to start reading for the law yet. My Papa's work in the Navy Yard doesn't pay all that much. As he said, he was lucky to get that since he doesn't have any building skills. He had some friends from Germany who already worked at the Navy Yard, and they helped him get the job.

"I give the money I earn in the Navy Yard to my parents. Between the two salaries, we live okay. I know a bit about clerking in a law office. A clerkship is hard to get and most don't pay much if anything. My family can't afford to have me clerking for nothing just to be able to read for the law. When I signed up with the army, my parents didn't say anything about money, but I know they must be worried about how they'll make ends meet.

I plan on sending my folks most of my army pay. That should be enough, with my father's wages, to let them keep on living the way they have been."

Michael seemed genuinely impressed. "I hope your plans work out. I know it's hard to get one of those clerkships in a law office because it often goes to relatives or friends of the attorney. But maybe I can help you. My father-in-law knows a lot of important people."

He motioned to a nearby log where we could sit and continue our conversation. "Before the war the 14th Brooklyn was much smaller than it is now, with most of the men from Brooklyn Heights." I recognized the Heights as the area where the wealthy lived. "With President Lincoln's call for volunteers, we've already increased in size seven times, and we're getting German and Irish immigrants and the sons of those immigrant families. Having those kinds of different backgrounds in the group is a good thing. We used to be all pretty much the same, and that's just not the way life is. I like the different kinds of recruits that we're getting. I think it will make us a better outfit."

"Well, I'm proud to be in the 14th," I said earnestly. "I've heard great things about it, and I hope I do right by the regiment."

"I'm sure you will, Jack. If you're interested, I can tell you about our history."

"Sure, I'd like to hear that."

"About fifteen years ago, the New York State militia was re-organized by combining units to reduce the number of regiments. The 14th Brooklyn was created with two companies. A company has about a hundred men in it. Colonel Willets and then Colonel Phillip Crook were appointed as colonels. After that, it became like other militia regiments, electing its own officers." Michael again sounded like a teacher speaking to his class, but I didn't mind. He was giving me a lot of information, and I was interested.

"Crook was followed by Jesse Smith as elected colonels. About a year ago, Smith was promoted to brigadier general, and A. M. Wood, who had been a major, jumped up to colonel. Below Wood is our lieutenant colonel E. B. Fowlerand and James Jourdan is our major. Right now there are eight companies in the regiment, each with its own elected officers.

"Before the war, the 14th Brooklyn was kind of a social club for well-off men. Our old armory was on Henry and Cranbury Streets in Brooklyn Heights. The men would get together on evenings or weekends for recreation and to show that they were ready to serve if the need arose.

"Now that the war has started and President Lincoln has requested volunteers, we are seeing the number of men in the regiment increase many fold, and, like I said before, they come from all walks of life, unlike the old social club. You know Brooklyn is the third largest city in the country, and many of the people in it are immigrants so I think we'll see Irish, Germans, Italians, English, French and Canadians in the group real soon."

Michael continued, "Don't let all this confuse you. What you should know is that the 14th has a proud history. The men know this, and nobody wants to let the regiment down. We've done real service for the country. We were called out to suppress riots in Brooklyn after some crazy person calling himself the Angel Gabriel had whipped the people into a frenzy." Now he really sounded like a teacher. "Just recently we were sent out to the Navy Yard where you worked, when people thought that rebel sympathizers were going to attack it. Do you remember seeing us there?"

"I do. I thought you boys were grand. That day was one of the reasons I wanted to join this regiment."

Michael nodded his head like he understood and said, "The 14th Brooklyn also has been a show piece for the militia. We took part in the reception for the Prince of Wales when he visited America, and whenever there is a military parade, we are asked to be in it.

"I think that once you settle in here, you'll be as proud of the outfit as I am. Let's keep walking so I can show you more of the camp."

CHAPTER TWO

April 17, 1861

As we were walking along, two fellows approached us.

"Jack, I'd like you to meet Peter Glasson and Robert Lewis. They've been in the regiment for a while."

Peter was heavyset with the beginning of a pot belly. He had a mustache and curly blonde hair atop his six-foot frame. Although big, Peter looked soft, like he wasn't used to doing heavy work, or even a lot of activity.

Robert, on the other hand, was medium height, medium build with brown hair and brown eyes. Nothing about him stood out.

Peter was the first to speak. "Good day to you, Michael. It's a pleasure to meet you, Jack. Any friend of Michael's is a friend of mine."

"Yeah, me too," said Robert.

"We were just taking a constitutional around the camp, noting many of the new faces like yours, Jack."

"Yeah," said Robert, who looked bored.

"I was explaining to Robert how medieval art has shaped today's architecture." I then understood why Robert looked so uninterested.

"Yeah," repeated Robert, this time rolling his eyes. Peter couldn't see the movement, but Michael and I could.

"I believe we shall continue our little stroll, and allow you two to continue whatever it is you were doing."

"Yeah, sure," said Robert in a resigned tone. And the two of them walked on.

Michael turned to me. "I hope you'll get to know them better. Peter is very well educated, and I am afraid he likes to show it off whenever he can. He'll never use a small word when he can find a big one. His father is a doctor from a wealthy family, so Peter has been able to attend a number of colleges, looking for the area that interests him. I feel kind of sorry for him, because he hasn't found his subject yet. When the war broke out, he was studying medieval history which he said was his passion. Unfortunately, he has also said that about a number of other fields that he's studied, like law, music and art."

"I can't feel sorry for someone who's had the opportunity to study law, and rejected it. If anything, I feel jealous."

Michael responded quickly. "Don't be jealous of anyone in this outfit. They all have their problems, believe me. Peter may have had every opportunity to find whatever he wants to do, but that's not to be envied. Rather, pity him for his inability to find his calling." I didn't understand what Michael meant. People in my neighborhood couldn't turn down a job just because they didn't like it. Before I could say this Michael was moving on to Robert.

"Robert's family controls Brooklyn politics. Robert can have anything he wants. But he doesn't want anything from his family. So where does that leave him? Again, don't envy the opportunity. Rather, feel sorry for a life at sea, not knowing what he wants to do. Robert's efforts to find his own way have led him down some bad paths. People took advantage of him, and Robert made a number of bad investments. That's why he sometimes seems sad or angry. But Peter and Robert are both good men. I hope the army gives them the direction they need."

"You know, Michael, we've talked about me and some of the other boys, but I don't know anything about you."

"Jack, I'm far less interesting than you. I'm an only child, too, but I always wanted a little brother. My parents were well-to-do, but unfortunately they both died of influenza in June 1857. I'm blessed that they were around as long as they were, and that they left me well provided for.

"Peter, who you just met, introduced me to my wife, Elizabeth, who is the finest woman in the world. I never get tired of telling the story. It was pretty funny at the time. I was working in the Brooklyn Savings Bank, and Elizabeth's father is the president of the bank. But I didn't know Elizabeth. So when Peter found out where I was working he introduced me to Elizabeth, who had known Peter since they were children. Peter thought the whole thing was very amusing, meeting the boss's daughter and all. Peter arranged it so that he and I were walking down Henry Street in Brooklyn Heights at the same time that

Elizabeth takes her Sunday stroll there. I think Peter believed it would be funny to introduce us and say, 'Michael, meet your boss's daughter, Elizabeth.'

Well, I fell in love with her as soon as I saw her and I guess she fell in love with me, because we were married within the year. I'm a very fortunate man: a wonderful wife at home, and a great career opportunity at the bank. Then war broke out and the 14th Brooklyn was called on to do its duty."

Michael reminded me of my father. He wasn't bitter about getting pulled away from his wife and job, just as my father was not bitter about being a laborer even though he had been an attorney in Germany. Rather, both of them were grateful for the lives they had.

Without even realizing where we had walked, we were back at the captain's tent. This time Lieutenant Uffendill led us inside. Michael introduced me to Captain Mallory, who welcomed me to Company B. The captain directed Lieutenant Uffendill to get me quartered. The lieutenant told me that I would be sharing a tent with Bernard Carney, and that he would show me where it was. Michael offered to take care of that.

Michael, Captain Mallory and Lieutenant Uffendill all seemed comfortable together. This must have been the informality Michael told me about. In thinking about it some more, I realized it wasn't so surprising given that these people had known each other socially for years outside of the army.

Michael and I walked out of the captain's tent so he could show me where I would be sleeping.

"As long as we've got the time, Jack, let me tell you what the routine is around camp. They run this camp like a regular military outpost. You'll learn to react to the sounds of bugles and drums. There are about sixteen different signals that the bugles and drums use to tell the soldiers in camp what to do."

"SIXTEEN! I can't remember all that!" I felt a little panicked.

"Don't worry, you'll get used to it. The army is all repetition and drill, drill, drill.

"At five o'clock in the morning, reveille is blown by the head bugler to alert the drummers. That's the signal to prepare for the morning roll call. Fifteen minutes later, the drummers sound reveille for the regiment to assemble."

"What do you mean by assemble?" I asked.

"That's where men gather for roll call. And before you ask, roll call is where they make sure no one has left camp without authorization, by counting who is present or has a good reason not to be present. When assembly is sounded you'll see men rushing out of their tents, some of them half-dressed, to form up on the drill field over there," Michael said in his teacher tone, pointing to an open field at the end of camp, "so that they can be noted as present. All soldiers except for those on guard duty and those on sick call must be at roll call unless they're excused for a really good reason. After the men have formed up in line, the duty sergeants, each of whom is in charge of about twenty-five men, call the names of everyone in that group. The sergeants then report to the orderly sergeant that all the men are present or accounted for. The orderly sergeant reports that information to the officer of the day. If any of the men are not there or accounted for, they are considered deserters unless some good explanation can be given. That's why all the men race out when assembly is sounded.

"What happens after roll call?" I asked. "Can we do whatever we want?"

"Following roll call, if there are no special orders or instructions, the line is dismissed. Then during the day, the drummers will signal us to do whatever activity is scheduled.

"We have different duties for which we are responsible until breakfast call is sounded. When we hear that, a representative from each tent goes to the cook house to get the food for his tent."

"Why don't the men just line up and get their own food?" I asked.

"The whole process would just take too long if every soldier had to line up to get his own food. Imagine eight hundred or a thousand men lined up for their food. The line would stretch on through the whole camp, and the wait for food would be terrible. Instead, one representative gets the food for his tent, takes it back, and distributes the food to his tent mates."

"How does each tent decide who has to get the food?" I asked.

"Oh, each tent has its own system for dividing up responsibilities, like who gets the food, who gets water, or who cleans up. That system has worked pretty well so far.

"When sick call is sounded, if someone is not well," Michael continued, "this is the time where the ill soldier would go to the hospital tent to see the surgeon. After breakfast call comes fatigue call where we are assigned things like cleaning up the camp, getting wood for the cook house or the officers, or doing other things that have to be done in an army camp."

"Sounds like we're going to be pretty busy. What's next?"

"Drill call. In the mornings we usually do squad drill rather than company or regimental drill. You should know that a squad will have about twenty-five men in it, while a company like Company B will have about a hundred men at full strength, and then the regiment is made up of eight to ten companies so it will have 800 to 1000 men in it. That's about what I expect we'll have when we are at full strength."

"So you're saying that even though you and I are both in Company B, we might not be in the same squad?"

"Exactly! You catch on quickly."

Michael continued explaining the various daily calls. I wondered how I would ever remember all of this information and shivered at the thought of being punished for forgetting something. "At twelve o'clock dinner call is sounded, and the representatives report again to the cook house tent for their food. In the afternoons, the drilling is for the entire regiment to practice the maneuvers that it will have to use in battle. Five o'clock is supper call, and at about six o'clock assembly is blown again so that the men can line up for roll call again. This roll call is also known as the dress parade where all general orders are read and lectures may be given to the soldiers."

I interrupted. "Is that roll call done the same way as the morning one?"

Michael nodded his head. "Exactly the same. Then at about eight thirty, assembly is sounded again for the final roll call of the day. It is done just the same way it is done in the morning and in the afternoon, and then the company is dismissed. After the evening roll call, the men have half an hour to make their beds and get ready for sleep. At nine o'clock, retreat is sounded, and then all lights are supposed to be put out, all talking and other noises stop, and every man except the guards should be inside his quarters. That's about what your days will look like, Jack."

"That sounds like a really long and busy day. But earlier, we saw a lot of boys that were just lolling around. There seems to be a lot of time when people aren't doing anything."

"Yes, that's true. You'll be surprised at how much free time there is, and that's what separates good soldiers from the others," Michael said. "You can use that free time to play cards, joke around with the men, or do an awful lot of other things that aren't going to make you a better soldier. I try to read manuals so I know what we're going to be doing when we get into battle. That's what I was doing when we met. You really helped me a lot with that German book I was reading. You might want to think about becoming familiar with some of the manuals that tell you why you're doing the things you're doing in training to prepare you for battle."

"I don't have any manuals."

"That's no problem. I could lend you some if you're interested."

"Sure, since I signed on to be a soldier, I might as well be a good one."

"I thought you'd feel that way," said Michael. "Let me get you the first volume of Rifle and Light Infantry Tactics which is a basic training manual. It will show you the way an army fights as an army. If you finish it and want to look at the second volume, I'll be happy to lend you that one, too."

"Thanks, Michael. I really appreciate the offer, and I'll certainly read the manuals."

By then we were in front of my tent. Michael said, "You'll be sharing this tent with Bernard Carney and some other new recruits. Bernard is a good man, but he spends most of his time trying to find out camp gossip. The problem, though, is that you can't trust Bernard to keep a secret. He would be a better soldier if he spent more time soldiering and less time gossiping. I'm telling you this in advance because from what you say, you're serious about becoming a good soldier. You'll get along fine with Bernard, but just don't get caught up in all the gossip."

When we looked in the tent, Bernard was lying down. Michael introduced me, then said he had to be going. He told me that we'd see each other soon, and promised that he would get me the manual.

Michael left, and I threw my sack containing all of my spare clothes on the floor.

The tent was more spacious than I expected. It was shaped like the Indian teepees I'd seen in pictures, and was about fifteen to eighteen feet in diameter and about twelve feet high. The tent was supported by only one long pole in the middle that used a tripod about three foot high at the bottom to hold the pole up. At the top was an opening about a foot in diameter. I guessed that the hole at the top was how air got into and out of the tent.

I introduced myself to Bernard, who immediately asked, "Well, Jack, what do you think so far?"

"Michael was just showing me around and explaining how things worked around here. It looks pretty good to me. Say, how many boys can sleep in this tent?"

"It can hold about a dozen if they lay like the spokes on a wheel, with their feet at the center. But I don't think we'll have nearly that number. The regiment is not at full strength. We're still recruiting."

"I see. But one question, though. What do we do when it rains, with that hole at the top of the tent?" I asked.

"Oh, that's no problem. We have a flap that we put up there to cover the hole when it rains. In cold weather we can use a stove in here, and run the stove pipe through the hole. It should all work pretty well. I don't think we're going to be here in cold weather anyhow. I suspect we'll be moving south pretty soon.

"I have to tell you, Jack, that Michael is a strange man. He could have been an officer if he wanted. The men like him and respect him. He would have been elected easily. Instead, he just wants to be a private along with us other soldiers. There's some story there, and I don't know what it is."

I could see what Michael meant when he said Bernard was a gossip. I vowed not to give Bernard any information that I didn't want made public. "Maybe that's just the way Michael wants it. Maybe he thinks just being a soldier is how he can do the most for the regiment, and himself. Not everyone wants to be an officer. I figure most of what the officers do is to stay back behind the line and send other boys out to do their fighting for them. That's not something Michael would want, I bet."

"Maybe," Bernard replied. "But before the war I was a reporter for the Brooklyn Eagle so I kind of see stories everywhere. Funny thing about the Eagle. Do you know what happened? Before the war it was pretty much pro South. I suspect that was because of all the trade that was done with the South coming into the Brooklyn ports. But for whatever reason, the Eagle was of the opinion that the South should be left alone. But once those rebs fired on Fort Sumter, boy did the Eagle change its mind. Now the Eagle wants the South whipped fast and whipped good. That's my view, too. I figure if some newsworthy story comes along while I'm here helping to beat the South, that's all to my benefit. I can send a letter to the Eagle, which publishes soldiers' letters. Then I sort of get credit for the story. That will help me after the war when I try to get my job back."

As he talked, Bernard kept stroking his brown mustache which was really just some wispy hairs on top of his lip. He was thin and of medium height. You could see that he'd worked indoors before the war because there were no sun lines, or any kind of lines on his face. In fact he had kind of a baby face, and I guess he grew the mustache to make him look older. Even with the mustache, however, he still had a boyish look about him.

I played along with his role as a reporter. "If a story comes in, I'm sure you'll be the first to hear about it."

"That's my idea," Bernard replied. "You have to keep alert to find out everything you can. Most of the stuff isn't worth the effort, but when that nugget comes along, you want to be there to get it. I'm going out now to talk with the boys some more, and see if there's any news about what we're going to do. If you need anything, just let me know. My stuff is over there, and you can feel free to share my razor."

I think Bernard made me that offer to point out that he "used" a razor. I hadn't brought one because I didn't really need it yet. But it was a nice enough gesture anyway.

"I'll see you later then, Bernard. I'm just going to stay here and get settled in."

"See ya later," Bernard said as he left.

I spread out the bedroll, which was part of the equipment I was given by the quartermaster, and lay down to try and think about army life so far. Before I had much of a chance to think, two men came into the tent.

Actually it was more like one older man, bald but with a full beard, and one young boy. The older man introduced himself as Patrick Murphy, and the young one was Davey O'Connor.

Patrick looked old enough to be my father. He was stocky, but it looked to be all muscle. I thought he was in pretty good shape for a man his age--fit as a fiddle. Davey, on the other hand, was thin, small, no more than five feet three inches. I'm seventeen and he looked much younger than me. They both looked about as nervous as I felt before I met Michael. I supposed they hadn't had the good fortune to meet someone like Michael to show them around and take the edge off their nervousness.

"I'm Jack Muller," I said. "Today is my first day here."

"Me, too," Patrick and Davey replied almost as one.

Davey continued speaking as if he was excited to tell me something. "I got to the tent a while back, and I seen Patrick just sitting there. We got to talking. Turns out Patrick and me are both Irish, although my family's been in Brooklyn a lot longer. Ain't it something to run into another Irishman my first day?"

"It sure is," I replied. "Wonder what else we might have in common. I worked in the Brooklyn Navy Yard before I signed up, and one day I hope to be a lawyer. I've got no brothers or sisters. My parents didn't really want me going off to fight this war, but I thought I should. What about you, Patrick?"

"I have me a wife and three children. Sure I couldn't find work so I signed up thinkin' that even if this was only ninety days long, I could get some money for me to take care of my family. I had to lie about my age to get in, didn't I now? Told them I was thirty-eight when truth be told I'm fifty-seven."

"I lied about my age, too," Davey chimed in proudly. "Told 'em I was eighteen, when I'm really fourteen."

31

They both spoke with lilting Irish brogues, but Davey's was much less noticeable than Patrick's. I figured that Davey had come to this country when he was very young, while Patrick was probably a more recent arrival. I could easily understand what they said, and I was concerned for them. "Be careful. You don't want the fact that you lied about your ages to get around."

"Why not?" Davey asked. "We're already in the regiment. They can't kick us out. Anyways, why would they give a hoot?" Patrick and Davey were chuckling like they had gotten away with something.

"Yes, they can kick you out!" I was shocked at how unaware they were. It was one thing for fourteen-year-old Davey to be so innocent, but Patrick was a grown man. "The army has rules that they stick to. If someone breaks those rules the army can, and probably will, take action. If an officer finds out about your lies and doesn't do anything, then he has lied, too. No one is going to take a chance on being punished for helping you lie to the army. Have you boys told anyone else about your real ages?"

"No, we just got here," responded Patrick. His eyes, like Davey's, were wide open, and they had lost some color in their faces, and their smiles were gone.

"That's good, and you should keep it that way. Don't worry about me, I won't tell anyone."

Patrick's eyes narrowed suspiciously. "Why would you not tell 'em our secret? Did you not just say that you must be telling them or else you lied about our ages, too?"

"That's only for officers." I may have made that up, but it sounded right. I didn't see myself as a stool pigeon and had no reason to turn them in. As far as I could tell from our brief conversation, they seemed like decent fellows who would make good tent mates. "What you have to worry about is someone else, for whatever reason, telling one of the officers about your real ages. We've got another tentmate named Bernard Carney who seems nice enough, but he's quite a gossip. He was a reporter for the Brooklyn Eagle, and he's always looking for information that he thinks would make a good story. By my judgment he doesn't particularly care who he tells this information to. So you boys better keep your real ages a secret."

"Why would he tell on us?" Davey asked.

"I think he just likes to show off whatever he knows. Or maybe he's a stickler for the rules; or maybe he thinks it will make the officers like him more. I don't know what his reason might be, but you boys can't take the chance." I called them boys, even though Patrick was older than my father, because that's what I called all the soldiers who weren't officers.

They considered what I had said, and apparently decided that I was worthy of their trust. They both thanked me for helping them, looking sincerely grateful.

"How come you couldn't find work?" I asked Patrick.

"Well, if you need to ask that question, you ain't been much outside of your own neighborhood in Brooklyn. The Irish don't have it too easy in New York. It began when me and my family first came to this country. I had an uncle livin' in New York who

I was tryin' to get to. As soon as we got off the boat, a young Irish lad steps up and asked if he could help. I told him about my kinfolk, and he asked if I had any money to get there. Sure, I said that I did. He asked me how much, and I told him. He said that's what it costs to get to my kinfolk's place. I thought to myself, if I can't trust a fellow Irishman, who can I trust, so I gave him all my money like a damn fool. He told me he would bring his wagon 'round to make it easier to load our baggage, and that I should wait there. Sure he never came back. If I ever see him again, I'll make him wish he'd never been born!" Patrick's eyes still blazed with anger and shame.

My shock earlier about how a grown man could be so innocent about lying to the army was answered. Patrick was too trusting. He thought everyone would do what he thought was the right thing. The army wanted soldiers, and he was ready to sign up to fight. So the army should welcome him, regardless of his age. He could do the job, and that's all that mattered.

Listening to Patrick speak, I could tell that he was not used to talking so much. I was getting used to his brogue. And I noticed that he paused between words like he was thinking about what he was going to say before he said it. But now he seemed to want to confide in me and share his experiences. Then I realized that Patrick just wanted to show me that he was a friend, and that he trusted me and Davey.

Patrick continued, "We ended up walkin' several miles to my uncle's home on the east end of 42nd Street in New York. The first time I laid me eyes on it, I thought I would be sick. I didn't expect the streets to be paved with gold, but I didn't figure them to be paved with garbage either. The slopes on the east end of 42nd Street are filled with shanties. People live on small plots, raising goats and growing potatoes. The old women there still speak the Irish and smoke clay pipes.

"Businesses in the city, they don't hire the Irish." Patrick was getting more and more worked up, and his hands were moving up and down while he talked. "So we line up at the docks day after day looking for work unloading ships, and never get picked. You can walk around the streets going into every business and askin' if they would give you a job, losin' all your self-respect, and the answer is always, 'get out of here, Paddy.' Paddy is what they call us, and a friendly name it is not. Anyway, I still got to support my family, and I ain't been able to get a job that lets me do it. So when President Lincoln called for ninety-day volunteers, I signed up. It pays more than I can get begging for jobs sweepin' out bars. If it's for only ninety days, well that's ninety days more than I had before."

"Don't you believe in the Union?"

"No, can't say I have an opinion on that one way or the other. But I signed on to fight for the Union, and so I will. That's my job."

I started to try to convince Patrick of the righteousness of our cause. "But Patrick, this country became great because it joined the different states into one nation. Now the south is trying to break up these United States."

"Well, Jack, my boy, this country ain't been that great to me and the Irish, has it now?" I hadn't thought about that before, and I couldn't really say Patrick was wrong about how the Irish were treated. At that point Davey interrupted in support of Patrick. "I didn't think much about the Union either when I signed up. My family has a small farm in Brooklyn which gives us barely enough to live on. I figured they'd have one less mouth to feed if I joined up, and maybe I could send some money home to them. My folks told me it was a real good idea. I got two older sisters and three younger brothers. All of 'em have to be fed too. So my ma and pa liked the idea of one less mouth to feed a whole lot. And that's okay by me. I suspect I'm going to eat better here than I ever did back home. And fighting for the Union ain't such a bad cause so that don't bother me none either."

At first I was put off by Patrick and Davey's lack of commitment to the Union cause. But I just couldn't help myself. I liked them. They were good boys. As we talked more, I started to appreciate that there were all sorts of different reasons to join the army: fighting for your country; fighting to free the slaves in the south; fighting to re-unite the states. It was all so complicated. But Davey and Patrick were going to fight simply because it was a job and they needed the money. If the job required them to fight, they were ready to fight. It was simple, and I liked it. I figured that most of the boys in camp wanted to get into action before the war was over so they could say they fought in a battle. I know that applied to me. Davey and Patrick figured that they would get into a battle if the war didn't end soon, but they didn't really care one way or the other. All they really wanted was work and pay.

As our talk continued, I felt that the three of us would become great friends. I liked their straightforwardness. They said what they thought, whether you wanted to hear it or not. I also liked the simple way they viewed life. You had to make a living before you could worry about causes. You did what you had to do to meet your responsibilities. For Patrick and Davey that meant joining the army.

I told Patrick and Davey more about my hopes of becoming a lawyer, how my father left Germany, and how he insisted that I read a lot in English and learn to speak like an American to help me become a lawyer. I didn't detect any envy of my grand hopes. Nor did I detect any jealousy because my parents didn't want me to go into the war, while their families supported them enlisting and risking their lives for the money it would bring to their homes. Instead, Patrick and Davey listened, and told me that they were sure I would get what I wanted because they could tell I was smart and would work hard and earn it. I felt an immediate bond with them. They really did want me to get what I hoped for. And I really wanted them to get whatever they could from the army. We talked for quite a while, and the more we talked, the more we got to like each other.

Then we heard the drummers. Patrick and Davey looked alarmed. I guessed that no one had told them what drum calls mean.

I tried to remember what I had learned from Michael. "That's the signal to do something, but I don't remember what. It's the way they do things in the army. The bugle blows or the drummers drum, and that means you have to either wake up, line up, eat, or go to sleep. Let's go find out what it is we should be doing."

CHAPTER THREE

April 18, 1861

After drill the next morning, Michael brought over the manual on tactics he'd offered to lend me. Bernard was already gone on his never-ending quest for news or gossip. But Patrick and Davey were still in the tent when Michael arrived. "Good morning, Jack," Michael said as he pulled back the flap on the tent, saw me and started to come in. "How did you like your first night in camp?"

"Fine!" I replied enthusiastically. "These are my tent mates, Patrick Murphy and Davey O'Connor. Patrick, Davey, this is Michael Gorman. He showed me around camp yesterday and explained how things work. Anything I told you two, I learned from Michael. He was really helpful, and made my first day a lot easier."

"Pleased to meet you," said Michael. "Although I think Jack exaggerates my help."

"Same here," said Davey. "Jack helped us a lot. If he knew all those things acause a you, I'm obliged."

"I'm grateful as well, aren't I now?" added Patrick.

"I hear your Irish brogue. I'm glad you could join our regiment." Patrick and Davey looked suspicious right away. Michael saw it, too, so he elaborated, "It's important that we have people from all different backgrounds here to show what I've always believed: that we can all work and live together. I know that's not the way life is out there. They call you Paddy, and won't give you jobs. They say you're drunk all the time and useless. Well, let me tell you, that's hogwash." Michael's hands were moving just like Patrick's hands had moved when he talked to me about the prejudice the Irish had to put up with. I was thinking about how these two fellows, who were so different, had the same views and spoke about them in the same way. Michael was right. Having people in the 14th Brooklyn from different groups and backgrounds is a good thing. We can learn from each other.

Michael continued, "The Irish people I've met through the bank where I work are hard-working, responsible people. And yes, we hire Irishmen, just like we lend money to Irishmen. If we believe they are a good risk, we take it.

I could see Patrick and Davey relax a bit. But they still didn't know if they could trust this wealthy, well-bred sweet talker. "That sounds mighty nice, but sure I've had some trouble with people what sounded nice, haven't I?" responded Patrick. "Yeah, me too," added Davey.

Patrick and Davey were as straightforward as ever. I still liked that trait. There was no need to guess where you stood with them.

Apparently Michael liked it, too. "That's fine. I wouldn't expect you to take my word for it. Just keep an open mind. If I can do anything for you, let me know. I've been in the outfit long enough to know the routine so I might be able to help make it easier."

Now Patrick and Davey visibly relaxed. It wasn't all Michael's words that put them at ease. Michael's tone and posture were easygoing like he was one of the boys talking to friends. He wasn't trying to sell them something or take something from them. They could tell that Michael's offer to help was sincere.

A drum roll rang out. "That's mealtime," Michael said. "You're supposed to have a representative from each tent go to get the food for all the men in the tent, but I know the cooks, so we can just get food for ourselves. Come on, let's all get some grub and pull up a nice spot of ground to sit on and eat."

"You'll be eatin' with us?" Patrick asked, unable to hide his surprise.

"If we're going to fight together, and maybe die together, I think we can eat together," Michael replied, grinning.

After we ate, Michael and I took a walk around camp. Patrick and Davey wanted to explore on their own, probably to talk about what they thought of Michael. They knew he was a friend of mine, so didn't want me there if they decided they couldn't trust him. I was confident that Patrick and Davey would conclude that Michael was one of the good ones and trustworthy.

While Michael and I were walking, two boys approached us. When we got close, Michael said, "Come on, Jack, I want to introduce you to two more of the old timers, Bill Shannon and Steve Cooper."

"Bill, Steve, meet Jack Muller. He's a new recruit." Michael said.

Bill was a big man, but slightly overweight with a baby face and curly red hair. He was clean shaven, and looked friendly. Steve, on the other hand, was a thin bearded man with slick backed hair. His eyes kept darting around making him look nervous, like he had something to hide. Steve shook my hand, and Bill gave me a friendly pat on the back. They both seemed pleased to meet me. Michael went on, "Did you know, Jack, that Company B has its own base ball team?"

"No, really? That sounds like fun."

Michael went on, "Well, Bill is the catcher on our team, and Steve is our second baseman. They're both really good players. Steve is fast, and covers a lot of ground, and Bill can hit the ball a long way."

Steve and Bill smiled at the compliments, and Steve said, "That's nice of Michael to say, but he is almost as good as me." Steve was looking around him as he was talking. It was as if we were discussing some secret, and he did not want someone to overhear us. I found it strange since we were only talking about base ball.

I saw Bill chuckle at Steve's remark. Bill said, "Michael is our star center fielder." Bill was patting Michael on the back as he talked. "He runs like a deer and takes away hits with some unbelievable catches. He always seems to be able to judge how the ball will bounce on the field, so he can catch it on one bounce for the out. But that's only when he can't catch it on the fly." Michael explained to me that when a ball is hit in the air, the batter will be out if the fielder catches it on the fly or on one bounce. Bill was nodding his head in agreement with what Michael was saying. Then he came over to me, patted my back and said, "Hey, Jack, do you play?"

"No, I'm afraid not. Between work and studying to prepare to be a lawyer, I just never had the time. I've seen a couple of games though, and I would like to try."

Bill suggested, "Why don't you watch some of our games and see if you still want to play? You look fast. How are your hands?"

I looked at my hands then looked at him like he was speaking a foreign language, so Bill tried again, "Can you catch a ball?"

Now I understood what he was asking. "Well, in the Navy Yard where I was a laborer, I was always throwing and catching packs of nails and other material. Beats walking back-and-forth. I never dropped the nails or had any complaints about my tosses. That what you mean?"

"Sure is, and that's great." Bill replied, patting my back again. "We have a full team now, but you never know what's going to happen. We may see action fighting the rebs pretty soon, and people might get hurt. If you still want to play, maybe we'll give it a try."

"That reminds me, Michael," Bill added, "do we have any games set up?"

Michael replied, "I'm trying to arrange something with the team from Company A. I should know soon."

"Great, looking forward to it." Bill and Steve walked off.

Michael turned to me and said, "They're good boys for the most part. They've been with the regiment for a couple of years. Bill's family owns taverns, one around the docks and one in Brooklyn Heights. Steve's family owns a drug store. Bill and Steve love the regiment, and love base ball. Come on, let's keep walking."

CHAPTER FOUR

April 22, 1861

It had been about a week since I joined the army, and the routine of life at the camp appealed to me. Drilling twice a day, meals with the rest of the outfit three times a day, work details every day, guard duty once every fourth day, and target practice as ordered. We were being trained to be soldiers, which meant living and fighting as a group.

Despite all of the activities, Michael was right that there was a lot of free time. In the beginning, I spent most of that time getting to know the routine in the camp and the other soldiers in my company. A number of the boys had been in the company for a couple of years. Raw recruits like me were at a real disadvantage. We didn't know the signal calls for meals or assembly, where to go, or when to go there. Fortunately for me, Michael had explained a number of the camp routines and was always there when I had questions.

I already knew some of the boys in the regiment like Joe Cramer and Hans Newman from my neighborhood. Both were big strapping boys about eighteen years old from German immigrant families like mine, and they worked at the docks loading and unloading ships. They were good, friendly fellows who enjoyed a beer or more and could hold their own in any barroom brawl. I was glad they were on our side. Michael also introduced me to some soldiers who were older and more refined. Their families came from the rich part of Brooklyn.

Michael arranged the base ball game with Company A for Monday, after regimental drill. I went over to the drill field to watch the game along with hundreds of other soldiers, not just those from Company A or Company B. Everyone seemed interested. I saw Michael and waved to him. He waved back, and walked over to me.

"Hi, Jack, glad you could make it."

"I wouldn't miss it! I'm hoping to learn more about the game and maybe even try playing one day. Actually, I can't stop thinking about getting in a game ever since Bill suggested I give it a try. But I have to tell you, I still find the plays on the field confusing. Maybe you could explain the rules to me, at least those I need to know as a beginner."

"Sure, I'll tell you the basics. If I miss something that confused you before, just ask me about it, all right? "

"Sounds good to me."

"Then here goes. There are a lot of specific rules like the size of the bat and ball that you really don't need to know. Last year the members of the National Association of Base-Ball Players adopted the rules I am going to give you. We met in New York City, and I can tell you, as a member, that it got pretty hot."

"Wait, are you telling me that you were on the committee that decided how the game should be played? So I'm having the game explained to me by one of the people that determined just that. Wow!" Michael's face reddened, and he stuttered something. I could tell that he was embarrassed at the way I was making such a big deal about him being on the rules committee. But to me it was a big deal.

Then Michael got down to the business of explaining the game to me. He started speaking as if he was teaching a class, and I was the student.

That's probably an accurate description of what it resembled. I liked it when Michael spoke to me that way. I always learned something, and I thought it brought us closer as friends.

Michael started the lecture. "The pitcher stands behind a line which is drawn at a right angle to the line between home base and the second base, forty five feet from home base. The striker stands at home base ready to hit the ball. The pitcher pitches the ball underhanded to the striker. The pitcher's throwing hand cannot go above his waist. Once the pitcher starts to pitch, he has to finish it. If he doesn't, that's a balk. In the case of a balk every player on base gets to move to the next base."

"Why is that rule needed?" I asked. "If the striker doesn't swing it doesn't count anyway."

"The rule is for the runners. Remember, a runner can be tagged out whenever he is not touching a base. So if the pitcher fakes the pitch, the runner may be fooled into thinking he can leave the base. Then the pitcher could throw the ball to his team mate on the base and tag the runner."

"I see. Now it makes sense."

"Anyway, the striker gets three swings. If he doesn't hit the ball in those three swings and the catcher catches the pitch on the third miss, either without the ball touching the ground, or on one bounce, then the striker is out. If the catcher does not catch the ball on the third miss, the striker can run to first base as if he had hit the ball. The catcher has to recover the ball and throw it to first base before the striker gets there for the striker to be out.

"As you can see, the catcher is a more difficult position than you would think. He has to catch that third strike, which isn't easy with the striker swinging the bat in front of him. And if the striker fouls the ball and it comes back to the catcher at a different angle, the catcher's reflexes have to be good enough to catch the ball for the out, or he might end up with a broken finger. You need great reflexes and Bill has them. He also has had some broken fingers from foul balls that caught him wrong.

"Although the striker gets an unlimited number of pitches, he can't stand there forever. If he doesn't swing at good balls, then the umpire will give him a warning, and then call the pitch a strike if it's a good ball, even if the striker does not try to hit it. The umpire will continue to call strikes after that."

I wondered what a good ball was so I asked Michael, who answered, "Anything that is in the fair reach of the striker's bat between a few inches off the ground to his shoulders."

Michael went on. "There's only one umpire and, generally, he is asked for decisions only when the players can't agree. His decision is final, and there's no arguing. The umpire doesn't wait to be asked in certain situations, like calling foul balls. That's when the ball is struck, but it lands outside the line from home base to first base, or home base to third base. The striker cannot get to first base on a foul ball. And the striker is out if a foul ball is caught without hitting the ground, or after one bounce. If no one catches it, the ball is dead, and doesn't count.

"After the striker hits the ball, and if it isn't foul, he runs the bases, touching as many as he can without being tagged. As I mentioned, the striker can be tagged out anytime he's not on a base. If he goes around all the bases and touches home base, that's a run.

"What if he touches the base and then can't stop?" I asked.

"Then the striker is out if he is tagged off the base. The only base you can over run is home base. Anything else, and you can be tagged out.

"Another way for the striker to be out is if a fielder catches the struck ball without it hitting the ground or after one bounce. Then no tag is needed."

"After three outs the striker's team goes into the field and the team in the field comes up to hit. Once each side has made three outs, that's an inning. The game lasts nine innings, unless it is tied at that point. Then the game continues until one team is ahead at the end of an inning."

"Thanks, Michael, that's really helpful. Is there anything else that you think I should know?" I asked.

"Now that you mention it, there is." Michael replied. "Remember there is only one umpire, who has to watch everything going on. Specific rules are important so the man who has to make the call, whether the person is safe or out, knows what to look for. One of those rules is that when you run from one base to the other, you do it in a direct line. If you run out of that line by three feet or more to avoid a tag by the opposing player, you will be declared out."

"I guess that makes sense, or the base ball game could turn into a free for all. And it's easy for the umpire to see."

Michael smiled at that. "Also," he said, "if you obstruct a striker from reaching a base, then he is entitled to that base, and is not put out."

"That makes sense, too," I said. "If you can block a player from reaching base, I can see the game turning into a brawl."

"I think that's pretty much all you need to know for now. Hope you have a good time. I'll see you after the game," Michael called as he walked over to join his team.

The game against Company A was exciting. The crowd loved it. We won, 17-16, and the result was in doubt until the end. The lead changed hands five times.

The score was 16-16 in the ninth inning. We were the home team, so Company A batted first. Company A's first striker to bat in the ninth inning was their first baseman, Nathan Teasdale, a very big fellow who had hit the ball well the previous times he went to the plate. On the first pitch, he hit a shot to center field that seemed like it was going to leave Brooklyn. Michael started running at the sound of the bat hitting the ball. He was really fast, and knew just where to go to catch up to the ball. At the last second, he reached out one arm and caught the ball one- handed. I could hardly believe he reached the ball, let alone caught it with just one hand. One out.

The second striker to bat was their shortstop, Dan Teasdale, Nathan's brother. He swung at the third pitch and foul tipped it. Bill Shannon moved like a cat and caught the ball for the second out. I saw what Michael meant about the challenges of the catcher's position.

The third striker to bat for Company A was their second baseman, Manus Geary, who got a one base hit. That was followed by another one base hit by John Mack, their left fielder. Now Company A had two men on base, with the tie-breaking run at second base. You could feel the tension. There must have been a couple of hundred boys in the crowd screaming their heads off. Half of them were yelling for Manus to score the run that would put Company A ahead, and the other half were shouting for Company B to stop him from scoring.

The next striker for Company A was their third baseman, Aaron Schwebel. He refused to swing at a number of pitches, obviously waiting for "his" pitch - one he knew he could smack. The umpire warned Aaron that he would start calling balls and strikes because Aaron had let a number of reachable balls pass without swinging. The umpire called two strikes on Aaron on the next two pitches. To avoid striking out, Aaron had to swing at the next ball if he could reach it, whether or not he liked the pitch. The crowd fell silent. You could hear Aaron tap the barrel top we used for home base with his bat as he waited for the ball. George McIntyre stepped up and pitched the ball underhanded. George was careful to comply with the rule that the pitcher's arm couldn't go above his belt, because he didn't want the umpire to call the toss a ball.

It was one of George's fastest throws of the game because he knew Aaron couldn't take a chance of striking out, and had to swing at it. The pitch was barely reachable, but Aaron managed to hit a slow roller to second base. The Company A half of the crowd groaned at the weak tap and started yelling at Aaron to run faster. The Company B half screamed with delight because it was an easy play for Steve Cooper, who picked up the ball and threw it to Peter Glasson at first base for the out. Then Steve raised his arms over his head as though he'd just won the game single- handedly. "Steve sure thinks a lot of himself," I thought.

But now it was our turn to bat in the ninth inning. If we scored, we would win the game. If not, we would play more innings. Our first striker hit a short fly ball that their second baseman caught on one bounce for the out. Our next three players each got one base hits so there were Company B runners on all three bases. It was Michael's turn now. He let three pitches go by, waiting for just the right one. The umpire, after a warning, started calling strikes. Michael had two strikes when he got his pitch. He hit it over the left fielder's head. It would easily have been a four base hit with Michael's speed, but after the runner on third base scored, the game was over. As soon as Michael touched first base, everyone in Company B, including the players, started celebrating. Anyone watching it would have thought we won the war.

While Company A was grumbling about the result, all the players on Company B kept talking about how well they played. Everyone got at least two hits and Robert Lewis, Steve Cooper, and Bill Shannon each had three. Michael had four.

It was a fun game, and I had a great time. I caught up with a few of the players on their way back to their tents.

"Great game. You really played well out there," I told them. "I did, didn't I?" said Steve Cooper.

"We all played well," Michael corrected.

Steve didn't give up. "Yeah, but I made some outstanding plays at second base."

Michael didn't give up either. "Bill Shannon was great behind the plate. He caught three foul tips for outs. And Peter Glasson at first had the presence of mind to tag those two runners who overran first base."

Peter couldn't help responding, "Thank you, but it was the rather obvious action for any thinking ball player."

Now Steve was getting angry, and his eyes were moving all over the place. "I've had enough of you always criticizing my play, Michael."

"I am not criticizing your play. I am only saying that other players contributed, too. Robert Lewis at shortstop made plays all over the field. Honford Hovey in right field made that diving catch that saved at least two runs. And George McIntyre not only pitched a good game but he fielded well too. I'd say it was a real team effort."

That was not good enough for Steve. He exclaimed, "You don't get it, do you? When you immediately bring up other players, you are saying I didn't contribute as much. Base ball is made up of individual plays. Sure there is a team, but when a striker is at bat, it's just him. And when a ball is hit to a player, he has to make the play. Those are individual efforts." Steve's eyes were still shifting from player to player. I couldn't tell if that was because of the way he talked or if he was looking for support from the others. "The team doesn't help the striker swing, or the player field the ball. If you think individuals like me don't count, get another second baseman, and see how the team does."

"That goes for me, too, Michael!" Robert Lewis added loudly. "You always have to say and do what you think is the proper thing, and I find it sickening. Team this and team that. If teammates are so important to you, I'm sure you would treat them better. As it is, a teammate means no more to you than a stranger. So all this talk about the team is just nonsense."

The usually friendly Bill Shannon was nodding his head in agreement with Robert. Bill didn't say anything, but he was clearly bothered about something. I got the idea that there was more going on here than base ball.

Robert continued his tirade. "If Steve wants to talk about his own accomplishments, that's fine. You don't always have to bring up the team."

It was Peter who stepped up to defend Michael. "Calm down, Steve, and you too, Robert. You know that's not what Michael was saying. We are a team, with everyone expected to do his share. You both did your shares exceptionally well. We're all proud of you, and grateful."

Steve and Robert started to calm down, but they still appeared to be a little put off by Michael. "Thanks, Peter," Steve said. "That's all I wanted to hear. If goody goody Michael had only said that in the beginning, we wouldn't have had this argument." I saw Robert and Bill nodding their heads in agreement. After that, the talk about individual efforts came back without the bickering, and continued all the way to the tents. I was relieved. I had felt uncomfortable hearing the criticism of Michael, but it seemed like I didn't know the whole story. I had thought that Michael was friends with Steve, Robert and Bill, but maybe not.

Company B played three more games at Fort Greene, won two and lost one. I went to all the games, and enjoyed every one of them. I grew to love base ball.

CHAPTER FIVE

April 24, 1861

The boys in the regiment filled up their free time in different ways, but they all seemed to be enjoying themselves. There were visitors to the camp all the time, including pretty girls from different neighborhoods in Brooklyn. Whenever we marched, there was a crowd watching us.

Initially, this bothered me because I didn't have a uniform and I didn't know what I was doing. The old-timers with the 14th Brooklyn wore beautiful uniforms and seemed to know exactly what to do.

The manual Michael loaned me helped with the marching, and eventually we recruits were issued uniforms. Then I could fit in and enjoy the attention as much as anyone.

Every day I met new people. One day while I was walking through camp I saw Michael talking with an older man. Michael caught my eye and motioned for me to come over. When I did, Michael introduced me to his father-in-law, Daniel Gault, the president of the Brooklyn Savings Bank. Mr. Gault was short with brown hair and a well-trimmed beard, and was very well dressed. He had a powerful look about him, but it wasn't physical power. His green eyes sent out the message that he was a man who was always in control of the situation. I could also see that he was very fond of Michael. Whenever Michael spoke, the corners of Mr. Gault's lips turned up and his eyes seemed to open wider.

"Jack, let me introduce Mr. Daniel Gault, my father-in-law. Sir, this is Jack Muller, one of our new recruits."

"How do you do, Jack."

"Nice to meet you, Mr. Gault."

Mr. Gault asked, "So, Jack, how are you handling army life?"

"Thanks to Michael, very well. He shows me what to do, and how to do it. Since I had no idea what to expect in camp, I can't tell you how helpful he's been. He even introduced me to a number of the old-timers in the 14th, and that's put me more at ease."

"Well, Jack," Mr. Gault responded, "Michael is a good man. However, I have trouble thinking of any of the boys in camp as 'old timers'."

We all laughed at that. Michael told Mr. Gault, "Jack wants to become a lawyer after the war."

I was a little embarrassed that Michael would say this, but then I found out why. He continued, "I have spent a lot of time with Jack recently and he's a very bright fellow. I loaned him one of my military manuals, and I can say that he's a quick study. I think he'd make a fine lawyer if he got the chance."

To my surprise and delight, Mr. Gault turned to me and said, "I know a number of lawyers professionally and socially.

This war should not last long. And when it's over, come see me and I'm sure I can arrange something for you."

"Thank you so much, Mr. Gault! I sure hope you're right about the war ending soon."

I was bowled over by Mr. Gault's generosity. But before I could say more, I saw a beautiful woman approaching us, accompanied by Peter Glasson. Michael went over and took her hand. "Jack, let me introduce you to my darling wife, Elizabeth. Peter was kind enough to show Elizabeth around camp while I was talking with her father. Sweetheart, this is Jack Muller, a recent addition to the 14th Brooklyn."

"It's nice to meet you, Mr. Muller," "Please, call me Jack."

"And you call me Elizabeth." She was beautiful. Slim but not skinny. About five feet three inches tall, with brown hair that hung in ringlets framing a lovely face. Her hazel eyes seemed to be sparkling, and when they looked at you, they made you feel important. And she had a flawless complexion. She wasn't merely beautiful, she was perfect.

Anyone could see that Elizabeth and Michael were in love. When she looked at him, it was with adoration. And when he looked at her, it was pure worship. Elizabeth broke my train of thought as she said, "Peter is an excellent tour guide. He showed me so many interesting things in camp. The commissary that prepares meals for all these boys is fascinating, as are the tents where the men live and the officers work.

"I've known Peter almost all my life," she laughed. "Walking with him reminds me of when we were children and Peter would show me all of the interesting sites in the neighborhood. Which trees were which, the architecture of the area, and all the plant life. Peter just knows so much."

"Thank you, my dear," Peter said. "My interests have always been varied. I think a gentleman should know a lot about a lot. Today, so many men believe it is sufficient to know a lot about a little, and nothing about everything else. I have always been fascinated with architecture, art, and many other subjects."

Although Michael had already told me how he met his wife, I was curious about Elizabeth's view of the event, so I asked her, "How did you meet Michael?"

She smiled and replied, "Actually, Peter introduced us, and I will tell you that I fell in love with Michael immediately. I was so hoping that he would ask father for permission to court me, but nothing happened.

Since Michael worked at Father's bank, I asked him about Michael." She smiled even brighter, lighting up her entire face.

Michael chimed in. "Elizabeth didn't know that I felt the same way about her. I was sort of tongue-tied when we met, so I figured she thought I was a fool."

Elizabeth interrupted. "It was adorable. He could barely form words."

Michael continued. "Anyway, I just couldn't ask to see her; I was too embarrassed at the way I had babbled on in our first conversation. When Mr. Gault approached me and suggested I see Elizabeth, I couldn't believe it! But he was my employer, so I couldn't say no. Not that I wanted to say no," he laughed. His eyes gleamed at the memory.

Mr. Gault interjected, "When Elizabeth asked me about Michael she was trying to appear uninterested. It was humorous because I could tell how she really felt. I knew that if I didn't step in, she would be very disappointed when Michael didn't call on her. After that, love took its course."

Peter said, "It was very fortunate that you were there to give love a little push." At this point the conversation broke up because we had to report for regimental drill. Mr. Gault and Elizabeth were anxious to see the drill so we said quick farewells and parted. I hurried to my tent to pick up my equipment, thrilled that my career prospects had improved so dramatically in a mere five minutes. I was so grateful to Michael for believing in me.

CHAPTER SIX

May 15, 1861

We camped in Fort Greene Park until mid-May, drilling and drilling and drilling. We felt so prepared to meet the foe and expected any day to receive orders to move out. The uniforms we had been issued were grand. The jackets were dark blue and triple breasted with three columns of tiny brass buttons. They appeared to have a red vest but it was really just flaps of red material that looked like a vest when the jacket was buttoned. The pants were red and we had red and white leggings. A red and blue cap was the finishing touch. I heard that the uniform was chasseur style like the Zouaves wore. It was wonderful.

Brooklyn was decorated for patriotism. The national colors were proudly displayed in stores, houses, flagpoles and even street crossings. Crowds thronged through the City trying to spot some marching company or some group on its way to war. Whenever they saw a soldier, people started cheering.

In the middle of all this excitement, however, the boys had to make a big decision. We were told that no more militia regiments would be accepted into the United States Army for a term of less than three years. That meant that our 90 day enlistments didn't qualify us for the regular army. If we wanted to fight in this war we had to agree to increase our time commitment to three years, twelve times what we originally agreed to.

I still believed in the cause and that the rebels had no right to try to tear apart this wonderful country. But it was one thing to leave my parents for three months, and quite another thing to go away for three years.

That was a serious commitment. I couldn't afford to go to law school, but another way to become a lawyer was to clerk in a lawyer's office like an apprentice. And Mr. Gault had told me that he could help get me such a position! I would draft routine contracts and wills while studying legal treatises. Then, when I was ready, I could be admitted to the local court in order to practice law. If I hadn't had this prospect, or if I had a better place in the regiment, my decision might have been easier.

I decided to speak with Michael. Since his prospects in civilian life were a whole lot better than mine, I wondered how he would react to the idea of committing himself for three years away from his lovely wife and his vice-presidency at the bank.

"Jack," he said to me, "the time doesn't matter. The 14th Brooklyn asked to be accepted into the regular Army for three months like the President first said. Now it has to be 3 years. We committed to put down the rebellion. If we haven't done it in three months, I wasn't going to go home anyway. This country should be preserved, and slavery should be abolished. The south wants to tear the country apart so it can keep slavery. Keeping people slaves is wrong, and so is destroying the Union."

"The war's not about slavery," I said. "It's about preserving the Union. I couldn't care less what the south does about slavery. That's not why I'm fighting. No, I'm fighting for my country, not some Negroes."

Michael didn't want to argue. He calmly explained, "Whatever your reasons are, a man is only as good as his word. When I gave my word, I wasn't giving it for three months. I agreed to help put down the rebellion, for as long as it took. I know that even if I live through the war, I won't see Elizabeth very much while the war is going on. Other men may move ahead of me at the bank. You may think that sounds strange, since I'm married to the president's daughter. But Mr. Gault has very strict views about earning your place. He told me that he did not make me a vice president because of his daughter, and I believe him. I respect him for that. So the time I lose at the bank could hurt my plans, and make it harder on my family. In fact, we'll have to put off having a family until I get back. But none of that matters. A man has to do what is right, and defending the Union is the right thing to do."

"Aren't you scared about not coming back at all?" I asked.

"Sure," he replied. "But I could just as easily get killed in three months as I could in three years."

That didn't make sense to me. "Hold on a second. Going into battle for three years is pushing luck a lot more than going into battle for three months. In three years you are going to be in a lot more fights than you would in three months."

Michael explained his logic. "If God determines that I won't make it through this war, then time doesn't matter." I couldn't really argue with the power of God, so I just kept quiet.

My conversation with Patrick and Davey was much shorter. They both had joined up to get a job to be able to send money home.

"Shoot," said Davey. "Time don't matter none to me. My family needs the money. They're gonna need it in two months and they're gonna need it in seven months. I got no other prospects anyway."

Patrick echoed Davey's sentiments. "We have to support our families, don't we now? Sure there ain't many jobs available for a fifty-seven year old Irish man with no skills. We'll be stayin' in the army for as long as they'll have us."

I thought a lot about what to do. Despite what Michael said, my gut told me that the chances of getting killed increased a whole lot between three months and three years. Also, my plans to read for the law would have to be put off. But when I enlisted, like Michael, I gave my word to fight to put down the rebellion. I didn't think of it as fighting for three months only. I truly expected this war to be over in less than three months.

That's the reason I was in such a hurry to join. I didn't want to miss the fight. I still expected the war would be over in three months, although the government's insistence on a promise to serve for three years made me wonder about my assumption. But I realized that if they had asked for a three year undertaking when I joined up, I would have given it. So why should I hesitate now?

I decided to accept the three years. I had to take another oath since the army didn't share my view that when I signed up it was for the duration of the war anyway. Next I had to face the awful task of telling my parents about my decision.

Families visited the camp regularly. During one of these visits, many, including mine, heard for the first time from their sons that they decided to enlist for three years, and not the three months the families had known about. I dreaded telling my parents about my longer obligation, but it had to be done. It was a beautiful spring day when I saw my mother and father. Warm but not hot with a nice breeze. But for me it might just as well have been a torrential rain, I was so afraid of this meeting.

My parents came over to me and I got the usual hugs and kisses from my mother. "Oh, mein baby," my mother almost shouted, "it's so good to see you."

"Please, Mama, don't call me baby in front of the other boys."

My father just smiled, but my mother said, maybe even louder, "And why not? You are mein baby."

I gave up. Instead I replied, "Mama, Papa, I have something important to tell you."

Before I could say another word, my mother practically yelled, "What? Are you sick? Did those other boys hurt you?"

"No, no. I'm not sick or hurt. The army has told us that we have to join up for at least three years, not just 90 days."

"Can you say no?" my father asked somberly.

"Yes, I can refuse, but then I won't be allowed in the army. The 14th Brooklyn is a militia unit. If we want to fight in the war, we have to be in the regular army and agree to the three years."

"I spit on the army!" my mother shouted and began to cry. "You are my only child, mein Kindela. They should be cursed forever before they take you for that long!"

I tried to be gentle and firm at the same time. "Mama, I'm going to do it. I signed up to fight in the war, and that's what I'm going to do. I'm sorry you feel this way."

"And how else should I feel? Three years is so long. More bad things can happen to you." She sobbed quietly.

Thank God for my father. He gently put his arm around my mother and said, "Son, I know you're doing what you believe is right. Your mother, she's upset, but she'll get over it. When I was your age, the same thing would I have done. We will hope and pray you'll come back from the war after it's over, just like we would have hoped and prayed you came back after three months."

I embraced my parents. My mother was still crying. Michael just happened to be walking by at the time, so I introduced him. My mother apologized for her tears, and said, "Ach, I'm sorry I am crying, but it's because now they want mein baby to agree to serve for three years." I was embarrassed again at being called her baby, but Michael seemed not to notice. Anyway, my mother wasn't finished. "We left behind our beautiful home in Vienna and came to America to find a safe place for us and our boy. Now he is agreeing to go to war for years. That is not safe! Three months is bad, three years is terrible! Did you agree to that, too?"

Michael answered her directly. "Mrs. Muller, I believed it was the right thing, so I did it." I had told my mother about Michael from the Brooklyn Savings Bank, and that he was from an old-time Brooklyn family. The news that he had signed on too seemed to calm her.

Whether it was because she thought he was smarter, or because he was richer and had better prospects, the fact that Michael signed up for three years made it easier for my mother to accept my decision to do the same.

We talked some more about home. Michael was charming and my mother was captivated. By the end of the conversation she seemed almost glad because the additional time would mean that I could be with Michael longer. I knew she was still afraid of losing me, but Michael's confident tone gave her assurance. Mama was also impressed that a man from such a family would treat me as an equal, and speak to her as an equal. Suddenly the army wasn't such a bad place.

Practically all of the boys in the regiment agreed to the additional time commitment. Bernard Carney told me that seventeen of the boys in the Regiment refused to sign up for three years, and that they would be left behind in Brooklyn while we went South. They would be discharged after their three month enlistments were up.

My first thought was that those seventeen lacked either patriotism or courage, or both. Then I thought about it more, and realized that I was wrong to jump to conclusions. Those boys may have had other commitments, or figured that their families could get along without them for three months, but not for three years. They may have needed the boys' earnings at home, or needed them to work farms or stores. My parents would be all right with the money I would be able to send home. The same might not be true for other boys. Each of us had to make our own decision based on our own circumstances. There was no right or wrong.

CHAPTER SEVEN

May 18, 1861

On the afternoon of May 18th, the drums sounded assembly and the regiment formed to head south. Since Colonel Wood was already in Washington, arranging for us to be inducted into the United States Army, Lieutenant Colonel Fowler was in command. He was a striking figure. His sword was drawn, and he looked like he could take on the entire southern army right then and there.

Everyone stood at rigid attention waiting for the direction to march. The order came and the ranks broke with the band playing "The Girl I Left Behind Me." The regiment moved out and the cheers from the crowd were deafening. We left Fort Greene Park and went onto Myrtle Avenue where the citizens were pushing as close as they could get to try to have one last look and a farewell word for a son or a neighbor.

The boys seemed to want to shake hands with everybody and bid them good-bye, even total strangers. The citizens seemed to want to touch us soldiers just as much. I must have greeted hundreds of people who I had never seen before. From Myrtle Avenue we marched on to Fulton Street and then to the ferry where we were to go to Jersey City to get the train heading south. All along the route people were shouting their good wishes.

When we boarded the ferry for Jersey City, people were yelling and waving like we were family members leaving home for a grand holiday. Everyone was smiling and laughing, including us. The ferry ride itself was wonderful. There was a cooling spring breeze with a refreshing scent that made you feel like everything was going to be fine today. As we cut across the Hudson River, the boys were in a great mood. We joked about how many secess we were going to kill. This wasn't a war, it was an adventure.

After we landed in Jersey City, we marched to the train station and got more greetings and congratulations along the route. The train station in Jersey City was an impressive two story brick building about 500 feet long. There were towers in each corner that added to its height and impressiveness. I was told it was only four years old, and it sure looked new. It was exciting to be there on my way to war, and the people's elation only added to my excitement. I approached the train with a bounce in my step. The other boys seemed to feel the same way.

It was strange getting all this attention. I realized that all the hoopla wasn't really for me. They didn't know me. It was for what me and all the other boys were doing: going to war to fight for the Union.

In the crowd of boys in the train station I lost sight of Michael, but I saw Bernard Carney waiting to get on the train. I made my way over to him to talk and see what information he had.

"Hey, Bernard, this is some crowd, huh?"

"Yeah, Jack, it's nice, but there was an even bigger crowd here earlier this year. Did you know that in February, President Lincoln stopped right here on his way to his inauguration? He came to New Jersey on a ferry just like us—only we came from Brooklyn, and Mr. Lincoln came from New York City. He spoke right here in Jersey City to a crowd of 25,000 people who gave him a huge ovation. That was a little surprising because Mr. Lincoln lost New Jersey to Stephen Douglas in the election. I think the people were telling him they supported a united nation. I still remember some of his speech that I read in the Brooklyn Eagle. Mr. Lincoln said something like, 'We desire to live in harmony with our brothers as of old, asking from them only what is fair, and giving them the same in return; this, I am sure, sir, is the unanimous sentiment of the people of New Jersey.' Isn't that powerful?" Bernard asked.

"It sure is," I replied. "How do you remember all that?"

"First of all," Bernard answered, "the message got to me. The man impressed me and so did his ideas. Second, reporters need good memories to be able to report accurately."

My opinions about Bernard and Mr. Lincoln both went up a lot.

Mr. Lincoln must be quite a man, I thought. I'll go to war for what he believes because that was what I believe too. As Bernard and I were speaking, we inched up to the train and I got a good look at it.

I'd never been on a train before. It was huge. Before I got on I could see that at its head was an old black engine. At the front of the engine were vertical bars angled forward and downward to move obstacles off the track. Behind the engine there was a car carrying logs of wood to fuel the engine, and then there were a number of passenger cars. I could see each car had rows of benches with an aisle down the middle. The benches were wooden and each one could probably seat two or three of us. If there weren't enough seats, the boys could sit in the aisle, which probably wasn't much less comfortable than the benches.

When Bernard and I entered the train car many of the seats were already filled, so we could not sit together. That was fine with me. I expected that I wouldn't be talking a lot on the ride because I wanted to look out the window and see everything I could. If I had been sitting next to Bernard, I suspect I would be doing more speaking; or more likely listening.

The train finally got going and the sights I saw were amazing. We passed by buildings, fields and some livestock. Now that I think about it, these sights themselves weren't so strange. But when you're speeding along at 15 to 20 miles an hour, everything looks different. When a shack flies by, it turns it into a grand house in my mind. I kept saying, "look at that" to no one in particular. When I looked around the train car at the other boys, I saw that I was not the only one whose mouth was hanging open in awe.

Some of the boys tried to act worldly, not showing any emotion. I thought this was because they were embarrassed to look like children on an outing. I wasn't embarrassed at all.

When we arrived at Newark Station in New Jersey, we had a small rear end collision with another train that bumped us. No one was hurt so we rode on. We were going to war, and there was no time to make a fuss. After leaving Newark, we were ordered to load our muskets. The word going around was that the officers were worried about trouble along the line. That made sense since we were at war, and loading our muskets sure was a reminder of that fact. The boys looked a little more serious after that.

Everything was peaceful as we pulled into Philadelphia station about 7 AM. We had to switch trains and there was a considerable wait while the baggage was moved to the other train. Instead of trouble, we were treated like heroes. The matrons of the city invited us into their homes for coffee and cakes that were made especially for us. They also let us use their washrooms to get rid of some of the dust we picked up on the trip. Clean and with full bellies, we gave the women three hearty cheers as we pulled out of the station.

The trip from Philadelphia to Baltimore was mostly uneventful. I continued to watch the scenery as we passed by. At first, there were still people applauding us and waving at our train, but when we crossed into Maryland, things changed. There were troops at all the bridges and other points along the rail line. Fewer people hurrahed as we passed, and I wondered what was going on.

I saw houses that were some of the finest I have ever seen. The view would've been beautiful, but it was marred by the large number of picket guards I could see from the train. I didn't understand why there were soldiers on guard duty when at least some people were yelling for us. If they were wishing us well, why did they have to be guarded? So I walked down the aisle of the train until I found Bernard Carney, my unfailing source of information, and asked him what was the story.

Bernard explained to me that the people of Maryland were divided between pro union and pro rebel beliefs. "I heard that they had to sneak President Lincoln into Washington because they were afraid there would be an assassination attempt. But it was actually because of a different incident in Baltimore that we now have all these Union soldiers guarding the train line."

"What incident?" I asked.

"You see, the train from Philadelphia doesn't go all the way to Washington. The last stop is Baltimore and our boys will have to march through the city to get to the other train line which will take us to Washington. Sometime in the middle of April, the Sixth Massachusetts was heading to Washington, just like us. In Baltimore they got off the train to take horse-drawn carriages to get across town to the other railroad station where the train to Washington was waiting for them. A mob of secessionists blocked the carriages. I guess they wanted to stop the Sixth Massachusetts from reaching the train to Washington. The boys ended up getting off the carriages and marching to the station. But the mob followed them through town. The boys were jeered and then the mob started throwing bricks and stones at them. The Sixth Massachusetts had to fight their way to the station, opening fire on the rioters in the mob. If I remember correctly, something like four soldiers and 12 rioters were killed."

"That's terrible!" I was shocked at the idea of American civilians attacking soldiers. That's not war where two armies fight honorably. That's just rioting. Innocent civilians, who didn't sign up to fight, could be killed. It made me think of the revolution and riots that had led my family to escape Austria.

"I know it is," said Bernard, sharing my view. "That's not fighting a war. That's having private citizens fight your war for you. It's cowardly. Those rebs will stop at nothing. Anyway, after the incident with the Sixth Massachusetts, bigwigs in Maryland demanded that the government stop sending soldiers through their state. Well, that wouldn't work because the train route from up north to Washington goes through Baltimore. So the soldiers kept going through Maryland. Secessionists burned bridges and cut telegraph lines, so we answered by sending in soldiers to occupy Baltimore. That's why you see so many soldiers out the windows. You probably also see some signs of burned bridges that had to be rebuilt."

"I did see that. Thanks for the information, but what are we going to do when we get to Baltimore?"

"You'll see," Bernard replied in a serious tone. After I got back to my seat and thought about his comments, I realized that he probably had no more idea of what was to come than I did.

Sure enough, as we approached Baltimore we received orders. We were told that after we got off the train in Baltimore we were to fix bayonets on our already loaded muskets. I hoped that the bayonets were for show to scare off the southern sympathizers, and that we wouldn't have to use them. I sure didn't like the idea of stabbing some civilians with my bayonet.

We were also ordered not to speak to anyone, unless it was to answer civil questions. And then, we were to use as few words as possible. Finally, we weren't to accept food or drink for fear of poisoning.

At Baltimore we got off the train and formed up as ordered in columns with four boys in each row. We marched down Pratt Street, east to Camden Station where we would get the train to Washington. Like our march through Brooklyn, the streets of Baltimore were crowded on both sides. Unlike Brooklyn, however, the crowds in Baltimore were much quieter. Children and ladies yelled and clapped for the union and waved flags, but the men seemed much more careful about showing Union sympathies. I guess they were scared of starting a fight with those on the southern side in the crowd. We heard a couple of shouts for Jeff Davis, the rebel president, but everything seemed peaceful enough. One pretty girl offered me some flowers, and if we were in Brooklyn I would've gone up to her and talked a bit. But here in Baltimore I wouldn't step out of formation. So she threw them to me. Because of what I learned from Bernard about Marylanders, and the orders we were given not to speak,

I was scared that she was just a ruse to get me out of line and alone. Then some southerner would kill himself a Union soldier. If the purpose of the orders we were given was to keep us watchful, they worked. We marched mostly in silence, and in excellent order.

There were no incidents during our march to Camden Station, where we got the train for Washington. We arrived in Washington on Sunday, May 19, about 24 hours after we left

Brooklyn. It amazed me. I thought about what it must have been like before railroads. During the Revolutionary War, this trip, with all our baggage, would've taken more than a week of marching. Times have changed, but I'm not sure if being better at making war is progress or not.

It was hot and raining when we got to Washington at about 7 o'clock in the evening. It had been getting warmer as we headed south. Now that we were in Washington, I thought spring here felt like summer in Brooklyn. We were quickly assigned barracks. I was put in one of the two vacant stores used by our regiment, on Pennsylvania Avenue near the Union Hotel. Companies C and E were assigned to stay at the home of Daniel Sickles, a politician who had been made an officer in the Union Army. Since I wanted to study law, I was familiar with Mr. Sickles' history, and would have loved to stay at his house. In 1859, Mr. Sickles was found not guilty of murder because of temporary insanity after he shot down his wife's lover in cold blood in the middle of the street. The victim, Barton Key, was a lawyer and the son of then Congressman Francis Scott Key who wrote the famous poem about the defense of Fort McHenry. This was the first time the legal defense of temporary insanity was used successfully, and I found the whole case fascinating. Despite Mr. Sickle's checkered past, he was made a Union officer and was presently away with his troops. So the Regiment was allowed to use his house for some of our troops.

Michael, Patrick, and Davey were all staying in the same vacant store as me. After settling into our temporary barracks, we were all tired from our trip and went to sleep. We didn't have to report for duty for a couple of days while the higher ups decided where we would camp. So in the morning, when we were refreshed, all the boys wanted to explore the area and see some sights. I knew what I wanted to see because I had heard about the Patent Office and the Post Office buildings and really wanted to go there. My friends, including Michael, offered to go with me. Over the next two days that we were in Washington, we did a lot of exploring. Since this was all new to them too, most of the time our mouths were hanging open and our eyes were wide.

We walked around a lot but eventually got to the Patent Office, a couple of blocks from Pennsylvania Avenue on West 7th Street. The building was more than just impressive. It reminded me of those ancient Greek temples I had read about. Steps led up to the entrance of a large two- story building, and ten columns surrounded the wide doors. On top of the building was a roof coming to a point with carvings done in it. The sides of the building were equally impressive with their own columns.

When we first saw it, Davey said, "This building is beautiful. And so big! It would take me ten minutes just to walk around it!"

Patrick agreed, "It seems to take up at least two blocks, don't it now?"

"It has to be big," I said, "because I read somewhere that patent law requires every inventor to submit a scale model of his invention. The patent office puts them on display here. That's why I was really interested in seeing this building. I thought it would be a great way to look at all the new things that we have around us."

"That's a great idea," Michael said. "One of the things I noticed about you right away was your curiosity. You seemed interested in everything, and I like that. We can all learn a whole bunch of things just by being around you as you satisfy your curiosity. Let's go in and see what's inside."

The building had skylights and interior lights that made it as bright as daylight. Models were everywhere. However, the biggest surprise came when we saw barracks on the top floor gallery. There were three tier bunk beds right next to glass display cases showing new inventions.

"Well, look at that," Davey almost shouted. "Boys are sleeping here! Them bunk beds don't look comfortable. We're better sleepin' on the floor than around displays that could fall on us in the middle of the night. I'll bet that glass ain't gonna last long with all them boys staying here. I hope they don't take them invention models as souvenirs."

"You seem more interested in the barracks than in the inventions," I teased.

"No," Davey said. "It's just that we ain't gotten to any farm equipment yet. I think that the telegraph and them other things we've been seeing are fine inventions, but I don't use them."

Patrick agreed with Davey's reasoning that what we were seeing didn't mean anything to him. Patrick was the most practical man I've ever met. If something didn't directly apply to his life, he didn't need to know about it. I was going to explain how the telegraph did affect his life, then thought better of it and kept quiet. Patrick was a good man, but set in his ways. Michael, however, was a born teacher and seemed to need to explain to Patrick how these inventions did apply to him.

"Patrick, these inventions do have an impact on you and Davey, even if you can't see it right away. Sometimes it's because the full effect hasn't been felt yet. Take the telegraph, for example. You think that it does not affect you, but it does, and it will. The telegraph can save your life. It can send information about the rebels, like where they are, how many men they have, and what direction they're going. That information would be really important to know when you're planning on fighting them. It could be the difference between you surviving the fight, or you walking into a trap and getting killed in the action. And when this war is over, you can still get useful information. Patrick and Davey, wouldn't you like to know where there are jobs to be had? If the telegraph sent word that the Navy Yard was hiring, wouldn't that be good to know? No telling what other information can be passed on and used by you. Information could be useful in ways you might not even think of now."

I could see Patrick thinking about what Michael said. "You know, Michael, you might be right, but we'll just stick to what we know, meanin' no disrespect." he said.

"None taken. You do whatever makes you comfortable, Patrick." Michael responded good-naturedly.

After Michael's comments, though, Davey became more interested in everything. He was like a curious child. Then I thought, he is a child; only 14 years old, and everything was new to him.

"What's this musket doing here?" Davey asked. "That's not a new invention."

I replied, "The whole musket may not be new. If some part of the musket like the trigger or the barrel has some new development, then that would be patented, and a scale model of the whole musket would be submitted to show how the new part works with the whole."

"Oh, what could be new about the barrel?" Davey asked. "Ain't it just a long tube?"

Here Michael came to my rescue. "I've read a number of military manuals so I know that aside from being made with a different metal, newer barrels are rifled which makes them shoot straighter and farther. The old barrels were just long tubes, but somebody found out that by cutting grooves inside it, the bullet or minie ball goes through straighter because the heat in the grooves from the gunpowder going off keeps the minie ball from rattling in the barrel. Old muskets were accurate for only 20 to 30 yards. With rifling, you can shoot accurately at more than 100 yards. That means you will be able to reload and shoot again at least once before the enemy is on you. The extra shots can really mean a lot when you are being attacked."

"Wow," Davey said, "I didn't know that. These things are more interestin' than I thought."

Michael wasn't done impressing Davey. "And look here. That's a paper cartridge. It doesn't look like much, but it makes a big difference. It used to be that men would carry around a pouch of musket balls and a separate container for the gunpowder, usually an animal's horn. When you were loading, you had to go from one to the other container, estimate how much gunpowder to use, and hope you got the right amount. Now we just bite into the paper holder to tear it open, and it's all there--the bullet and the right amount of gunpowder. It makes loading simpler and faster."

Davey practically bounced with enthusiasm. "Darn if you ain't right. It was a good idea to come here. This place is a lot more fun than I thought it would be. I got a real hankering to keep looking at stuff."

We walked around the patent office for a long time looking at the items in the display cases. Then we headed over to the post office which was just across the street.

"This is an awful big building, too," said Davey, "but not as big as the patent office. Why did ya want to come here?"

"One of the boys told me that the post office handles about 60 letters every day from each of the regiments, give or take. That's thousands of letters a day." I answered. "And the secessionists use Union postage so that even more letters come through here. I just wondered how they could handle all that. Now that I see the size of the building - about one whole block - I guess they have lots of people to do it."

We weren't allowed to see how the operation worked. They probably figured that we would interfere with what they were doing. So we walked around the block and continued exploring Washington.

The next day, Michael, Patrick, Davey and I continued our sightseeing.. We went to the Capitol which was also not far from where we were staying. Since the Senate was not in session we walked right into its chamber. I found the desk marked, "Sen. Stephen A. Douglas." I sat there and thought about him. Mr. Douglas was a favorite of my father, who believed Senator Douglas would have made a fine president. My father went to hear him speak, and when he got home, he laughingly said, "That little man had everyone in the room convinced that he was a giant, even though he was really only about 5 feet tall!" My father really admired him, and so I did too.

Michael, Patrick, and Davey came up to me while I was sitting at Mr. Douglas' desk, and Davey asked, "Jack, what are you doin'?"

I replied, "I'm sitting where a great Senator, Mr. Stephen A. Douglas, sits, just thinking about him and my home."

Patrick asked," Why'd it make you think of home?"

"Because my father spoke so highly of Senator Douglas. People call him the 'Little Giant' because he's only about 5 feet tall, but such a big force for good in the country. My father thought Mr. Douglas could've kept us out of the war by having states that entered the union vote on whether they wanted slavery or not. Now, when we need people like the Senator the most, he's very sick and can't help."

"That's sure a shame," said Davey.

"Yes, but we are in the war," said Patrick, "so there's no use in thinking about what might have been, is there now?" On that practical note, I got up, and we continued wandering.

Although there was plenty more to see in Washington, we didn't have the time because we moved to our camp after only two days. We left our temporary quarters on May 22nd, marching down Pennsylvania Avenue to 14th Street to Meridian Hill, where we went into camp with a number of other regiments.

Meridian Hill was like a tent city with row after row of tents and an open field for drilling. The tents were different from the ones at Fort Greene in Brooklyn, which were like Indian teepees, while the ones at Meridian Hill were shaped like the letter A, but with vertical sides at the bottom to give them greater height. There was a horizontal pole at the top and two vertical poles at each end to hold the canvas up.

Our tents on Meridian Hill could hold eight boys each. Much to my disappointment, I was not with Michael. Boys were assigned to tents based on the amount of time they had been with the 14th Brooklyn. My company had 12 tents, with two rows of six facing each other. Where your tent was placed mattered because some locations were better than others. They might be nearer to water or to the commissary. This made a difference when the boys whose job it was to get rations for everyone in the tent had to walk over to the commissary and carry the food back.

Each tent elected a captain, and the boys living there had to follow the orders of the captain just as if the captain was a real officer. The captain appointed two boys to get food, two to bring water, two to clean the tent, and two to wash the dishes.

So based on time with the 14th, Michael ended up sharing a tent with Steve Cooper, Robert Lewis, George Hudson, Peter Glasson, and Bill Shannon. All of those boys had been with the regiment for more than two years. Because of their length of service they received certain benefits. Their location was well placed nearer to the commissary and the creek. And although it was an eight person tent, the six of them were the only ones assigned to it.

I was lucky to be with Davey and Patrick. We had five other boys in the tent, all of whom were also new to the regiment. There was Bernard Carney, so we would know all the news in the regiment, and John McNamee, William Dakin, Lawrence Staunton, and Hugh Doharty.

Those four boys were all in their twenties, and seemed to be nice fellows. Even though I was not with Michael, I got to see him a lot, and our friendship continued to grow.

CHAPTER EIGHT

May 23, 1861

The day after we arrived in camp, on May 23rd, the 14th Brooklyn was mustered into the United States Army for the period of three years. General Irwin McDowell, the head of our army, swore us in. McDowell looked the part. He was a stocky man, about average height, in his mid 40's. His double-breasted uniform was clean and well pressed, and his saber was shining. The 14th formed three sides of a square around him as he led us in the oath. The flags of the United States and the regiment were at the head of the square. After the oath, the general told us that we were now the 14th New York State Militia.

This was the first time most of us realized that the name of our regiment would be changed, and we didn't like it. "That's horse crap!" said Robert Simmons, who was standing on one side of me. "I joined the 14th Brooklyn, and I'm gonna fight for it, not some outfit called the 14th New York State Militia." This sentiment was echoed throughout the ranks.

There was real grumbling among the boys about this renaming.

After we were dismissed from the ceremony the officers went around letting the boys know that the army had its own system for naming regiments, and they would not name one for a city. Regiments were named for states. The boys didn't care about customs or systems. We joined the 14th Brooklyn, and that was where our loyalty lay. Later on we heard that General McDowell himself ordered that the regiment could continue to be called the 14th Brooklyn. That was our first win in the war, and even though it was against our own army, it felt good.

We stayed at Camp Wood for almost 6 weeks, until July 2nd, and it was an easy time. The heat was a bother but we were getting used to it. We drilled, did guard and picket duty, and had a lot of free time. The drilling was mostly in the morning when it was not so hot. We practiced by squad, company and regiment. Just as Michael had told me that first day in camp, the squads had about ten to twenty five soldiers, while the companies were made up of a number of squads and had about 100 soldiers. The regiment was supposed to be about 10 companies with 1,000 fellows, but we were short of that number and expected more recruits any day.

I followed Michael around like a puppy dog, and he was a good sport about it. At times I wondered why he was so patient with me. Eventually I guessed that I was that longed-for kid brother that Michael never had. That was fine with me.

One day I spoke to Michael about it. "Michael, can I ask you something?"

"You can ask me anything."

"Do you think of me as sort of a little brother?"

He paused before his answer. "Well. I haven't thought about it at all until you just asked, but now that you mention it, I guess so. You make a good kid brother. You're smart, eager to learn, willing to fight for what you believe in, and good company. And your base ball is improving," he concluded with a grin.

"Thanks, I think you're a great brother, too. If I got to choose my brother, it would be you." I probably sounded pretty pompous, but I meant every word.

"Thanks, Jack."

If possible, my friendship with Michael was even stronger after our little talk. Michael explained things to me like how the drilling was necessary to practice moving the boys in battle. Marching looked like a fine parade to me, but I didn't see the need for it.

Michael asked me, "If you need a company of 100 men to move from one place to another, what would you do?" I replied, "I would tell them where to go, and to get moving." Michael chuckled and said, "And that would be a fine mess. Men would be running this way and that, unable to shoot at the enemy because their own men would be in front of them. Drilling teaches you how to move groups of men from one place to another so they can form up a line of fire in the shortest time, and not be shooting one another. The idea is to have the most guns firing at the enemy as possible. If the rebels turn out to be at your flank, or side, the officers can have you wheel right or wheel left so the men can change the direction of their firing quickly. We drill so much because you have to be able to do these movements in your sleep. Remember, the enemy will be shooting at you while you're doing these things, and you can't even fire back until you're in position. It takes courage to move like that under fire, as well as confidence that the other men are all doing the movements the right way. If some of them mess up, and your line doesn't wheel, the men are in danger of being flanked."

I learned a lot from Michael, and enjoyed the talks. Michael also helped me use all the free time. You could not leave camp without a pass. They were not hard to get, but there was a limit on how many boys could leave camp at one time. Also, getting a pass took time, mostly waiting in line. I heard a non-commissioned officer complaining about his lack of time because he was always dealing with passes. "Somebody comes for a pass to go for wood or water, and as soon as they are served another comes for a pass to go and wash himself in the brook."

Originally you needed a non-commissioned officer to accompany the boy with the pass wherever he went outside the lines, and to bring the boy back. But that just took too much time, since the brook where you got water was a half mile away, and you needed to go further and further from camp as the firewood close to camp was used up. Soon the pass itself was enough. But since there was usually a long line waiting to get a pass, most of the boys just stayed in camp. They talked, played cards, wrote letters, or had a catch with a bunch of rags tied up to be a base ball.

Base ball was one of the things Michael and I talked about a lot. I had watched the games Company B played at Fort Greene Park in Brooklyn. Michael organized that team and lined up games against other companies. Michael and I also played catch a lot, both at Fort Greene and here.

One day my secret wish came true. Michael asked me to join the team. "Jack, how'd you like to play for the company team? E. J. Blake accidentally shot himself in the leg while he was cleaning his musket, so we need a right fielder. The wound isn't that serious, and he should make a full recovery. But he certainly won't be playing base ball for at least a month or more. I've seen you catch and throw, and you're good. You have a strong arm, and it's accurate. I just know you'll be able to hit the ball. Also balls aren't hit to right field all that often. Most of the strikers are right handed so they generally hit it to left field or on the ground. So how about it? Will you play?"

I replied without hesitation, "Sure, sounds like fun." I also thought it would give me more time to spend with Michael.

"Great. We have a game tomorrow against Company C, who have a strong team. When the war started, they ended up with a few recruits from some of the best teams in Brooklyn. They have a great infield. Henry Libby played second base for the Excelsiors, Charley Pearce played first base for the Atlantics and Frank Marshall played third base for the Eckfords. Last year, the Excelsiors and the Atlantics played for the championship. What a series that was!"

"What happened? Who won?" I asked.

"Well, it was a three game series, and the Excelsiors and the Atlantics split the first two games. The Excelsiors won the first game handily, but lost the second game by one run. They played the third game at the Putnam Base Ball Club's field because it was supposed to be neutral territory. There must have been 15,000 people at the game."

"So what happened?"

"Unfortunately, the game was determined by the crowd."
"The crowd? That doesn't make any sense."

"Well, listen to what happened." Michael said in a tone that I had come to know when he was about to give me a lesson on some subject. I liked his lectures, so when he spoke like that I was anxious to hear the rest. "Early on in the game, the people started to get angry when one of the Atlantics refused to obey the umpire's call. Eventually, he did what the umpire said, but by then the crowd was getting loud and ugly. Then, in the top of the sixth inning the Excelsiors were ahead eight to six, but some of the people in the crowd, who supported the Atlantics, began again to curse the umpire about his earlier call, and generally act rowdy. Joseph Leggett, the captain of the Excelsiors, warned that his team would withdraw if the crowd's behavior continued. Members of the Atlantics asked their supporters to quiet down and let the game continue. It didn't help. The hooligans just got more disorderly. Finally, Leggett ordered his players off the field. A mob followed the Excelsiors and threw stones at their omnibus as they left. So the Atlantics won even though the Excelsiors were ahead when they left the field. I heard later that the cause of the trouble was gamblers who had a lot of money on the Atlantics and were not going to let the Excelsiors win a close game."

"Wow, that's some story." I said, "There was a lot of cheering and yelling at the games I saw, but nothing I would call roughneck."

Michael nodded his head. "That's right, and that's the way it should be." Michael's hands were moving as he talked, and became more excited with what he was talking about. I knew something about the game really bothered him because Michael wasn't usually so animated when he talked. "I believe that gamblers caused the trouble at the Atlantics - Excelsiors game, and that got me very angry. There's no place for gambling in sports. It leads to bad people trying to affect the results of the game by cheating. Thankfully, we don't have that problem here. The games are supposed to be fun. And if they turned into something else, the officers would put a stop to it."

"Thanks for giving me a chance to play."

"Happy to have you aboard. I know you'll do well!"

Easy enough for Michael to say, I thought. I was already getting scared just thinking about playing in the game tomorrow. Could this be what it felt like to go into battle? Actually, I thought I was more nervous now than I would be heading into battle. In battle, I could be killed and it would be over. Here, I could be humiliated in front of all my friends, and it would stay with me for the rest of my life. What had I been thinking, agreeing to play base ball? There were boys on the

Company teams who had played the game for years, and some had even been on championship teams.

The next day, there must have been three hundred soldiers standing around or sitting on the grass, waiting for the game to start. I saw Bernard Carney in the crowd and laughingly wondered if he thought he was reporting on the game for the Brooklyn Eagle.

We were on the drill field. Someone had laid out the base ball diamond, using rags for the bases with a stone on each to keep it from being moved by the wind—except home base. That one was a round piece of wood about the size of a barrel top. I looked closer. It actually was a barrel top. Michael saw me standing there, and came over to me. "You look a little nervous, Jack. Don't worry. I've seen you throw and catch, and I know that you're fast on your feet. Hitting the ball is just a matter of keeping your eye on it as it comes in, and swinging the bat around to hit it. It's like swinging a sledge hammer at a spike. I know you've done that in the shipyard. Only you're swinging even with the ground rather than down. You'll be fine. We'll be using the ball I brought from home, so you're used to it from our catches. And the bat I brought is just the same as a stick or the handle of a hammer like the ones you've used at the Navy Yard."

I don't know why, but as usual I felt better after Michael spoke to me. "Thanks, Michael. I'll do my best."

"That's all we can ask." Michael replied. "Let's get out in the field. I met with their captain, and we worked out that we will be the home team, so Company C bats first. Remember you're in right field. You should stand between first base and second base about forty feet behind the line between those bases. Just catch whatever is hit to you, then throw the ball to Steve Cooper who is playing second base. Got it?"

"Got it," I replied.

We went out to our positions as Company C came to bat. Our nine was composed mostly of Michael's tent mates, Peter Glasson, first base, Bill Shannon, catcher, Steve Cooper, second base and Robert Lewis, shortstop. The others were Hans Hovey, left field, Tom Abbott, third base, George McIntyre, pitcher, with Michael in center field, and me in right field.

The umpire, Captain Jordan from Company A, yelled "Play ball!" It was a good idea to have an officer umpire the game, so there would be no arguing with him about his calls. I'd heard that Jordan had been a lawyer and played for the Excelsiors before the war. Michael had told me about the make up of some of the Brooklyn teams. The Excelsiors were made up of doctors, lawyers, merchants and professional men. Other teams attracted different types of men. The Atlantics had a lot of players in the food preparation business, like butchers, while the Eckfords were mostly mechanics. Michael mentioned to me that after the war, if I got on a team with lawyers it could be good for my hoped-for legal career.

All these different types of people shared one thing—a love of base ball. I loved it too. But I wasn't sure I would continue to love it if I made a fool of myself today.

Company C's first batter was Rudy Smith, their shortstop. He singled to left field. I sighed in relief as the ball went to the other field. The next batter was Henry Libby, their second baseman. He hit a ball in the air--- oh my Lord, it was coming to me in right field. I thought that I could catch it, but then I remembered Michael telling me that if I caught it on one bounce the batter would be out anyway. So I thought I would make it easy on myself and let the ball bounce, and then catch it. I never thought that the ball could hit a pebble, take a crazy bounce and be out of my reach. But that's what happened. I recovered as quickly as I could and threw the ball to Steve Cooper, who then threw it sharply to Peter Glasson playing first base. I wondered what that was all about. Then I saw it. Libby had overrun first base. Peter casually tagged him just as easy as you please. Libby was out, and I was off the hook. The crowd was cheering Steve and Peter's great playing. They seemed, thankfully, to have forgotten my mess up that started it.

I learned some quick lessons. Don't overrun a base. Catch whatever you can. Don't try to out-think the ball or the ground. No short-cuts.

Steve and Peter showed me some fine fielding, and the other players seemed to be just as good—except me. We got two more outs on grounders to the infield, one to Tom Abbott at third and the other to Robert Lewis at shortstop. I was impressed, and worried even more about not messing up.

After the third out, we ran in to bat. Michael met me as soon as I reached our side of the field. "Don't worry about that missed ball. It happens to all of us, and we got the runner out anyway. This game is supposed to be fun and I want you to have fun playing it." I felt a little better.

Our side could hit, as well as play in the field. Our first four strikers all got hits. It seemed like no time before we had scored four runs, with two outs in between. Hans Hovey and Tom Abbott had hit the ball well, but Company C's center fielder Jim Swan made two nice catches. I found out later that Jim had played on the Atlantics before the war, and was considered a top base ball player. On our side, George Mcintyre and Peter Glasson both singled, and then it was up to the last man in the batting order—me. I watched two pitches come in, but I was too afraid to swing. The umpire gave me a warning after the third pitch. Now if there were three hittable pitches, and I didn't swing, I would be called out without even trying. I could not let that happen. The next pitch came in, and I saw that it was within my reach. I had to swing. So I made believe it was a spike on a wall and my bat was the hammer, like Michael had suggested. I swung with all my might. I must have just grazed the top of the ball because the result was a slow ground ball that stopped about half way to third base. I ran as fast as I could to first base, and it was not until I touched first that I remembered the lesson I thought I had learned; don't over-run the base. I tried stopping, but I had gone about five feet beyond first base before I could. I turned to run back, and saw that Company C's third baseman had thrown the ball wildly to first base. There was no way Charlie Pearce, Company C's first baseman, could hope to catch the ball. So I turned and headed for second base as the ball bounced into right field. I stopped at second base and saw that both base runners ahead of me had scored in the meantime. That was twice in one inning that I played badly, and each time I had been saved by chance.

How could I not love this game? We were ahead six to nothing, and the crowd was cheering for me. I was a base ball player.

Steve Cooper made the third out of the inning with a ground ball to first base that Charlie Pearce handled himself. We went back into the field, and I started to feel comfortable in the game. Both teams scored a number of runs, but Company C could not overcome the six run lead we got in the first inning. The final score was 16-12. I had three real hits in seven tries, and caught four balls that were hit to right field. There were a number of other hits to right field, and I fielded them and threw to Steve Cooper who knew what to do. All in all, I was very happy with the way the day turned out.

After the game we all received a lot of back slapping and congratulations from the boys in Company B. Even the boys in Company C were good sports, telling us we played a good game. The team itself got together later to relive the game and exchange stories. Steve started the conversation by telling everyone what a great game he had in the field, and at bat. He made it sound as if we would have lost the game without him. Steve looked in all directions. his eyes moving rapidly. I'd seen him do this before and I guessed it was a nervous habit. The other players knew Steve, and just chuckled. Bill blurted out with a big smile, "Yeah, Steve, you were great." Bill's big grin told everyone, except for Steve, that he was kidding. But Steve replied seriously, "Thanks, Bill." Robert Lewis was more of a trouble maker. He goaded Steve. "Come on, Steve, you know Michael is our best player, and he had a better game than you. More hits and great plays in the field. It's not even close."

Steve began fuming while Michael tried to deflect his temper. "Let's not argue, ok. We won the game and that's what's important."

"Oh, stop it!" Steve yelled. "You always try to say the proper thing, whether it's right or wrong. Be a man. If you think you are a better ball player than me, say so. If you think that you contributed more to our win today than I did, say that. But for God's sake, stop being Mister 'I am such a good person.' You're not. Friendship means little to you, for one thing." Steve stopped, almost as if he realized he had gone too far. Interestingly, no one came to Michael's defense. Bill, usually so friendly and back-slapping, looked serious and nodded his head. I saw Robert nod as well.

Everyone was quiet. This wasn't the first time I'd seen them argue after a game. And it wasn't friendly banter. It was mean, and they were practically all against Michael. Friends don't talk that way, and the nods from Bill and Robert made it worse.

I was about to say something when Peter spoke. "Alright, everyone, you act as if we lost the game. Arguing like this could adversely affect our performance in the next game. I suggest we change the topic to something we can all agree on, like how we are going to defeat the enemy in our upcoming confrontation." Thank goodness for Peter, I thought. He turned what could have been a brawl into a lively discussion about what good soldiers we are, and how we're going to crush the rebs.

After everyone calmed down and went their different ways, Michael came over to me and said, "You played well. I'm proud of you. For your first game it was very impressive. Did you have fun?" I replied that I did, and that I would like to keep playing on the team. "That's great." Michael said. "You'll only get better. As long as you enjoy it, you should keep playing."

"Thanks. Can I ask you something?"

"Of course. What do you want to know?" Michael probably thought that I was going to ask him some questions about base ball and the rules of the game. I must have surprised him when I asked, "What were those comments all about? You know, the ones where Steve said you weren't a good friend? And I think Bill and Robert were nodding their heads in agreement. What are they talking about?"

Michael hesitated. "Well, I had some run-ins with Steve, Bill, and Robert a while ago, and I'm surprised they still hold a grudge. I thought it was all forgotten. I know a little brother thinks his big brother is perfect, but I'm not. Some people think I've done some awful things. But they're personal, I won't talk about them. Just know that Steve, Bill and Robert are basically good fellows."

"It's just that I thought that those boys were your friends, and I didn't think friends talked that way to each other."

"Don't you worry about it. Everything is fine. I'm just glad you're part of the team. It will be a lot of fun."

Over the next couple of days, Michael's tent mates all told me that I had played well, especially for my first game. Bill Shannon gave me a bear hug, as his way of showing me that I was now part of the team. Steve, Peter, and Robert just shook my hand, which was fine with me. Tom, George, and Hans, the other members of the team, said they looked forward to playing with me again. I was feeling really good.

CHAPTER NINE

June 7, 1861

Camp life agreed with me. I liked the routine. Meals, drills, target practice, and base ball. We played more games and practiced when time allowed. I was seeing a lot of Michael. Besides regularly running into him in camp, the base ball practices and games also brought us together. He continued to be my example of what a good soldier and a good person should be. We talked a lot about home, our plans for the future, and, of course, the war.

"When do you think we'll move out?" I asked Michael for the tenth time. Or was it the twentieth time?

"I don't know, but it will probably be soon. People want this war to be over, and many of them believe that one big battle should do it."

"Don't you think that's true?"

"No, I don't," said Michael emphatically. "You know I've read a lot of books about military history and strategy. You helped me by translating the phrases that were in German. I think we have some good leaders in the Army. But I've also learned that it's the politicians, not the generals, who are making the decisions. The men in Washington will decide how to run the war, but they aren't fighting, and they won't feel it when the soldiers are hurt or tired. The politicos want to win, and as long as they have boys to use as cannon fodder, there's no reason for them to stop fighting. One big battle could lead to a lot of soldiers being hurt or killed, but there will be a lot more soldiers ready to go on fighting. And like I said, none of the government men will be injured, so the war will continue regardless of who wins the upcoming battle—which, of course, I hope we do."

"That's pretty depressing," I said. "You make it sound like I'm never going to get home to see my parents."

"That's not what I said," Michael replied. "I said the war is not going to end with the next battle. It will end when one side wins."

"What does that mean?" I asked.

"It means when one side gives up and surrenders all its armies. Right now the generals think that if you take the other side's capital, you win the war. So we're going to move out to capture Richmond. But I don't think that strategy is going to work. The war is fought by soldiers, and as long as there are men available for fighting, it's going to continue." Michael was getting more emotional than I had ever seen. His hands were moving fast as he talked. I knew that Michael did that when he was excited, but now his hands were going like crazy. "Come on, Jack. Why do you think they made us enlist for three years, and not for thirty days? The men in government know that this war is not going to be over quickly. I want to get home as much as you do. But we have to do our duty until the war is over. Then we'll both go home; you to your parents and a legal career, and me to my wonderful life with Elizabeth."

I always respected Michael's opinions but I really hoped that he was wrong this time. I didn't want to hear any more about the war dragging on, so I asked if he wanted to throw around the base ball. "Sure," he said, with a deep sigh. "Let's go get my ball."

We went to Michael's tent and ran into three other members of the Company B team, Robert Lewis, Steve Cooper, and Bill Shannon. Michael called to them. "Hi, boys. Jack and I were just going to throw around the base ball. Want to join us?"

"I can only play for a little while," Steve said. "I have a card game I have to get to." Steve seemed to be busy a lot with card games.

Both Bob and Bill agreed that throwing the ball around was a good idea. So the five of us walked on to the drill field. When we got there, we started to throw the ball in kind of a large circle, with each of us throwing it to the fellow to his right. We did this for a while, and then reversed the order. After that we changed again so that you could throw the ball to whoever you wanted. The idea was to keep everyone alert, because in a real game you never knew who the ball was going to be hit to. It was good practice to keep our reflexes sharp.

Of course, while this was going on we kept up a constant chatter like, "Get rid of that ball faster.' Or, "Come on, you can throw it harder!" Or, "The batter will be on first base before that throw gets there." Some of the chatter was directed to Steve, who kept trying to show off by making one handed catches. He ended up dropping the ball a lot so we started calling it his one handed misses. Every time he missed it, the boys would yell, "God gave you two hands, so use them." It was fun, and I said so.

Everyone agreed, but Bill added that an ale would make it even better. And Robert, not to be outdone, said it was too bad there were no women around to show off for. We laughed, and continued to have a good time.

Then we saw Bernard Carney running toward us, and the game stopped. The way he was running, we knew Bernard must have news, or at least the latest rumors. Bernard didn't disappoint. "Hey boys," he said, "did you hear? We're going to be on guard duty at the White House for President Lincoln!"

"Where did you hear that?" Michael asked.

"Oh, I just heard it around." Usually Bernard did not like to tell the sources of his information. It had to do with his reporter's training. He said that if your source found out that you gave his name, the source would not tell you anything after that. I think he just didn't want to share credit for the story.

Robert and Bill started firing questions at him. "When does it start?" "Will it be the whole regiment or just one company?" "If it's just one company, which one?" Bernard replied that he didn't know the details yet, but that it was supposed to start soon.

Then Michael asked, "Does this mean that we'll be staying in Washington and not be moving out to fight the rebels?" I couldn't tell by his tone if he thought that was a good thing or not. The other boys, including me, had not thought of that.

Bill said, "I sure don't want to miss the action." "Me neither." Robert agreed.

Michael told them, "Don't worry. This war's not going to be over quickly. There will be plenty of fighting for all of us." Bill and Robert both disagreed, saying the upcoming battle should take care of the secessionists once and for all. Michael gave them the same reasons he had given me earlier. We had a long talk about it, and like most other arguments, nobody changed anybody else's mind.

With this news, the game of catch broke up and we went back to our tents to talk some more.

CHAPTER TEN

June 9, 1861

Sure enough, on June 9th, the 14th Brooklyn drew special guard duty for the President. The White House was an impressive building. Two stories high with tall windows everywhere, and wide columns in the front that went the whole height of the building. Each column was as big around as three men with their arms stretched out, holding hands. The thought that a family lived in a building like that one made me dizzy, even if it was the President's family. It was several days before I stopped being awed by that building.

We were positioned on the west side of the White House. Squads from another regiment were positioned on the east side. There was a very fancy dining room on our side of the building that you could see through the big windows. Sometimes we could view people all dressed up, many of the men in dress uniforms, just eating. I figured they must be important people, but I didn't recognize most of them. Of course, I recognized the President. I also recognized Generals Scott and McDowell. General Scott, the head of the whole army, was easy to recognize because he was one of the fattest men I had ever seen. And I remembered General McDowell from our swearing-in ceremony, when we joined the regular army.

Our job seemed to be to look good. Our fancy uniforms were probably one of the reasons we were chosen to guard the White House. The red pants and chasseur style uniforms set us off from most of the other regiments. The other regiment on the east side of the building also had chasseur style uniforms.

The guard duty was pretty easy, and after I got used to the White House itself, kind of boring. We rotated squads and companies so guards were there all day and night. It was only about a twenty minute march from our camp to the White House, so it was not hard to get there. Each group's shift was six hours, so guard duty was really just a lot of standing around.

One day, however, made up for all the boring times. The President himself came out of the White House to thank us! I never thought I would get to see him other than through the window into the dining room. But there he was; really tall, over six feet, with a beard. I had not realized how tall he was from the glimpses I had gotten. This was not surprising since he was mostly sitting down when I saw him. He was kind of skinny, but you could sense that under his coat he was a powerful man. My bigger impression was how sad he looked. I couldn't understand that, because he was the President of the whole country, and we were going to war. That was exciting, so why was he so sad? I wondered if he knew something I didn't.

"Hello, boys," President Lincoln said. "I just came out here to thank you for guarding the White House." To my surprise, he then went down the line and spoke to each of us, and shook our hands. When he got to me, I thought I might pass out, I was so nervous. My hand must have been wet from nerves, but the

President seemed not to notice. I thought that he was probably just being polite.

"Hello, son, what's your name?" the President asked me. Thank goodness, I remembered, and even though my tongue felt twisted in a knot, I managed to answer. "Jack Muller, Mr. President."

"What did you do before the war?" Again I was somehow able to reply. "I was a laborer at the Brooklyn Navy Yard with my father." The President responded, "That's important work. How was it working with your father?"

"It was fine, Mr. President." Then I started jabbering. "My father was a lawyer in Germany, but after the failed revolt there, he had to leave. He brought my mother and me to America. Although he's a laborer here, he's grateful to the country for giving him a safe home. He's happy here, and wants me to become a lawyer." That's when I realized that I had gone from being too nervous to speak, to running my mouth off and taking up the valuable time of the President. But he just seemed so genuinely interested that I felt at ease in a matter of seconds.

"That's fine, son. It's a shame that he came here to keep his family safe, and now his son is going to war."

"I don't mind, Mr. President. It's a good cause, and almost everyone says it will be over soon."

"I pray that they are right, but I fear they are not. You know, I was an attorney before I got into politics. I rode the circuit representing parties in all kinds of actions. I do hope you get to be a lawyer after the war, and make your father proud. Thank you again, son." And he walked on to the next boy.

Guard duty may be boring, but I knew I would remember my meeting with the President for the rest of my life. Shortly after President Lincoln went back inside the White House, Michael came up to me. "He's a great man, isn't he?" Michael said.

"He seems to have some power I can't explain," I replied. "When he first came up to me, I didn't think I would even be able to speak. But then looking in his eyes I found myself telling him about my father, and just talking to him."

"That's because he cares about you." Michael observed. "He's a decent man, and it comes out. You can tell he's sincere. He doesn't try to hide his belief that the war would not be over soon. I really like him."

"I like him, too. I guess that's a good thing since we are going to war for him."

"We are not going to war for him," Michael corrected me. "We are going to war for the Union. But he's our leader so it's important that we respect him, and I do."

"I do, too. How much longer do we have to be here?"

Michael laughed. "About an hour. I know it's boring being on guard duty, but it has to be done."

"It's not boring anymore. I just want to get back to camp, and write to my parents that I met the President. By the way, I heard some of the boys complaining that we would be on permanent guard duty, and miss the action. What do you think?"

Michael replied, "I don't know how much longer we'll be on guard duty, but I don't think we're going to miss the action. Like the President, I hope the war will end quickly, but I don't think it will. So we won't miss anything."

I didn't know whether to feel relieved or worried, so I just said, "Thanks," and we went back to our posts. I thought about the numerous motives that had led the boys of the 14th to volunteer to be in the army for three years. Michael believed in the cause. The rebels were trying to leave the Union, and that was wrong. President Lincoln was trying to hold the Union together, and that was right. Given Michael's beliefs, abolishing slavery was a major part of his thinking too. That certainly was the motive for some of the boys. Then there were others, like Patrick and Davey, who just needed jobs, and the army was a place that gave them meals, shelter, and pay that they could send home to their families. And finally there were fellows who signed up for glory. They dreamed of battles where neither they nor their friends were injured and only the traitors got killed. Of course our soldiers would be heroes, and come home to the cheers of their families and neighbors.

My motivation was a combination of several of these notions. I believed in the Union cause, and would fight for it. And the money was helpful for my parents. But I also had dreams of glory where the rebels fell before me. The drive to be a hero was what made me and many other boys in the regiment worry that we would have to continue with guard duty at the White House, and miss the action.

We needn't have worried. We broke camp on July 2nd, and marched down to Maryland Avenue near 14th Street and then crossed the Potomac River by way of the Long Bridge, going from Washington to Virginia. The bridge was impressive. Made of wood, with beams on its sides and across the top, the bridge had a six-foot wide section for pedestrians, set off by a four-foot high railing. The rest of the surface was for horses, carriages, or in our case cannon. The noise from all those feet and wheels and horses' hooves was very loud.

After we crossed the bridge, we were in enemy territory. At first, it didn't feel any different, but soon I became more watchful, looking out for enemy soldiers. I could see the other boys tense up, too. We were getting closer and closer to seeing action.

We made camp near a place called the Arlington House. The set up was similar to what we had in Washington. To make things as orderly as possible, we kept the same tent mates. That suited me just fine. Outside of Michael, Davey and Patrick were my best friends in the regiment.

Bernard Carney, it turned out, was a nice fellow, and I didn't mind his gossiping because I was sure to know all the latest news of the camp from him. William Dakin, Hugh Doharty, John McNamee, and Lawrence Staunton were also fine fellows. They did their fair share of the chores, and didn't complain much.

Two companies were added to the regiment bringing the total number of boys to 960. The two companies, called fresh fish, were separate from the rest of us, including sleeping in separate tents, except during free time when we all got to know each other. They were separated because they needed a lot more work to catch up to the rest of us in drilling and target practice. When I looked at the fresh fish drilling, I thought about how we must have looked in the beginning. When they marched, it was like they didn't know their right from their left.

We were assigned to the brigade of Brigadier General Andrew Porter. I only saw him twice in the two weeks we stayed there. The General was a stocky man with a full beard and a piercing stare, about forty years old. He looked like a leader, and that made me feel good. We named the area "Camp Porter" in honor of him.

The two weeks we spent at Camp Porter followed the same routine as when we were in Washington, with two big exceptions. We had more boys out on guard and picket duty. While boys on guard duty are closer to the camp, pickets go about a mile outside of camp and patrol the surrounding area. If the rebels attacked, the first thing they would run into would be the pickets, who were supposed to get off a couple of rounds and run quickly back to camp. That way the rest of the boys would be warned of the attack and could form a line of battle. None of the pickets ran into any southern soldiers. Camp routine was not disturbed, and the two new companies continued to do extra drill.

On July 16, we moved toward Richmond, Virginia. We were now even deeper into enemy country. The warm, sweet winds, the beautiful scenery, and the peaceful rolling hills made me forget for periods of time that this was war and that we were close to the enemy. There were no peaceful periods like that the next day when we went into battle.

CHAPTER ELEVEN

July 21, 1861

"**M**y God, this is real," I thought as I heard the rebel shells shrieking overhead. I'm really in the war, and scared to death! My heart pounded. I could feel the pulsing from my chest to my head. It was a beautiful summer day; the lush, green rolling hills with clumps of trees and open fields had been so impressive to a boy from Brooklyn, but I barely noticed them now. This was the moment I'd been waiting for since the day I signed up. Back then, I had worried that the action would be over before I could get into the fight. Now the fight was here, and I was right in the middle of it. Be careful what you wish for, I thought.

Earlier in the day, my brigade had moved closer to the battle and crossed Bull Run Creek at Sudley's Ford. After that we rested for half an hour and had all the canteens filled. Then we re-crossed the ford and moved up a railroad grade, where we heard the rebel shells for the first time. I don't know why we crossed Bull Run Creek only to come back to the same side we had started from, but I figured the officers knew what they were doing. At least, I hoped they did.

No one spoke. Before we heard the shells, there had been excited chatter about what we were going to do to those traitors. Now everyone was quiet, waiting for orders.

I made up my mind to stick close to Michael. I knew he would do whatever was right and I would just copy his movements.

We moved out, me staying near Michael. When we reached an open field, we stopped to throw off our blankets and haversacks. That's when we first saw rebel soldiers yelling and shooting. I saw boys from both sides getting shot. Some screamed in pain, and some were missing parts of their bodies. I saw blood. Suddenly all I could see was blood. I quickly went from excited and eager to get into the fight to being close to terrified. This was real -- not like the dress parades back in Brooklyn where the people would turn out to watch us march and to cheer.

The uniform I had been so proud of now made me feel like an enormous target. Back in Brooklyn, I'd thought that this was the finest outfit I'd ever worn. Now the red, white, and blue uniform seemed like a bright sign screaming "Shoot Here."

I looked over at Michael again. His expression still hadn't changed. He hadn't appeared to be excited before, and he didn't look scared now. He just seemed determined. On the other hand, I was terrified of getting shot. I was also afraid of not being able to fight. I was even anxious about running away and letting down the boys of the 14th Brooklyn. Just at that moment, Michael looked at me and winked. I instantly felt calmer.

The regiment moved out quickly and took shelter to the right of a battery of cannon, behind the old "Henry House," a modest wooden frame house. I had been told that the widow of a navy surgeon named Isaac Henry lived there with her children. That thought surprised me. In the middle of the battle what was I doing thinking about who resided in a little one story building with an attic above? To me, though, the structure was like a port in a storm. I felt safe because the house blocked the enemy fire. I briefly wondered if the widow and her children had left their home. It was strange. My thoughts ran all over the place. One moment I was scared to death, thinking only about getting shot, and the next moment I was fixed on who lived in a building and whether they were still there.

Then I heard small knocking sounds as bullets hit the structure, and fear drove all other thoughts from my mind. I looked out and saw smoke coming from both rebel and Union guns. I smelled the gunpowder carried by the breeze. The smell made me want to throw up. I would have been happy to hide behind that house forever but Captain Mallory, our commander, pointed and shouted, "All right, boys, fall in over there to the left!" We had just been ordered to move out from behind the house into the enemy fire. That seemed crazy. I was safe behind the house, while there was nothing between me and the rebs out there.

Our regiment was supposed to support a group of cannons that were in danger of being overrun. We had to form a line of battle. We had done this countless times before in drills, but never under fire. In a line of battle, the soldiers line up abreast and keep that formation. This is the way an army maximizes its firepower. If the soldiers bunch up, the ones in the rear cannot shoot at the enemy. Besides, a clump of soldiers makes an easy target. I appreciated that those manuals Michael loaned me did help me understand what was going on. Then I realized that my brain was jumping around again from being terrified to thinking about manuals.

Michael walked out, and I followed him. The whole regiment just marched out from behind the shelter of the house and got into line, one next to the other, while the Confederates were shooting at us. I didn't know how the other boys did it, unless they were following Michael, too. I couldn't believe I was walking like I might have done on a street back in Brooklyn, while people were trying to kill me. Michael turned to me and said, "This is it. Let's give it to them." His words were meaningless, but his tone meant everything. He spoke plainly and confidently. I felt better again.

At first, we lined up too close to the battery of cannons. By shooting at us, the enemy was also shooting at the battery. So we moved out to the front, and then our colorful uniforms made us easy targets for the reb fire. They shot at us, and we shot back. No one in the 14th Brooklyn hesitated. I think that there is no greater test of bravery than to take part in one of these fights: two rows of men shooting at each other, with no shelter or cover between them. We were about 300 yards from the rebels, which was just in rifle range for both of us. Even over the sounds of the shooting, I heard the screams from the boys who were shot.

The only protections we had were the smoke from the guns that made us hard to see, and the amount of time it took the enemy to load and fire. A soldier just can't get off that many shots because of the time-consuming process of loading a musket. I went through the drill of loading and firing my musket just like I'd been trained to do. When I was first taught to load and fire back in camp in Brooklyn, I kept getting confused about all the steps. But after all the practice we went through, the process came back to me without thinking, just like it was supposed to. I reached into my cartridge box to pull out the paper-enclosed bullet and powder. I bit through the paper so I could pour the powder into the barrel, then freed the minie ball from the paper and placed it into the barrel before ramming them both home with my ramrod. I then replaced the ramrod in its slots in the rifle. I half-cocked the rifle so I could take off the old percussion cap, which is struck by the hammer to fire the gun, and put on a new cap I got from my pouch. I hadn't thought that I could do all these steps in the heat of battle, but I did them. And I kept doing them, even with all the carnage around me.

My first thought was that everyone was being shot. Actually, most of the boys were doing just what I was doing, loading and firing their rifles.

But my eyes always seemed to find someone being wounded or killed. I was grateful it wasn't me getting shot, so far anyway, but that made me feel guilty. How could I feel glad about one of my friends being shot?

We just stood there, loading and firing, over and over. Every once in a while, one of the boys was wounded but able to keep shooting–– as if that was going to make it better. With all of the noise I couldn't really hear the individual muskets firing; I must have been imagining it. But I did not imagine the boys dropping around me. I saw Augustus Brown get shot and drop. John Ryan fared no better. Ernest Seidel and Robert Simmons were also killed.

By then the batteries we had been supporting had moved off, supported by other regiments. But we kept fighting. Michael was on my left side, and on my right was Jesse Pietro, a big dark-complexioned boy from Italy who I met in camp. Jesse took a bullet in the face, which seemed to blow off his entire jaw. His blood splattered me. In fact, the blood hitting my hand was what made me look at him. At first, I thought I was shot. Then I realized it was Jesse, felt relief, and then guilt that I felt relief. Up until then I had been like a machine, loading and firing. After seeing Jesse get shot, I looked around at the other men in our regiment. Tim Burton was on the ground with blood coming out of his chest. Alex Turnbull was on his knees with his left arm hanging limply at his side. I shook myself and went back to my loading and firing.

The commanders must have decided that our position was not good enough. We were ordered forward. There were flag bearers on both ends of the line so it stayed straight as we charged. Here too, the idea was to maximize your fire power and not bunch up.

We marched up a hill right at the enemy's position. I didn't even feel my legs moving, but they must have been because I went forward. I saw more boys falling, either stumbling or being shot. I knew they had been shot if I saw blood. I heard the thud of bullets slamming into flesh. I smelled the gunpowder from the enemy's guns and saw their smoke. It seemed like I was sleep-walking right into the cloud of smoke.

I saw a unit of Zouaves come running down the same hill we were going up. The Zouaves had crazy looks on their faces. They were beyond scared. I thought that the Zouaves would kill anyone who tried to stop them, whether it was a rebel or a Union soldier. This wasn't a retreat, it was a panic.

I realized that the Zouaves were one of the regiments that had taken over for us, supporting the battery. The enemy must have captured the cannon and now we had to take it back. For a moment I felt like joining the fellows running down the hill. They were heading for safety, and I was going into a line of Confederates shooting at me. Then I looked at Michael. He didn't even seem to notice the cowards running down the hill. He just kept moving at the same pace. The moment passed for me. I don't know if anyone else even felt it, because the 14th Brooklyn kept moving up the hill into the enemy fire.

The 14th held up wonderfully for a group that had never been in a fight before. From time to time we stopped to load and fire when we got close enough for it to have some effect. I noticed that some of the boys sometimes forgot to shoot. They just loaded and reloaded instead of firing. They must have had 3 or 4 balls in their guns waiting to be fired. I supposed that when they finally pulled the trigger, all three or four balls would shoot out, or the muzzle would explode. If the muzzle exploded, and the soldier wasn't hurt, he would probably pick up another musket from one of the boys who had been shot. The injured boy sure wouldn't need his rifle anymore.

The shots we got off seemed to be doing their job as we watched reb soldiers fall. Near me, Major Jourdan emptied his pistol into the enemy front, then grabbed the edge of the flag held by Color Sergeant Head of Company C and shouted "Follow me!" I heard the Sergeant reply, "I'll follow you, Major!" Head was shot almost immediately after, and the last words I heard him saying were about saving the Colors, asking someone to make sure the flag was safe. Michael moved to take hold of the colors but George Blake of our company beat him to it. I wondered how long it would be before George was shot. I heard later that he was killed in the fight.

Then the Confederates executed a maneuver that I had only read about. In the middle of this battle they deployed out on either side so that they had us in a crossfire. I watched them do this as if it were a dream. They seemed to be moving so slowly. But once they were done, both ends of their lines overlapped ours, and the enemy could just pick off soldiers at each end of our line. Most of our fellows weren't able to return the rebel fire without hitting our own soldiers. When you're lined up in a battle formation, someone in the middle of the line can't just turn sideways and shoot; his own soldiers are in the way. As I had learned from the military strategy books Michael had loaned me, you never want to be out-flanked. And yet here we were: out-flanked and getting shot at from both ends. We couldn't stay in that position.

I wanted to scream "run" or actually start running down the hill. Even though our position was hopeless, and the longer I stayed here, the more likely I'd be shot, I didn't do either. I couldn't skedaddle as long as Michael and the 14th Brooklyn stayed.

Finally, we got orders to retreat. I could hardly hear Lieutenant Pearce of our company, going around and telling everyone to fall back. The regiment retreated in good order, not the running panic we'd seen from the Zouave unit. We would fall back for a short distance, turn, load, and shoot. It took as much guts for me to do this as it did to charge up the hill. Every time we stopped, it seemed like I saw another boy get shot. I heard, or imagined that I heard, the sound of the bullet hitting him, then his scream or groan. Then I looked, and saw more blood. Maybe if we didn't stop, no one else would get shot? But Michael stopped, so I stopped. And Michael loaded and fired, so I did too.

After we got out of range, we rallied, formed a line of battle and tried again to take the hill. We walked forward under a hail of bullets. The enemy seemed to have more boys and more spirit. I learned later that rebel soldiers under Gen. Johnson arrived from the Shenandoah Valley late in the battle and turned the tide. I heard the sound of a bullet hitting flesh, and checked myself to see if I was shot. It was John Bradley of our company standing by me holding his side. His scream told me that it wasn't me who was wounded. Despite the murderous fire coming at us, we kept going for a while, but then we had to pull back because we didn't have support from other units, who all seemed to have disappeared. The same thing happened on our third try to take the hill, and we were ready to give it a go a fourth time, even though we didn't stand a chance of getting up that hill.

Like most of the soldiers in the ranks, I didn't know what was going on in the rest of the battle. But I could see that most of the Union forces behind us were running away. We seemed to be the last regiment to hear about the retreat. Since the 14th couldn't stay alone in the middle of all this shooting, I knew that we would be pulling out soon as well, and that was what happened. The Union army lost the battle, but the 14th Brooklyn stood up to the fight, and I did not run away.

CHAPTER TWELVE

July 21, 1861

The retreat became a rout, and then mayhem. We needed to get back to Washington. Our fellows might have kept some form of order if the situation hadn't been made so much worse by all the civilians also trying to get back to Washington. They were running over soldiers, or getting trampled by soldiers, as everybody competed for the limited roadways.

Before the fighting started, the residents of Washington believed the upcoming battle was going to be something worth watching. Other than veterans of the war with Mexico, nobody had seen a real live battle before. Everybody thought it would be more entertaining than a play, and it was free. People poured out of Washington in their carriages for the 25 mile drive. They packed picnic lunches, expecting to see a show, have a bite to eat and then go back home with a great story to tell.

Unfortunately for all concerned, instead of seeing a spectacle, they became part of it. And their single-minded goal was to avoid being shot or captured by the rebels, and they believed that would best be accomplished by beating the army back to Washington.

Since there were very few roads and bridges that could be used by carriages, vehicles of all types backed up. The wounded in wagons were trying to get by as well. One small accident would turn individuals into a crazy mob. People tried to turn over carriages with men and women still in them in order to clear the path. It was an impossible situation.

Soldiers and civilians each believed they had priority on the roads. There probably would have been more fights, but everyone was too scared to take the time. Instead, there was just a lot of cursing as folks climbed over each other.

Michael and I stuck together. Or rather, I stayed with Michael. While others seemed to be running in panic, Michael walked along purposefully. He knew that he had to get back to camp, and that he would do it. There was no reason to run. If we met roadblocks, we walked around them. If a bridge was crowded, we waded through the water.

While we kept up a steady pace, boys from different units were running by us. You could see fear in their eyes. When we tried to talk with one of them to find out if he knew what was happening, he just said, "All I know is that we lost bad. Get out of my way. The rebs are coming." I didn't see any rebels, and Michael told me not to pay the fellows running by us any mind. So I didn't.

The scene was terrible. Every so often panicked soldiers would stumble or fall. No one stopped to help them. By the time we went over to see if we could help, they had gotten up and were running again. Michael tried telling them that there was no sign that the enemy was following us, but the boys didn't believe him. "You're crazy," they said. "Them sons of bitches are coming for sure. Get out of my way. Leave me alone." And they ran off.

I noticed that the soldiers running away looked so defeated and afraid. Also, they weren't carrying rifles or any equipment. Realizing that I was still carrying a lot of heavy equipment, I said to Michael, "Why don't we get rid of these guns? We're not going to need them."

"You don't think so? You're a soldier, Jack, and soldiers carry their guns. You want to be a lawyer. Would you go to court without something to write with?"

I wasn't sure I followed Michael's reasoning since a musket weighs an awful lot more than a pencil, and in court I wouldn't be running for my life. But since it was Michael, I just said, "I understand." As more and more fellows passed us, it became obvious that there was no organization left. It wasn't just Michael and me who had been separated from our regiment; there were no more regiments. We were just one big herd stampeding to Washington.

We walked for hours. It started to rain, and that made me feel worse. On top of everything else, I was wet. The trees and bushes may have been beautiful during a summer's day. Now they were just more obstacles to go around. We stayed on the road as much as we could, but when there was something blocking our way, like an abandoned carriage with no horses, we would go into the woods to get around it. In the woods, it seemed like I managed to find every thorn and bramble that could stick to me. I was soaked by then and tired, and the equipment I was carrying seemed to be getting heavier. I thought again about simply shedding my rifle, like the other soldiers running past us. I didn't though, because I wouldn't raise the issue again with Michael.

Night had fallen, but fortunately moonlight gave us enough light to keep going even when we had to go off the road and into the woods. The moonlight also created shadows that made the area look real scary.

Michael said the enemy was not coming, and I believed him, but the shadows sure looked like Confederates to me. But Michael just kept walking, so I did too.

I was thinking about what this disastrous battle meant. "Michael, do you think this army will fight again?"

Michael nodded. "Of course it will. This was just one battle. The politicians will make some general the scapegoat for what happened, and the army will go on. We'll lick our wounds, and the government will re-outfit the boys and send them out again."

"What do you think happened?"

"I don't know. I don't think any line soldier ever really knows. We have such a small view of what's going on in a battle that we can't know what happened, or what determined who won and who lost. The only thing that's clear now is that we lost."

"I heard the enemy doesn't take prisoners," I said, remembering some of the stories I heard in camp before we left for the fight. "The fellows said they kill the Union soldiers that they find so they can take their uniforms and all their possessions. That really makes me sick seeing as how we treat prisoners so well. I tell you, I'd just as soon commit suicide as have some reb make believe he's taking me prisoner only to murder me to steal all my stuff."

"Jack, that's all stories. Don't you think that the rebels say the same thing about us? Both armies use those tall tales to make the soldiers hate each other. That's important when you expect the men on one side to go kill the men on the other side. Killing people isn't natural. You have to be trained to do it as an army. Stories like the ones about the enemy not taking prisoners make it easier to get us to pull the trigger when we get one in our sights. Do you think you killed anyone today?"

"I believe I did."

"Did you ever kill anyone before today?"

"No, of course not." The question made me stop in my tracks. "I may have been mad at some people, but I would never even think of killing them."

"Exactly. Have you ever thought about what it takes to make a man kill another man, or for that matter to stand up in the open while the other person is shooting at him and trying to kill him?"

"Michael, what are you saying? We're not killers. We're fighting to save the Union."

"I know what we're fighting for. But what's hard to figure out is how fighting for the Union turns a peaceful fellow like you into a killer."

"I'm not a killer. I'm a soldier. I'm doing my duty."

"That you are, Jack, and you did it fine. But you can't get around the fact that you killed other men today, and that you never killed anybody before. All I'm saying is that stories that make you hate the enemy help you become a killer or, in other words, a soldier doing his duty."

We walked on. More people ran past us. I considered what Michael had said. I didn't understand all of it, and I wasn't sure I wanted to. It made things too complicated. When I was told to stand in a line of battle out where I could get shot, I did it because I was ordered to. When I was directed to shoot and kill the rebels, I did that too because I was ordered to. I thought of it as "kill or be killed." Almost self-defense. That was simple, and that was good enough for me.

As we were walking, I thought I saw two boys who looked familiar. Actually, even in the moonlight I could spot Bill Shannon's bright red hair. He was walking with someone who looked a lot like Steve Cooper.

"Say, isn't that Bill and Steve up ahead?"

"Yes, it definitely is," Michael replied.

"Bill! Steve!" Michael shouted to get their attention. They both turned and walked closer to us so we could see each other pretty clearly in the moonlight.

When we got closer, I could see that they looked scared and confused. Their shoulders were slumped forward and their eyes were wide open in a look of pure terror. As soon as Bill recognized us, he came running over and started smacking our backs. "Great to see you fellows," he said. "I sure am glad you made it through the fight." Steve came near, relaxed a bit, and said in a surprised tone, "What are you doing here?" I thought that he was referring to the fact that I was still with Michael, and hadn't run away from the battle. Michael acted as if Steve was just surprised that the four of us would get together in the middle of all this chaos.

"We're heading back to camp, same as you, I guess," answered Michael. I saw that neither Steve nor Bill had their guns or equipment. Steve noticed me staring at where his equipment would be. Being the pompous person he was, Steve had to make up a story quickly.

"There were some boys back there who couldn't keep up, and they had thrown away their equipment. So we gave them ours in case the enemy caught up with them."

Bill laughed at what must have been the worst lie Steve told in a week. Bill obviously had no trouble with the idea of throwing away his equipment, so he didn't say anything. Michael was too much of a gentleman to call Steve a liar. I didn't respond out of deference to Michael's friendship with Steve. In order to break the awkward silence, Michael asked, "So, have you boys heard anything? What's the enemy doing? Are we re-forming anywhere? Have you seen any of the others from the 14th?"

Before they could answer, I asked if they had seen Patrick Murphy or Davey O'Connor. I was worried since I hadn't seen them since the beginning of the battle.

Bill answered first. "You're the first fellows from the regiment we've seen since we started running. That is retreating, I mean," looking at Steve with a grin. "We would've made a whole lot better time, but we got caught up in that bridge incident back there."

"What bridge incident?" I asked.

"There's this bridge along the Warrenton Turnpike, a direct route back to Arlington," Bill said. "Maybe you remember it. A whole bunch of our boys were about to cross the bridge when a cannon shell landed right smack in the middle of it. The explosion turned over a wagon and blocked anyone from crossing. I tell you, the people about to cross that bridge, including us, hightailed it back as fast as we could."

Steve interrupted, embarrassed that someone implied he had run away from anything. "What the hell are you talking about? What really happened was after the shell exploded so we couldn't get across, we backtracked 'til we found a place where we could wade across the stream and continue the retreat."

Bill couldn't help laughing. "Backtracked? We skedaddled. We did have to go back the same way we'd come, but ran like hell doing it. We ended up losing a lot of time, though."

Talking about the chaos on the bridge made Steve very nervous. His eyes were darting left and right as though he was looking for someone. This was worse than his usual habit of looking everywhere but at the person he was talking to. "We don't know what the rebels are doing," Steve said. "But it doesn't take a general to figure out that they're going to come after us. They beat us, and people are running away. Now's the time for them to finish us off." As he spoke, Steve's voice took on a tone of panic, and his eyes never stopped moving.

Michael calmed him quickly. "They're as confused as we are. Once we left the Bull Run area, their organization wasn't any better than ours. You just told us that they exploded a shell in the middle of the bridge, delaying a number of our soldiers. Did they attack?"

"No," Steve admitted.

"See?" Michael said. "Both sides had a hard fight, and they're just as tired as we are. Maybe even more so because they don't have the fear of being caught that we do."

"What fear?" Steve dared Michael. Steve had recovered from his earlier slip and was back to his old bravado. But his eyes never stopped moving. He looked at people running past us and seemed to want to join them. But he couldn't without looking scared. Instead, he suggested, "Shouldn't we be moving on? We do want to get back to the 14th, after all."

"Yes, we do," Michael replied. "I was just wondering if you boys had heard anything about where General McDowell was going to re-form."

"Re-form?" Bill asked. "We've been beaten. I can't see this army fighting again."

Michael looked offended. "You're wrong. This war isn't over. I expect that both sides are going to sit back and lick their wounds for a while. Then the fighting will pick up again."

Steve didn't buy it. "Since they attacked us out in the battle, why shouldn't they attack us in our camp? Finish us off, end the war. If anything, they have to feel more confident now that they've beaten us."

Bill agreed, "That makes sense."

Michael didn't agree at all. "They didn't attack us. We came at them. Individual rebel units charged, but that's not an all-out assault on our army. Remember, we were the ones that moved out from camp and advanced on them? Besides, General McDowell has units covering our retreat. He's a good officer and good leaders always prepare for something like this."

"If he's such a good leader, how come we got beat?" Steve said in an accusing tone.

"For the reason you said. There were thousands of them. They had us outnumbered. There was nothing General McDowell could do," Michael answered calmly. I realized his argument made no sense, because we couldn't see much of the battlefield through the smoke and Michael had no idea if the enemy outnumbered us. Also, if they had us outnumbered before, they still did. But Michael's answer seemed to calm Steve, which I thought was probably why he said it.

Soldiers were still passing us, looking gloomy and demoralized. But we walked on with Michael setting a steady pace. It might have been because it was dark and rainy, but I couldn't help contrasting the difference in how I saw the scenery between when I was heading off to battle, and when I was running away after it. On the march to the battle, everything seemed really beautiful and smelled fresh. When the fight started, I didn't notice much about the scenery around me, but during the retreat everything looked dismal and grim and smelled bad. I didn't think it was entirely due to the rain and the dark. At least some of the bleakness reflected the mood of the boys. Nobody likes to get beaten, and everybody knew that we had been beaten badly.

CHAPTER THIRTEEN

July 22, 1861

As we walked in the moonlight with the rain falling constantly, I thought about life back home in Brooklyn. My family worked hard. My mother made our home clean and comfortable.

Bill must have read my thoughts because he said, "Hey, Jack, you're from Germany, right?"

"Yes, I am."

"Well, how did you end up in Brooklyn?"

"It's kind of a long story, but I guess we don't have anything else to do," I said as I shifted my rifle from one shoulder to the other to ease the pain. "My family came over from Germany in 1850 after the revolutions of 1848. I was only six at the time, but I heard the stories often enough to know what happened. In 1848, people revolted against the leaders in a number of countries in Europe. The people were seeking the right to vote for all men and other rights men should have. In some countries like England, Belgium, and Denmark, the demonstrations seeking reforms were peaceful. But in other countries like Italy, France, and Germany, there were violent revolutions." Now I was talking like a teacher, the same way Michael explained things to me. But Bill seemed interested, and talking helped to ease the tension.

"We lived in Vienna, Austria. Germany was made up of a number of separate states, like Austria, with an all powerful ruler in each. Vienna was the most important city in Germany because it was considered the successor to the Holy Roman Empire. In Vienna, students protested, demanding a new constitution where all men could vote to elect the assembly. The young people were fired on by troops, and several of them were killed. Working-class people then joined the movement to prepare for an armed revolt. Emperor Ferdinand of Austria appointed new ministers who were supposedly more liberal. But when these ministers wrote the new constitution, they did not include the right to vote. So the people returned to the streets, and Ferdinand fled the country. After that, the leaders of the revolt and the ministers met to try to resolve their differences."

Bill wasn't complaining about my rambling on, maybe because he was busy trying to avoid puddles in the road. "That sounds great, Jack," he said, actually listening to me. "You fellows got what you wanted. Why did you leave?"

"The story isn't over. Before anything could be done, everything changed for the worse. The military from the German state of Prussia violently put down the uprising there. Prussia then sent troops to other German states to defeat the rebellions in those areas. All of the accomplishments were lost, and absolute monarchy was reestablished.

"My papa had supported the movement's liberal ideas in Austria, so my parents knew we had to leave or he would be persecuted, arrested, or maybe even executed. He said we would go to America where they already have a constitution and the right to vote.

"My folks learned that a lot of German immigrants had settled in the eastern section of Brooklyn, in Greenpoint, Williamsburg, and Bushwick. They decided we would live in Williamsburg because it was close to the Navy Yard, where my father thought he could get a job. My parents had some friends who had moved to America, and we had kept in contact with them. They worked in the Navy Yard and wrote that they could get my dad a job there. So we came to Williamsburg."

"Boy, that's some interesting story!" said Bill.

"Wait, I'm not finished." I took a deep breath and went on. "My papa knew he couldn't be a lawyer in America like he was in Vienna, so he told me that I would be the attorney in the family. He decided that when we arrived in America, I would learn English, speak like an American, and read all of the books I needed to prepare myself. And that's what happened. My father and I got jobs at the Navy Yard, and I read out loud to my parents every night so they could work on making sure I didn't speak like an immigrant. I read everything - the Bible, Shakespeare, and even newspapers."

"You do sound just like a man from Brooklyn," commented Bill, and Steve nodded in agreement. "I'm sorry you had to leave your home, but I'm glad to have your company now."

"Thanks. It could be worse. At least we made it through the fight." In the midst of this downpour, it occurred to me that without this war, I would never have even met upper class people like Michael, Bill and Steve, let alone have them treat me as an equal. After all, we were all just privates in the Union army. Then I thought fondly of the quiet evenings reading or talking with my family, even though at the time the nights seemed dull. I missed sitting around outside on the street talking with my friends, finding out what was going on in the neighborhood. And we would never have stayed out in the rain like I was doing now!

I soon found out that I wasn't the only one thinking of home.

"You know," Steve said, "working in my father's drugstore wasn't so bad. At least I was dry and comfortable. We argued a lot because he wouldn't listen to my ideas. We could have made a lot more money if only my dad knew how to run a business. It doesn't take a genius to realize that it saves money if you dilute the medicine. It would still be effective, no one would get hurt! It was so frustrating trying to make him see what was obvious." Steve paused to shake some mud off his boots. "But there were fun times, too. All the business deals, and the card games. I was so close to hitting it big so many times. It was exciting. If I got just a bit more support from my family, I would be a rich man."

I didn't know what anyone else was thinking, but what Steve was saying sounded crazy to me. His folks were rich compared to mine, and Steve had been living off of them all of his life. I could just imagine Steve telling his father what to do when his father had already built a good business while Steve had done nothing. I could picture Steve's dad saying, "You couldn't find your rear end with both hands." It must have been no fun being in that drugstore. If Steve could speak fondly of those days, my homesickness was nothing compared to his.

"So you'd be a rich private, retreating in the mud, soaked to the skin," Bill jeered.

"That's not what I'm saying," Steve shouted back. "I miss home and I'm big enough to admit it. Sure, there were some annoying things, but home sure seems nice right about now." Steve wiped his face with his hands to try to get some of the rain out of his eyes.

"I know," Bill agreed in a softer tone. "I miss it, too. Working in my parents' taverns was fun, except when they had people spying on me to make sure I wasn't drinking more beer than I was pouring. I like beer! If liking beer was a problem, my folks wouldn't have customers. Anyways, I could always find ways to get the beer I wanted. And the girls in Brooklyn were great. They'd do just about anything if you made like you were going to marry them. They saw me as a real catch: good family business, prospects guaranteed. What they didn't know, and I sure wasn't going to tell them, was that I wasn't going to get caught.

"My mother and father took on some airs after their first tavern was so successful and they bought a second one. The first tavern is by the docks. We have a lot of sailors as customers. They're a rough crowd. And when they got out of hand we knew what to do with 'em: slip something in their drinks to quiet them down, and deposit them on the street minus their cash. They wouldn't remember what happened anyway. It was kind of fun and very profitable. The second tavern is in Brooklyn Heights and the customers are upper crust. My parents jumped from saloon owners, catering to anyone with the price of a drink, to society snobs. But life didn't change for me. I still drank what I could, and fooled around with the girls. Actually, the more successful we got, the more girls wanted me. My folks tried to make me change, but I think they finally kind of gave up. I sure miss that life."

There was silence as we digested each other's memories. We were all so interested in what the others had to say that we hardly noticed the other people running by us, still looking jittery and defeated. It was not like the panic had eased up. We were just thinking about other things and Michael was setting a steady and determined pace.

Then Bill added, "Gee, all this talk about the taverns is making me thirsty! Does anyone have a canteen? I seem to have lost mine in the heat of the battle." Michael and I knew full well that he had tossed it away after the battle to avoid having to carry it all the way back to camp, but neither of us said anything. We both held out our canteens; Bill grabbed Michael's first and took a big swig. We passed the canteens around and everyone felt a little better, at least for a few minutes.

Talking about home was like priming a pump. One person's memories led to another. Even Michael forgot about soldiering for a moment to talk about his life back in Brooklyn.

"I think about Elizabeth every hour of the day. She made our home on Hicks Street perfect." I knew Hicks Street, and I could easily imagine the houses there being like heaven. Of course, that wasn't exactly what Michael was talking about.

"Working in the bank for Mr. Gault was great. You know the Brooklyn Savings Bank was started years ago to help the people of Brooklyn."

Michael couldn't resist acting like a teacher. "Mr. Gault and the original officers weren't even paid until the bank became profitable. He's a fair man who respects the people who work for him. And I know they respect him. But coming home to Elizabeth at the end of the day was my greatest pleasure. I was never happier, whether we were reading, talking, or I was just watching her do needlepoint or listening to her play the piano.

"Our brownstone on Hicks Street was like an oasis where the worries of the world would disappear. I love our home. The lots in Brooklyn Heights are narrow, but it's ideal for us. We have a bay window that lets us look out onto the street. We can see the steeple of The Plymouth Church of the Pilgrims on the corner of Hicks and Orange Streets, where we worship.

"It's a very well known church. Our leader there, Henry Ward Beecher, is a rousing reformer and abolitionist. His sister, Harriet Beecher Stowe, wrote that famous book 'Uncle Tom's Cabin,' about the evils of slavery. Our church is part of the Underground Railroad. Escaping slaves on their way to Canada hide in the tunnel under the church. Elizabeth and I are abolitionists. We believe that slavery is wrong, plain and simple. I don't understand why the rebels are fighting. Most of them don't even own slaves and never will. I think every slave owner should be punished for his sins. Jail is too good for them. If they whipped their slaves, they should be whipped! If they hung a runaway, they should be hanged."

I had never heard Michael talk this way. It made me nervous. Steve and Bill were staring at him with their mouths open. Michael had always been the voice of reason. Now he was practically ranting. I was fighting to preserve the Union, to keep a great country together. I didn't want to hear that my "big brother," my "idol," was such an extremist that he could whip or hang civilians. I wanted to talk with Michael about his abolitionist tirade before my feelings about him changed. But now was not the time.

Then Michael seemed to snap out of his mood and remember that we were trudging through the mud and rain. "But, we have a job to do," he said in a sudden change of topic. "Right now we have to get back to camp so the 14th can regroup. This war's only started. We lost the battle, that's all. There's a lot more fighting to do."

Michael's words about getting back to camp were both inspirational and depressing. Everyone must have realized that any hopes of a short war were gone. But we didn't necessarily want to face the fact that we were sloshing through the mud only to regroup and go on fighting. We just had a taste of real war, and the prospect of doing this for years to come was scary. Thinking about home made it easier for me because I didn't have to think about what was really going on.

"Michael, you're right, but I enjoy thinking about my life in Brooklyn," I said, contradicting Michael for the first time I could remember. "It doesn't mean I won't fight. It just means that I feel good when I remember things about home. Reading to my parents, talking with them, playing with my friends, were all fun. It wasn't that things were so great in Brooklyn. We worked hard and we didn't have a lot of money. But that doesn't mean I don't have fond memories. Maybe they seem even better now, compared to being wet, dirty, hungry, and having lost my first fight. Whatever the reason, thinking about my life in Brooklyn makes me feel better, not worse. The regrouping and fighting will come later, and I'll deal with that then."

"I'm sorry, you're right." Michael agreed in his usual reassuring manner. "Everyone has his own way of handling this situation and it isn't my place to tell anyone how to do it." It was like the earlier rant hadn't happened. This was the Michael I knew.

Despite the apology, conversation lagged after that.

CHAPTER FOURTEEN

July 22, 1861

We walked through the night. We were close to our old camp in Arlington when Michael suddenly said, "I don't feel well." He started to stagger. He looked like he was getting weak and having trouble breathing.

Steve cried, "Has he been shot? Are the rebels coming? We better get out of here!" His eyes darted from side to side and it looked like he was going to run off.

Before I could speak, Bill said, "Stop crying like a baby. We can't just leave him here. If you run, I'll tell people what a coward you were." Steve was more afraid of being branded a coward than staying, so he stood still. Bill continued, "What's wrong with Michael?"

"I don't know," I replied. "But he hasn't been shot. It looks like he's just not feeling well."

Everyone relaxed a bit knowing that Michael had not been shot, but Michael kept getting worse by the minute. He was trying to swallow, and his eyes looked strange. The dark parts of his eyes were very big. "Michael, what's wrong?" I asked, trying to keep the worry out of my voice.

Michael replied with difficulty, "I feel dizzy. My chest hurts," he paused to catch his breath, "and my skin feels strange, like someone's sticking me with pins."

"Don't talk," I advised. I gave Michael my canteen to drink some water. Michael took the water, but it did no good. He still looked terrible.

He tried to talk again. "I haven't been feeling well for a while, but it just got worse instead of better." Michael's legs then seemed to give out, and he collapsed at my feet. He was lying on his back looking up at us. I leaned over him to block the rain that was falling on his face. He seemed so weak and fragile. I could not understand how or why he was deteriorating so fast.

It was an eerie scene. The rain was falling steadily, and the moonlight cast gloomy shadows from the trees all around us. Everyone stood around him, stunned. He was our leader. The force that had gotten us here. And now he looked to be dying right in front of us, even though there had been no shooting. There was nothing we could do but try to make him comfortable. Everyone was asking questions Michael couldn't answer. Steve asked if Michael wanted a blanket which we didn't have anyway. Bill asked if Michael wanted his head propped up. Steve kept muttering, "We have to do something."

Finally, I couldn't take it anymore. Since no one else was offering any useful advice, I said, "Bill, you come with me. I can't carry Michael alone. Together we'll bring Michael to camp and find a surgeon. Wagons of wounded have been passing us since the battle. They must be going to a hospital tent. Let's hurry on ahead and get Michael to the doctor. Steve, you can stay or move on when you're ready. Camp shouldn't be far from here."

Steve had no objection to getting away from us. This way he could make up his own story about what happened and his role in it.

Bill and I propped Michael up between us. Each of us put an arm around his waist and we put his arms over our shoulders. In that way we half walked and half carried Michael along. We hurried in the direction we had seen the wagons with the wounded go.

Michael was going downhill fast. His breathing was tortured. And when he could speak, all that he could say was that there was a pain in his chest and his head was spinning. For a while his legs were moving as if he were walking. Then he couldn't seem to put any weight on his legs at all, so Bill and I were dragging him with his shoes scraping along the ground. We passed through a line of our soldiers that had been formed to repulse any confederate attack. Michael had been right. General McDowell had taken precautions in case the rebels decided to have at us again. The soldiers we passed had the look of tired veterans. These boys, or rather men, weren't going to run at the first sign of the enemy.

It turned out that the remaining distance to our old camp-- Camp Porter-- was not that great, but we took a long time getting there. We went as fast as we could, but carrying Michael between us slowed our progress. As soon as we came within sight of our old encampment, I saw boys from Companies I and K who had been left there to guard the camp.

There were no greetings. Some of the stragglers barely had the energy to take another step by the time they got there. The soldiers from Companies I and K helped get them settled, or if the stragglers were wounded, helped them to the hospital.

I refused any assistance from them. Bill stayed with me. I had to make sure that we got to see a doctor quickly. I remembered where the hospital was; it was hard to miss, being much bigger than the other tents. The tents that we slept in just looked like an upside down "V." The hospital, in contrast, had four upright sides that let you stand up straight even at the sides of the tent. From the looks of it, the place was already jammed with about forty boys in beds. I thought that these fellows had seen some sort of surgeon because they had bandages and most of their blood had been wiped off of them. I couldn't help noticing that many of the boys were missing arms or legs.

I only looked for a moment because my one thought was to get Michael to the surgeon. We walked through the hospital tent without finding anyone to help. At the back end, we went through another entrance only to find that the regiment had erected another structure as an addition to the first one to fit more wounded. Despite my need to get Michael to a doctor, I couldn't help thinking that this looked to be a pretty simple process because all you had to do was rip the seams of the two tents and set them up back to back. It was a good idea because that way you could double the number of patients you could shelter, and still keep them together and more or less comfortable. After going through the second hospital tent I saw a shelter that had been set up for the doctors to work in, protected from the rain but otherwise exposed to the elements.

It was pretty much just a roof on poles, with lanterns strung all around it to give enough light to work. And work they did.

I saw three surgeons dealing with three patients. Each of the doctors had a saw in his hand, and was getting ready to cut off some poor boy's arm or leg. There were two soldiers with each of the wounded. Their job seemed to be to hold down the wounded soldier while the surgeon worked. Around each of the tables were limbs from the previous patients who'd been treated there, if you can call it that. The blood I hadn't seen in the hospital was all over the operating area. Even though it was outdoors, you could smell the rot and the blood and the chloroform they used to try to ease the pain of the poor fellow who was about to lose one of his limbs.

I felt sick, but I didn't have time for that. I looked over at Bill who also looked like he was going to be sick. "Stay with me, Bill," I said. "We have to get Michael examined, and it won't be much longer." Bill looked at me, nodded and said, "I'm not going anywhere." Any doubts I had about Bill's backbone in a bad situation disappeared. I knew he wanted to run out of there, but he didn't.

I saw one of the doctors was finishing up, and they were taking the boy he had been working on, minus one arm, back to the main area. Before the next victim could be brought in, Bill and I dragged Michael up to the doctor's table and put him on it.

The surgeon was a heavy set man with brown hair and a full beard to match. His green eyes looked exhausted, and his manner and posture showed his disgust with what he was having to do. His apron must have been white once, but was now red with blood.

"You'll have to wait your turn, son, " the doctor said to me. I was not about to leave, and I was glad when I looked over and saw that Bill wasn't going anywhere either.

"I can't wait, doctor," I stated. "This man is like a brother to me, and he hasn't been shot. You have to look him over and tell me what I can do for him." The doctor sighed and seemed too tired to object. He walked over, scalpel in hand, and took a look at Michael. He propped open Michael's right eye and grabbed his wrist. He sighed again. "Son, I can't help you. This man is dead."

I collapsed to my knees, mindless of the blood there from countless soldiers who had been given medical attention. "But he wasn't shot."

"Son, I've got living soldiers to worry about. I don't know what killed him, and I don't have the time to find out now. Get him out of here. I've got work to do."

Bill and I looked at Michael and finally understood that there was nothing more we could do to help him. We picked Michael up off of the table, and carried him out of the tent. We didn't know what to do with him. There was a neat line of bodies outside the tent, but I wouldn't leave Michael there.

We took Michael to a deserted portion of the camp and laid him down as gently as possible. Since, thanks to Michael, I had kept my equipment, I had my canvas traveling tent with me. Actually, it was only a sheet of canvas that would connect with another boy's canvas to form a tent when they were put on two poles. I placed my sheet over Michael's body to protect him from the rain. Even though Michael was dead, for some reason I wanted him to be comfortable.

I felt wet, cold, and lost. I could no longer think about the fact that the 14th Brooklyn did well in the battle, or that I had done well. Michael was dead. Nothing else mattered. Even though I had seen a lot of carnage during the battle, I had been able to do my job. But now I was paralyzed because Michael was gone. I had no idea what killed him, but I was going to find out.

Bill brought me out of my stupor. "What do we do now?" he asked.

I thought about that question. We could bring him back to the hospital where he would be put with the rest of the dead, and disposed of in the same way as the others, but I couldn't bring myself to let him just get dumped with all the other bodies. He was my big brother. Then I realized that Michael wasn't just special to me. His family was important. His father-in-law was the President of the Brooklyn Savings Bank. He would want to bring his son-in-law home for burial, and he had the power to make that happen.

I decided to make sure the body wasn't mixed in with the others. Then, when I reported to Captain Mallory, I would convince him to let Michael's family come to take his body back to Brooklyn. I told Bill, "I'll take care of Michael's body. But first, I want to wait here until I can go back to the doctor and find out what killed Michael. I'll gather up his personal effects and equipment to send to his family. You can go and find the other boys from the 14th."

Bill nodded, seeming to understand that there was no way in hell that I was going to leave Michael. He said, "I'll go and find the regiment and I'll let them know what happened. You do what you have to do."

I looked down at Michael lying under the tarp and could hardly believe he was dead. At six feet, he was taller than me by three inches. We're both lean and have brown eyes and black hair. Other people might have thought we were truly brothers, we were together so much and looked so much alike. He seemed to know everything about everything, and did not mind sharing it with me. He never got mad at me and his brown eyes always shone with interest at what I had to say. I knew I would never have a better friend.

I figured I had a lot of time to wait before I could go back to find out what killed Michael. So I sat on the wet ground with his body and dug into my memories of Michael. I didn't even notice the rain that was still falling.

CHAPTER FIFTEEN

July 22, 1861

I thought about meeting Michael on my first day in camp. I remembered the good times Michael and I shared; seeing the sights of Washington, guarding the White House, playing base ball, and just talking with him almost daily in camp. They were such good memories. He was my friend, my teacher, my brother.

Then I thought of today's events and was instantly jarred back to reality. How foolish I had been: my dreams of glory with enemy soldiers dropping in front of me while none of our boys even got hurt. That wasn't war at all. Here I was, sitting in the rain with Michael's body, not even caring about the water coming down on me. I had protected his body with a tent sheet, and that was all that mattered. I could get wet, but not Michael.

I couldn't help wondering about what might have killed him. Could it have been a heart attack? No, Michael was healthy and fit. Could he have caught a fever from the rain we were drenched in during the retreat? No, it came on too fast to be a fever. I lifted the tarp covering Michael's body to take a close look at him. There were no wounds that I could see. He had some blood on his uniform and face, but a close look showed me that the blood had not come from Michael. Like many of us, he had been splattered by the blood of his comrades. So Michael shouldn't have died.

Suddenly I knew what I had to do; find out what or who killed Michael. Something happened to him that made no sense. Someone other than a Reb caused this to happen. I needed to investigate how he died.

I saw Davey O'Connor and Patrick Murphy come straggling down the road. Both were dirty and staggering, but unwounded. I was glad they were alive. They made such an odd pair. An old man and a young boy, two generations at war together.

They didn't notice me until I yelled to them. When they saw me they staggered up to me and we embraced. We were all so happy to be alive. They saw me standing next to a body covered by canvas. I told them that it was Michael's body and they jumped back. Davey was the first to speak. "Where'd he get shot?"

"He wasn't shot," I responded.

Davey asked, "Then how'd he die?"

"I don't know, but I'm going to find out. Would you boys mind staying with Michael's body while I go to the medical tent? There was a doctor there that was too busy to talk to me when I brought Michael in. I need to talk to him to find out what happened to Michael."

Davey and Patrick hesitated, and I could tell they wanted to get back to the regiment. Before they could respond I said, "Michael was my friend, and he always treated you boys well. He was a good man, and we owe it to his memory, and his family, to find out how he died. I would do the same for you."

Davey spoke first again. "It's pretty plain this means a whole lot to you. Outside of Patrick, you're my best friend in the 14th. Nobody else knows how old me and Patrick are. You didn't tell no one. I trust you, and I know that when you say you'd do it for me, that's the God's honest truth. So I'll stay." Patrick nodded his head in agreement with more energy than I thought he had, to show me that he would stay with Michael, too.

I went back to the medical tent and found the same surgeon who had told me Michael was dead. The man looked exhausted. His apron and his arms had more blood on them than before, which I wouldn't have believed possible. The wounded were continuing to arrive, but at a slower rate than when I had been there before.

I went up to the surgeon and reminded him, "Sir, I was here before with a friend. You told me he was dead and that you didn't have time to spend on a dead man, when there were so many wounded around. I understand that, but I have to ask you some questions. I need to know the answers."

The surgeon responded. "I remember you. I feel bad for you because your friend's death obviously affected you so much. I was sorry that I didn't have the time to talk to you, but I still don't have the time. The wounded have to take priority over the dead."

I couldn't let him go. "It won't take long," I said. "My friend wasn't shot. He told me before he died that he felt dizzy, his legs got weak, his chest hurt and his skin felt like someone was sticking him with pins. Oh yeah, and a couple of other things I noticed. The dark parts of his eyes were really big, and when we gave him water, it didn't help at all."

"How was his health before the fight?" the surgeon asked.

"Really good," I responded.

"Well, if he wasn't shot, then it must have been something else. Are you sure about the symptoms you described to me?"

"Yes, sir. That's exactly what he looked like and what happened."

"You say he got worse gradually? At first, he could keep walking, and after a while he couldn't use his legs?"

"Yes, doctor. It seemed pretty quick, but it probably took fifteen or twenty minutes."

"Well, son, that doesn't sound like a problem with his heart, or a stroke. The symptoms would have progressed faster. Same thing for some kind of allergic reaction. On the other hand, the onset of the symptoms was too fast for a fever. It doesn't sound like any of the diseases I've seen around camp. Was he bitten by a snake or some animal?"

"No sir. I was with him the whole time, and nothing like that happened."

"Then it wasn't venom. It seems to me he must have ingested something toxic."

"You mean he was poisoned?" I was shocked. "How could that be? You know what it's like in the army. Everybody eats the same food and drinks the same water. How could that have happened?"

"Son, I don't know, and I haven't got the time to find out. Maybe it was something he ate that he found on the road." The surgeon sounded exhausted. "I'm sorry to be kicking you out, but I've got more wounded to tend to. I've given you more time than I should have, but I understand what you are going through. It's one thing to lose a friend to an enemy bullet. Then you have someone to blame. It's another thing to watch a friend die and not know what killed him." He sighed deeply. "I've told you what I can. Now get out of here and let me do my job." I must have looked crushed. When I turned to go, the doctor said sincerely, "Good luck, son."

I was stunned. This couldn't be. I was with Michael the whole time. I knew he didn't eat anything while on the road that I didn't eat. That couldn't have been it. But then, what killed him? In a daze, I went back to Michael, and found Davey and Patrick faithfully watching the body.

"The surgeon says he was probably poisoned," I told them as I approached. Their reaction was the same as mine. "That's plum crazy. You can't get poisoned in the middle of a battle." Davey said.

"It's not like nobody eats or drinks anything different, is it now?" Patrick echoed.

"Could be the rebs. They won't stop at nothing." Davey suggested.

"I don't think so. First, even the Confederates wouldn't stoop so low. Second, if they were going to use poison, it wouldn't be to kill one private. A group of soldiers would have been killed, and the doctor would have heard about it and told me. No, I don't think it was the rebs, but I do suspect someone killed Michael. Nothing else makes sense."

"So what would you be doing about it?" Patrick asked.

"I don't know, but I'm going to find out what happened. I think it would be best if you both didn't tell anyone about the poisoning, especially Bernard. You know what a gossip he is. If someone murdered Michael, it's best no one knows. If the killer finds out I know, it will be harder to catch him, and he might try to stop me by doing the same to me.

"Hold up," Patrick blurted. "You're not saying 'twas one of our own boys what killed Michael, are you?"

"I don't know. It could be. Someone murdered him. I can't think of any other answer. You said yourself everyone eats and drinks the same food and water. I was with Michael the whole time, and he didn't pick up anything on the road to eat or drink. So what's left? Someone, somehow poisoned Michael. I'm going to find out how and who did it."

"Why not just tell the officers, and let themselves do it by the rules? Then sure you wouldn't have to worry about anyone trying to kill you, would you now?"

"Yeah," Davey piped in, "it would be a whole lot safer."

"I know it would, but I can't do that. I don't know for a certainty if it is someone in the regiment. If I start an official investigation, it has to hurt our reputation even if the killer is not in the 14th Brooklyn. Just the thought that one of our boys might have murdered Michael is enough to start people talking. Michael would not have wanted that, and I don't either. But I don't want to put you boys in danger, so stay out of it."

"To hell I will!" Davey almost yelled. "I've already told you that you're my friend, and I don't desert my friends no how. I'll help with this--what did you call it--investigation. I surely hope it ain't one of the boys in the 14th, but if it is, hell, so be it. Patrick, just cause I said I would help don't mean you have to. Like Jack said, this could be dangerous."

"I'm in," Patrick said as forcefully as I had ever heard him speak. "Jack's my friend too, and Michael was a good man. If he didn't need to die, then don't I want to find out who killed him? We won't tell no one how Michael died." Davey nodded in agreement.

Patrick added, "Sure, I can't believe one of our own boys is a killer."

"That's a funny thing to say, since we've just come back from a fight where I hoped I killed a bunch of rebs."

"You know what it is I mean," he said.

I asked them to stay with the body a bit longer while I asked about how to get it back home to his family, assuming I was right that they would want to bury him. Patrick and Davey agreed.

I located Captain Mallory and reported in. My voice broke as I told him that we had brought back the body of Michael Gorman. "Sir, I know that there are a lot of dead soldiers out there, but given who Michael's family is, they may want his body shipped back to Brooklyn rather than buried here." Mallory took some time to consider what I was suggesting.

Michael was a friend of the Captain's so I had a strong feeling that he would want to do the right thing. I hoped that I wouldn't have to try to convince him to send the body home.

"Private Muller, you're right about his family probably wanting the body. Bring his body to the hospital tent. I'll give you an order for the surgeon to prepare and hold the body until it can be claimed by his family. They'll have to get here quickly because in this heat, the body will decay rapidly. I don't think that will be a problem. If anyone can arrange for Michael's body to be shipped back to Brooklyn right away, it's Daniel Gault."

I told Captain Mallory that I would keep Michael's personal effects and equipment until the family told me what to do with them. Mallory agreed.

After we brought Michael's body to the hospital tent and relayed the Captain's order, I thanked Davey and Patrick for their help. "If I find anything out, I'll let you know. Remember, don't say anything to anyone about the way Michael died."

They nodded their agreement and walked away to find out who else had survived the battle. I went back to the tent because I had a lot of thinking to do. Now that I was pretty sure I knew what had killed Michael, I had to figure out how it was done, who did it, and why. I needed to revisit every action that we had taken between the beginning of the battle and Michael's death to determine how he could have been poisoned, but I also suspected that secrets providing answers to the "who" and "why" might lie in Michael's past.

CHAPTER SIXTEEN

July 23, 1861

When I got back to my tent, no one else was there. I realized that I had changed my thinking about my fellow soldiers. Before the battle, the officers were men, and the rest of us were boys. After going through what we went through, I couldn't think of us as boys anymore. We were men bloodied in battle, and would never be the same.

I knew Patrick and Davey were alive, but I wondered about my other tent mates, Bill Dakin, Hugh Doharty, John McNamee, Larry Staunton, and Bernard Carney. I hadn't seen any of them since the middle of the fight.

With no one around, I could think in peace about what I knew and what I didn't know about Michael's death. It didn't take me long, since I didn't know much. He was poisoned. I knew that. Everything else, I didn't know. How could that happen to a soldier in the middle of a battle? What did he eat or drink during the battle that no one else ate or drank? Who was close to him during the battle, or who had access to whatever it was that killed him? How did everyone else avoid it? Who would want to murder Michael, and how could that person be sure Michael was the one who ate or drank the toxic substance? Was Michael even the killer's intended target?

The questions nagged at me. How could Michael have gotten whatever it was that killed him? We'd had breakfast together. Even though he was not in the same tent as me, Michael had come to my place to share our breakfast. I like to think that he wanted to talk with me before we moved out to make sure I was ready for the fight. So, he and I ate and drank the same things from the same pot. If I wasn't poisoned by breakfast, he couldn't have been. I pictured our actions during the battle. I saw all of us loading and firing, loading and firing, and loading and firing. We ate nothing during the fighting.

We did drink water, but that couldn't have been what did Michael in. Before the battle, five men were assigned to fill all the company's canteens, so the killer couldn't have known who would get which canteen. During the battle, the men shared their water with others who had run out. I remembered drinking from Michael's canteen myself after mine was empty, but I'm alive and healthy so it couldn't have been the water. I had no answers.

I felt myself getting more and more sleepy. Everything was catching up with me: the brutal fight, the endless trip back to camp, Michael dying, and all those unanswered questions. I drifted off to sleep and saw the battle again in a dream. Through the smoke from the gunpowder everyone seemed to be getting shot. Pieces of bodies were flying up in the air. Blood was pouring out of bullet holes. The beautiful uniforms of the 14th Brooklyn were smeared in blood. I saw the same people die that I'd seen shot in the real battle: John Ryan, Ernest Seidel, Robert Simmons, Jesse Pietro, Sergeant Head. And even some men I hadn't seen shot in the battle died in my dream.

Before the battle, I had very different dreams about the fighting. In those dreams, none of the men from the 14th Brooklyn ever got shot. I was always in the lead carrying the colors of the regiment. We would march up to the rebel soldiers, shoot a bunch of them, and they would run away. I would never have those dreams again because now I knew what war was really like. It was not a glorious dream. It was a nightmare.

When I woke up, Bernard Carney was there looking tired, but excited. I was just glad to see him alive and unhurt. "Did you hear?" Bernard said. "Colonel Wood was captured. A lieutenant found him lying on the ground and took the Colonel to an ambulance. The ambulance was captured by the enemy. What d'ya think is going to happen?"

"Nothing's going to happen," I said groggily. "The regiment will be commanded by Lieutenant Colonel Fowler, and we'll do our duty. What else do you know?"

"Bill Dakin from our tent was captured, too. And John Ryan was killed." "I saw John get shot. It was horrible. That's really too bad about Bill. Did you hear that Michael Gorman was killed?"

"No," Bernard said, surprised. "I didn't know that."

"He wasn't shot. He died on the way back to the camp after the battle." I thought it was safe to say that because Bill Shannon and Steve Cooper saw him die on the road from the battle, and must have told others.

Bernard was shocked. "No! After the battle?"

"I think so."

"But how?"

"I don't know," I lied. "Did you hear anything else?" Given Bernard's reputation as a gossip, I was not going to tell him any more.

Bernard responded right away. "Everything about the fight was strange. I never dreamed it could be like that. Boys were getting shot and dying all around me. I just kept trying to load and fire. I thought the war would all be over after this fight. I thought we'd whip the secessionists and be heading home by now. We could have whipped them too. I heard all about the fight. We were doing fine, pushing the enemy back to Richmond."

Bernard was getting more excited as he prepared to report on the news he had obtained. "It was General Patterson's fault," Bernard pronounced with authority.

"What do you mean? General Patterson wasn't even in the fight," I interrupted. "His army's up north in the Shenandoah Valley."

"Exactly," Bernard replied. "General Patterson was supposed to be keeping General Johnston's Confederate army busy there. Instead, Patterson let Johnston slip away and four brigades of Johnston's army made it here for the fight and turned the tide. We fought well, and could have beat the army we were supposed to fight. General McDowell had a good plan, and our boys were whipping them in the beginning. But the rebels kept getting reinforcements during the fight. Remember that?"

"Sure," I said, even though I hadn't seen any of that because with all the smoke I couldn't see much of anything except what was near me.

"Well, that was Johnston's army coming in brigade by brigade. They arrived by train to Manassas Junction. Near as I can tell from all I heard, this is the first time railroads have been used to shuffle soldiers around like that in the middle of a battle. If not for that, no way Johnston's army could have gotten here in time for the fight. But that's beside the point. If General Patterson had kept Johnston busy in the Shenandoah, we would have won.

"We fought like hell, but they kept getting more men. Our boys were ready and wanted to fight. You remember Lieutenant Scholes of Company I? When Company I was left behind with Company K to guard the camps, Scholes volunteered to fight with Company B as a private. Scholes isn't back yet, and we think he was killed in the battle. Heck, I heard that some Congressman from Illinois named Logan joined a Michigan regiment because there was no Illinois regiment in the field. That Logan went into the struggle in his civilian clothes. Our people were ready for the fight and did all they could. If only Patterson had kept the rebs from outnumbering us so bad."

I figured it was only a matter of time before people started blaming others for the loss, just as Michael had predicted. But this was really fast. General Patterson was perfect to blame because he wasn't even in our army. Others, not in our army, would probably blame General McDowell or some of the units that didn't fight too well. It would be weeks or months before things got sorted out.

Bernard didn't have any more information for me. I suggested that he should get some sleep, and he agreed. I decided that I would ask everyone I could if they noticed anything strange in the battle or after the battle, in the hopes that the piece that I was missing would come to me.

I went outside our tent and sat down to write to my parents about the battle and about Michael's death. I thought it would be helpful for me to pull my thoughts together about what I had to do.

July 23, 1861

Dear Mama and Papa,

Although I wrote to you only a few days ago, I write this letter because of the importance of the news it sends. First, I am well, so please do not worry. I do, however, have some tragic news. My best friend, Michael, who you met at camp, is dead.

By now you have gotten news of our disastrous defeat at Bull Run. It was horrible. My idea of war will never be the same again. Instead of gallantry and heroics, there was only blood and death.

I will not give you the details of the fight because you probably know more about it from the newspapers than I do. All I do know is that we lost. You could tell that from all of our soldiers running away after the fight. I did not run. *I followed all of the orders, and retreated only when I was ordered to. Michael was with me the whole time.*

Since Michael was with me after the battle, you are probably wondering how he died. That's the strange thing. The surgeon thinks that he was probably poisoned. I think someone in our regiment might have killed Michael. Right now I do not know who or even how the killer did it.

We all ate the same food and shared the same canteens.

I feel like I have to find out what happened to Michael. I owe it to him. It is so unfair to have lived through the horrible battle, only to die afterward without being shot. If it were me who died that way, Michael would not rest until he found out what happened.

I have to stand on my own now. Michael was not only my best friend in the 14th, he was my teacher, protector and everything else. It was like I had a big brother, and I relied on his quiet confidence to get me through the battle. I do not have that anymore. Your son has to grow up.

Only two other soldiers in the regiment know Michael was poisoned. I have sworn them to secrecy. I think if the killer knows I am looking for him, it could be dangerous for me. So if you want to protect me, don't tell anyone about how Micheal died. There are a few soldiers here from the neighborhood. If their parents hear about it and write to their sons, it will be all over camp in no time. Gossip spreads fast here.

Please don't worry about me. My dreams of heroics are over. I will be careful, both in looking into Michael's murder and in battle.

I remain your loving son,

Jack

I read over the letter I had just written and immediately tore it up. It wasn't right to worry my parents about the danger of me investigating a murder. It was bad enough they had to worry about the "normal" danger of me getting shot in battle.

I wrote another letter to them just letting them know that I was safe, and not to worry. I also told them that I did well in the fight, as did the 14th Brooklyn. It was no fault of ours that we lost the battle.

CHAPTER SEVENTEEN

July 25, 1861

We were back at Camp Porter around Arlington House, and camp life picked up where it had left off. We started back into the routine of squad, company and regimental drill and picket and guard duty.

I don't know how many men I asked about seeing anything odd in the battle. All I could think about was finding the missing clue that would tell me how Michael died.

Everyone I talked to had some camp gossip he wanted to share. But when I asked about what they saw in the battle you could tell they didn't want to talk about it. Like me, they had their ideas about what war was supposed to be like. The smoke, blood and death in the fight just wasn't what they expected. They lost their innocence in that fight, and remembering it was hard for them.

I saw Joe Cramer, who was from my neighborhood in Brooklyn, coming up to me after drill one day with a look on his face that told me he had some news. "Jack," he said, "did you hear about the reb general who was in charge of the soldiers we kept attackin'?"

"No," I said. "What about him?"

Joe replied, "It turns out that was a General Jackson who the papers are saying became famous from the fight. Some other secess general by the name of Bee was yelling at his soldiers to fight harder. This General Bee pointed over at Jackson's brigade and shouted that they should look at Jackson whose brigade was standing there like a stone wall. Jackson's boys put up such a good fight they nicknamed General Jackson "Stonewall." Ain't that something?"

I agreed that was something, but I didn't really want to talk about some enemy general. I then asked Joe if he saw anything strange during the battle. Joe couldn't give me any information I did not already have. "I don't know what you mean by strange. All that shootin' and killin' was strange, at least as far as I figured what would happen. I was thinkin' we'd walk through those traitors and straight on to Richmond. It didn't happen like that and I'm afraid this war is going to last a while. If you mean something else, then I didn't see nothing odd."

I talked with Hans Newman, who was also from my neighborhood in Brooklyn, later in the day. He too was no help in providing me with the missing piece about Michael's death, but he had a very different version of the Stonewall Jackson story. "Did you hear about that General Jackson who led them troops we went up against, the one they nicknamed Stonewall?"

"Yeah," I replied. "I heard that story."

"Well, I bet you didn't hear this. According to some enemy prisoners, the story going around is all wrong. Jackson didn't get his nickname Stonewall because he was fighting so well. As I hear it, this General Bee was being pressed real hard, so he asked Jackson for reinforcements. Jackson wouldn't move his soldiers to lend a hand, so Bee got angry and started yelling at Jackson for standing there like a stone wall instead of coming to assist other soldiers. That's some different story, huh? The fact is, no one's going to know for sure what happened, since this General Bee got himself killed."

I agreed with Hans that the story was interesting, but once I found out that Hans couldn't help me with information, I didn't really feel like talking about the battle.

It was only a couple of days later that I received word that Captain Mallory wanted to see me. When I got to the Captain's tent, I was more than a little surprised to see Mr. Gault there. As soon as he saw me, he stepped forward to shake my hand and said, "Jack, I came for Michael's body as soon as I heard."

The Captain must have telegraphed Mr. Gault the news about Michael right away for him to be here so fast. I guess when you're an important man, people make an effort to get you the news fast. The families of the other men who were killed probably hadn't even heard yet, since they would be sent letters by post, and that wouldn't even be done until after the paperwork was finished. The names of the dead may eventually get published in the newspapers, but that too would not happen until after the Army finished its paperwork. If I had been killed in the fight, I thought, my parents wouldn't even know about it yet. I supposed the army could have telegraphed the wives or parents of each of the boys killed as soon as it confirmed the death, but that would tie up the telegraph lines. But didn't the army owe it to the men who had given their lives for their country?

Mr. Gault hadn't stopped talking, and I might have missed some of the things he said while I was thinking about how quickly he had been informed about Michae's death.

"I heard about you bringing Michael's body back to camp. Elizabeth and I are truly grateful. The Captain was telling me how close you and Michael were. I'm sorry for your loss."

"I'm sorry for your loss, too, sir," I said. "And please send my condolences to Elizabeth."

"I'll do that," he said. Mr. Gault spoke very fast, as if talking quickly would make the words hurt less.

"I understand that you have Michael's personal effects, and I'd like to bring them back home, too. You know, it feels like I lost my own son. I don't think I have to tell you how Elizabeth feels. This whole thing is just horrible. She wanted to come to help bring Michael's body back. My wife and I finally convinced her not to make the trip. She's taken the loss so hard that her health isn't good. Traveling would be very difficult for her."

"I can imagine what Elizabeth is going through," I said. "We'll all miss Michael. If you come with me back to my tent, I can give you Michael's things." I wanted to be alone with Mr. Gault to tell him about how Michael died. Captain Mallory was obviously uncomfortable with the relative of a dead soldier, especially an important relative. The Captain jumped at my suggestion.

"I think that's a good idea. You two should have some time together so Jack can tell you about Michael's last moments."

Mr. Gault and I walked toward my tent. When we were out of ear shot I said, "Sir, I did want to talk to you alone. There's something you have to know. Michael was not shot in the battle. I think he was poisoned."

Mr. Gault turned pale, staggered back a step or two and gasped, "What are you talking about? Are you saying that Michael wasn't killed by the rebels? That he may have been murdered by someone here?"

"That's exactly what I'm saying. Ever since Michael died, I have been trying to work out how he could have been done in, and by whom."

"What makes you say that?"

"I know Michael wasn't shot, you can see that for yourself when you pick up the body. You and I both know that Michael was as healthy as a horse going into the fight. And when I finally got someone's attention in the hospital, and told him the symptoms, he said it sounded like Michael ingested something toxic." I described the symptoms to Mr. Gault and asked that he confirm what the surgeon had said with medical men back in Brooklyn. He agreed to do so immediately. "The doctor said Michael might have picked up some tainted food on the road. But I was close to Michael the whole time, and he didn't eat or drink anything that I didn't eat or drink. And he didn't pick up anything on the trail."

Although I didn't like talking about the battle, I felt that I owed it to Michael's family. "During the fight, I can't tell you how many times I wanted to run away. I believe what kept me there was Michael. I decided going into the fight that I would stick close to him, and I did. During the fighting he didn't hesitate. He was the first to start marching toward the enemy, and the last to retreat. He would load and fire just as smooth as can be, while all around him bullets were flying, men were getting shot, and blood was being spilled. He was my hero, and I'm going to miss him more than I can tell you.

"Mr. Gault, if Michael was murdered, I'm not going to stop until I find out who did it, and see that the person is punished. That is my pledge to you and Elizabeth, on my word of honor.

"I've told only two people that Michael may have been poisoned. And I guess if the surgeon figures out who I was talking about that would be three people. I haven't told anyone else because if Michael was murdered and whoever did it finds out that I'm after him, I'll be the next soldier in this regiment to die. Anyway, I'd appreciate it if you wouldn't spread the word either until I tell you." I was talking to Mr. Gault as an equal, even though back in Brooklyn I probably couldn't even get his attention. I thought for a moment about how I'd changed since the battle. I would never have dreamed of suggesting anything to someone so important, let alone asking for him not to do something.

Mr. Gault didn't seem to notice anything unusual in the way I was addressing him. He was a man of decision and he didn't hesitate now. "All right, the first thing I'm going to do when I get back to Brooklyn is to ask some doctors about the symptoms you described. I'll have Michael's body checked, and if they confirm what you say, I want that perpetrator found as much as you do. I'm not going to tell Elizabeth about it now, because it would upset her too much. But if Michael was slain outside of the battle, I want an official inquiry to punish whoever did it."

"I know how you feel, sir, but I would prefer not to have an investigation. It would be a scandal for the regiment. Michael loved the 14th Brooklyn. He would not want that kind of shame brought on us. If the killer is someone in the 14th, I can't imagine how Elizabeth would take that. Let me find out what happened." The mention of Elizabeth's reaction had a real effect on him. I could see it in his eyes, and the way his shoulders tensed up more than they already were.

"Jack, I suppose you're probably in the best position to find the answers, so I'll abide by your wishes. I want you to keep me informed about what is happening, and I will help any way I can. I know that the mail is slow, so if there is something urgent, you can send me a telegram. I'll reimburse you whatever it costs.

"I'm giving you four months to complete the work. I think that should be enough time, even with the mail being so slow, and the difficulty with what you are trying to do. I suppose there's no harm in my waiting four months, since we will always know where the soldiers are. And if the murderer gets killed in battle or deserts so that they catch him and hang him, so much the better. Then we don't have to tell Elizabeth the whole story.

However, after the four months are up, I'm going to contact Washington and all hell is going to break loose."

When we got to my tent I gave Michael's personal possessions to Mr. Gault. There were three books on military drill and strategy; a bible; Michael's plate, knife, fork and spoon; a picture of Elizabeth in a small frame; a bundle of letters which I never looked at, but would guess were from Elizabeth; pencil, paper and a spiked candle holder that you could stick in the ground for light to write letters at night; a razor, comb, money; and finally a locket with Elizabeth's picture in it. Everything screamed of Michael and his love for Mr. Gault's daughter.

I had put them all in a sack, which I handed to him. I saw his eyes start to water as he gripped the sack. "Sir, I also took some of Michael's equipment; his rifle, cartridge case, bayonet, and the box of firing caps. I would appreciate it if I could keep these. When I go into a fight again, I'd like to be able to use Michael's things. If he can't be with me for inspiration, at least I'll be able to use his rifle." I knew it sounded stupid when I said it, but Mr. Gault seemed to know what I meant.

"You can have them. Use them well. I don't think Elizabeth wants reminders of the military right now. I hope you come home safely, and can bring those items to her then."

"One more thing, Mr. Gault. Michael was the captain of the Company B base ball team. He had the bat and ball. I would like to borrow them to continue his base ball team. I'll return them after the war if I make it through alive. I suppose we could make another ball from some rags, and a bat from a piece of wood, but

Michael's were regulation size and weight. It would help continue his memory in Company B."

"Of course you can keep the bat and ball. I like the idea of Michael's team continuing. As to his death, as I said, I want to help you any way I can. If you need any information, or you can think of anything else I can do for you, write or telegraph me. Whatever I'm doing, I'll stop and take care of you first."

"Thank you, sir. I'll take you up on that offer as soon as I can figure out how only one person can get poisoned in the middle of a battle. If you can figure that out, please let me know."

Mr. Gault left to go back to Brooklyn. If possible, the pressure of finding Michael's killer was even greater. Now I had his father-in-law counting on me as well. And I knew he wouldn't go beyond those four months before he started that investigation, even though it would scandalize the regiment.

CHAPTER EIGHTEEN

———

July 28, 1861

Three days after I met with Mr. Gault, I learned that General McDowell had been replaced by General McClellan as the head of all the soldiers around Washington. Not surprisingly, I heard it from Bernard Carney.

"Boys, have I got news," Bernard shouted as he ran into our tent. Davey, Patrick, and I were the only ones there at the time. Bernard almost fell over Davey and Patrick, who were lying down trying to get some sleep. I was writing a letter home. We were all startled by Bernard. "Have you heard? General McClellan is the new general in charge."

"Who's General McClellan?" We all asked at just about the same time.

"He's replacing General McDowell as top general." None of us had to ask Bernard what he knew about McClellan, because we all knew that he would tell us. And so he did.

"Here's what I know about McClellan. He's a West Pointer and kind of short. Some of the boys that served under him called him Little Mac because of his height. But he seems to be a good soldier. After West Point, he was sent to Mexico to fight in that war. Little Mac got sick really bad. It might have been malaria.

He spent a couple of months in the hospital, and missed a lot of the fighting, but got well in time to see enough action to get promoted a couple of times. After his army time, McClellan went to work for a railroad and became its president. So Little Mac seems to do well in whatever he tries.

"When war broke out, Mac became a major general of volunteers, commanding the Ohio militia. Then he went back into the regular army, and got a big job as commander of the Department of Ohio, responsible for defending Ohio, Indiana, and Illinois. Later they added western Pennsylvania, western Virginia, and Missouri to his responsibilities.

Little Mac was made a major general in the regular army. So this fellow really seems to know his business."

"Has he done any real fightin' in this war?" Davey asked.

"He's fought two battles in western Virginia; the battle of Philippi, and the battle of Rich Mountain. He won them both. Those fights were not nearly as big as the one we fought, but at least he won them. From what I've heard, he's a good choice."

I couldn't help myself from saying angrily, "I hope so. A lot of good men died in that last fight, and for nothing." Patrick and Davey nodded their heads in agreement. "Michael was right. This war is not going to be over quickly, so we better have a good general in charge."

Bernard reacted defensively. "You're right about losing some good boys, but we sure fought well. I heard some things about that too. Remember those charges we made up that hill? Well, that general Stonewall Jackson was heard yelling to his men, "Hold on, boys. Here come those red legged devils again." And that reb general Beauregard, who was in charge of their whole army, well he told this visiting officer from another country that the 14th Brooklyn did more damage to the rebel army than any other regiment in the Union army. That foreign officer could go between the lines, and when he got to our camp, he told General McDowell what Beauregard had said. Since McDowell always liked the 14th, he sent for our Lieutenant Colonel Fowler to tell him about it. The boys should be really proud."

"That's nice, but sure it's not going to bring the dead boys back, is it?" Patrick grumbled. Always practical, Patrick recognized the information for what it was -- a pat on the back to make you feel better about going out and risking your life again in the next fight.

Davey, a lot younger and not as mature, said, "I think it's great that people know that the 14th did itself proud. We did fight good, and it don't hurt none that people know it."

I saw that this conversation wasn't going to help me with my problem of finding Michael's murderer. And it was murder. I had received a telegram from Mr. Gault earlier in the day that I hadn't even had a chance to tell Patrick and Davey about because they were sleeping when it came. The telegram read simply, "Doctors confirm poisoning." I had no idea how Mr. Gault could have brought the body back to Brooklyn and had it examined so quickly. I guess that when a powerful man wants something to happen, it does.

I noticed that the telegram was worded in such a vague way that someone else reading it would not have known that it referred to Michael's death. That was smart, since I had asked Mr. Gault to keep the circumstances surrounding Michael's death secret.

Given that the way Michael died was now confirmed, I thought about how I could use Bernard and his knowledge of everything going on in camp to get some information. Bernard was the most informed soldier in the regiment. He would know if anyone else died suspiciously. I had asked him right after the battle, and he hadn't heard anything. But some time had passed by now, and he may have learned something new.

I still didn't want to tell him about how Michael had been killed. If I did, it would be all over the camp in no time. When the murderer heard about it, he would cover his tracks even more. And if he also heard that I was trying to find out who did it, I might as well put a target on my back. I had to approach Bernard carefully.

"Bernard, however people feel about the battle and the casualties, we sure appreciate all the news you pass on. You hear more than any of the rest of us." You could see Bernard beaming with pride. His eyes literally sparkled, and his smile went from one cheek to the other. He put his hand over his mouth to flatten the few hairs that made up his mustache. I figured that with Bernard feeling so full of himself, he would try his best to tell me whatever he knew. So I continued. "Did you hear about any of the boys dying from something other than a bullet wound?"

Bernard looked at me like I had two heads. "What are you talking about? Why are you asking that?"

"Well, I just wanted to know if the rebs used any other weapons, like knives or bayonets, or if they strangled our boys, or anything else. I want to know what I may be facing in the next battle."

Bernard, still puffed with pride, bought my explanation. "Oh, that's a good idea. No, the only casualties I know about were from bullet wounds except for what you told me about Michael Gorman." I was surprised he remembered our earlier conversation where I told him about Michael's death. I was trying to find out what I could, and figured that Steve Cooper and Bill Shannon knew that Michael wasn't shot, so there was no harm in asking Bernard about it. But now I didn't want to have the biggest gossip in the regiment talking about Michael. I was about to try to change the subject when Bernard eased my fears by saying, "I have to go and pass on the news I gave you boys about General McClellan. The other fellows will want to hear it."

"Thanks again, Bernard, for letting us know," we all shouted at his back.

After Bernard left, I told Patrick and Davey about Mr. Gault's telegram. Patrick spoke first. He saw what I had been trying to learn from Bernard, but he had enough sense not to say anything until now. "Sure, it looks like Michael was the only one poisoned."

Davey looked surprised, "So that's why you asked Bernard about people dying who wasn't shot. That was plum smart."

I acknowledged Davey's compliment, "We don't want to tell anyone else about how Michael died. If we do, pretty soon everyone will know about it. News travels fast through camp. If this got out, at best, the murderer will be on his guard, and at worst he'll try to kill the people looking into Michael's death. Since this could get dangerous I'll ask you again: if you fellows don't want to help me find the killer, just say so now. I'll understand. There's enough risk of dying in this war without adding to it."

To their credit, Davey and Patrick didn't hesitate. "I'll help," Patrick said. "He was your friend, and a good man, wasn't he now? You and me are friends. Sure, I know you would help me if I needed it, even if it were dangerous." Davey agreed with Patrick.

"So what is it we do now?" Patrick asked.

"I have to think about our next steps. I'll let you know when I have a plan."

Things changed after Little Mac was made our general. The spirits of the soldiers improved. The men had felt really down after the battle. Instead of whipping the Confederates, we had been whipped. Although the routine of camp life had immediately picked up where it left off, spirits were sagging. Fellows went through the drills without enthusiasm.

Supplies were short because so many things were left on the battlefield. Many of the men didn't even have guns because they'd dropped them on the run back from the fight.

After Little Mac was made top general, supplies started coming in. Soldiers got new guns. Food got better. And we had regular dress parades. Instead of just drilling, everyone would spruce up and march before Little Mac and the other officers. There was a spring in their steps which had been missing before. The regular inspections that Little Mac started didn't bother the fellows so much.

A couple of weeks passed, and I could see the changes in the men, but they didn't affect me so much. All I could think about was Michael being murdered. I asked everyone I spoke to about the battle, hoping someone would say something that gave me an idea about what could have happened. I was getting nowhere. I knew I was missing something.

We finally started to have target practice again. Little Mac made sure that everyone had rifles, and that there were enough cartridges to allow for fire arms training.

One afternoon, Second Lieutenant Ed Pearce stuck his head in our tent and told us that Company B was ordered to report for target practice on the parade ground where drills were held. After Pearce left our tent, I reached for Michael's cartridge case, then stopped. I did not want to use Michael's equipment when all we were doing was practicing. So I took my own cartridge box and rifle and headed out.

When we arrived, Lieutenant Pearce explained the drill. "Okay, boys, line up in columns with six men abreast. The first line will march up to here," he pointed to a branch lying by his feet, "and when ordered, start firing at will. Each boy will fire four shots at the target over there." He pointed to some stacked logs about two hundred yards away. I guess they were supposed to represent the front line of a rebel company. "After each soldier in the group has fired his four rounds, all six will march back to the end of the column, and a new group of six will march up to the firing line."

I saw that beyond the logs were some woods, so if you missed the target, your shot would go harmlessly into the trees. Of course, everyone had been told to stay clear of that area of the woods during the shooting drill.

I watched the boys in front of me take their turns loading and firing. I thought to myself that this practice was useful, but it was nothing like war. The day was clear and bright, and you could see for miles. I could hear other companies drilling in the background. The sound and smoke from six guns firing at the same time was nothing. Since there wasn't much shooting going on, the air still smelled fresh. Not like in battle where the air reeked of gunpowder. And of course, no one was trying to kill you during target practice.

During our battle, the smoke from the guns didn't let you see very far at all. The sound of the muskets was deafening, and you had to watch your friends getting wounded or killed. I wondered how many of the boys who had no problem loading and firing here had been able to do it in the battle a week ago.

How many of them ended up loading and not firing, or loading and shooting their ramrod because they forgot to take it out of the rifle? I shook my head to get rid of those thoughts. I would do what I was trained to do, while I tried to figure out how Michael was done in, and who did it.

Steve Cooper, Peter Glasson and Robert Lewis were in the line with me. They were friendlier to me ever since I had joined the Company B base ball team. "Hey, Jack," Steve said, "I'll bet you a dollar I can out-shoot you. Pick a spot on those logs and I'll hit it. I don't need target practice."

"No thanks, Steve. I don't gamble. I send my money home."

"You're missing out on a lot of fun!" Steve couldn't help it, he was just so full of himself. Robert and Peter just grinned. This was typical behavior for Steve, and I knew they found it funny.

"Keep quiet, you two!" yelled Lieutenant Pearce. "You're here to shoot, not talk."

"Damn officers," Steve whispered. "We should use them as targets. I'd never miss."

My turn finally came. I went through the process of loading and firing just like I'd been taught. I grabbed the musket with my left hand, putting the butt between my feet. Then I reached into my case and grabbed a paper cartridge between my thumb and the next two fingers. I took out the cartridge, brought it to my mouth and tore the paper between my teeth. I emptied the powder into the barrel of the rifle. Then I took out the minie ball from the paper and put it into the muzzle with the pointed end of the minie ball up. I drew the rammer and placed its head on the bullet. Holding the rammer with the thumb and forefinger of my right hand, I pressed down hard, pushing the bullet deep into the barrel of the rifle. I pulled out the rammer and returned it to the groove of my rifle.

Then I primed the rifle by half-cocking the hammer of the gun, removing the old percussion cap, taking a new one from my pouch, and putting it on the nipple and pressing it down. Then I fully cocked the rifle, brought it up to my shoulder, aimed and fired. I repeated this process for the next two of my shots.

Something was bothering me while I loaded and fired my first three rounds. I was missing something important. It was a thought I couldn't identify, but knew that I should be able to. I was so close. It was like looking through roiling water and seeing something at the bottom. I could barely make it out, but I knew that if and when the water cleared I would be able to see exactly what it was.

I thought about the cartridge display we saw at the Patent Office; what a great invention it was for soldiers. It allowed each soldier to load and fire so much faster because he had practically everything he needed in one packet he could tear with his teeth.

I started to load my musket for my fourth round when suddenly I froze. I knew what I had been missing. I knew how Michael could have been murdered. It was the one thing Michael had put in his mouth that no one else did.

I was brought out of my stupor by a shout. "Muller, what the hell are you doing there?" yelled Pearce. "Are you going to stop firing when the enemy is coming at you? No one said 'cease fire.' You keep shooting until ordered to stop. You got that?"

"Yes, sir!" I replied.

Steve Cooper snickered softly. "I told you! Damn officers, we should be shooting at them." Robert nodded his head while Peter calmly said, "Don't get upset, Pearce is merely doing his job."

I finished loading and fired my fourth shot. After that I and the five other men in my group marched to the end of the line. I watched the other fellows take their turns, but I wasn't thinking about the target practice. I just wanted to tell Davey and Patrick what I figured out.

Michael could have been poisoned by the cartridges! Every time he fired a shot, he had to bite off the paper cartridge to reload. During the fighting, the smoke was so thick you could taste it. This meant three things. First, any taste of the poison on the cartridge would be hidden. Second, the smoke made you swallow and drink water to try and keep your mouth wet. So whatever was on the paper cartridge would be swallowed. And third, only Michael would be using his cartridges. That would explain why only Michael was affected.

It was brilliant! I now believed that I knew how Michael, and only Michael, could have been poisoned. If you wanted to make sure a specific soldier didn't make it through a battle, the best way to do it was by tampering with his cartridges. If he wasn't shot, he would die from the poison. I figured the fact that Michael didn't die until after the battle was because whoever killed him didn't figure the dosage right. The day before the battle we were issued sixty rounds each. It was not likely that any of the soldiers would share their cartridges. Given the amount of time it took to load and fire, he probably wouldn't run out before he was killed or the fight was over.

I had another thought. When Company B was ordered to report for target practice, I had reached for Michael's cartridge box, then decided against it. I wanted to save Michael's equipment for use in battle, and that superstition may have saved my life. Michael was still looking out for me.

CHAPTER NINETEEN

August 8, 1861

I had to be sure that the cartridges were what killed Michael before I went on. I thought about how to do that while waiting for the other boys to finish up their target shooting. I couldn't come up with any plan, and hoped that Patrick or Davey might have an idea when I told them how I thought Michael was murdered.

After the practice, I found Bernard Carney in our tent. Patrick, Davey, Hugh Doharty, and John McNamee were there too. Bernard was all fired up to talk to anyone who would listen. "Boys, I have big news to tell you. It will make you feel a whole lot better about how the war is going."

"Well, that kind of news is always welcome." John said.

That was all the encouragement that Bernard needed. "You boys know about the rebel pirate ships, don't you?"

Our looks told him that we didn't. "Well, when the war started, that traitor southern president Jefferson Davis invited people to apply for commissions or what they call letters of marque, which allow privately owned boats to be armed and sent to sea to attack Northern ships. Those are just fancy words for pirates."

"What do you mean?" Davey asked.

"I'll tell you what I mean," Bernard continued with an angry tone in his voice. I think he was upset with the pirates, not Davey. "Northern trading vessels are no match for these damned armed Confederate ships. The rebs carry extra men so when they capture one of our merchantmen, the traitors take over the ship and sail it to a Southern port. Then they sell it and its cargo as what they call prizes. It's a real money-maker for the south."

"That's not good news, is it?" Patrick wanted to know.

"The good news is that it blew up on them. An unarmed merchantman named the S.J. Waring left New York on a long commercial voyage to ports in South America. It had a crew of eight including a free Negro cook named William Tillman, and one passenger. After about three days at sea, the Waring was taken by a southern vessel called the Jefferson Davis, which was armed with five guns. The Jefferson Davis had been flying a French flag just to fool Union boats.

"After the capture, those damned pirates put five of their men on the Waring to sail it to Charleston, and five of the crew of the Waring were taken to the Jefferson Davis as prisoners. One of the three original crew that was left on the Waring was the Negro cook, Tillman. Well, boys, Tillman knew that as soon as they got to Charleston, he would be sold as a slave. Tillman even heard some of the prize crew guessing the price that they would get for him."

Everyone was quiet. This was a good story. Bernard continued, "Tillman made up his mind that he was not going to Charleston. So one night, Tillman took the galley hatchet that he had hidden when the Waring was captured. With that hatchet and the help of one of the original crew, Tillman killed the prize crew captain, first mate, and second mate. Tillman put the other two rebel sailors in irons.

"That Negro and the others then sailed the Waring away from Charleston, and all the way to New York. Some story, huh, boys? Tillman is a real hero."

"Wow," said Hugh Doharty. "But he was just a cook. He ever sail a ship before?"

"No," replied Bernard. "But he had spent a lot of time at sea as a cook. I guess he just picked up enough to be able to sail the ship. That southern trash about Negros all being stupid is crap. This fellow was smart enough to kill three rebel sailors, capture two more, and sail a ship."

Someone yelled, "Hurrah for Tillman!"

"What happened to him?" asked John McNamee.

Bernard replied, "In New York they treated him like the hero he is. He'll probably get a reward for returning the ship and cargo."

Davey was smiling broadly. "Darn, that was some story. That Negro has grit. The story has everything: pirates, a hero, and a happy ending."

Everyone wanted to give their comments on the story, but Bernard cut them off. "Sorry, boys, but I have to get going. There's a lot more folks to tell this news to."

It was a great story, but I was only half listening. I needed to tell Patrick and Davey what I figured out. We also needed to talk about what to do from here. As soon as I could, I signaled to them to come outside with me where we could talk without being overheard.

When we were all outside, I started to walk towards a deserted area and Patrick and Davey walked with me. I told them that I did not want anyone overhearing us because I had big news.

"It was at target practice that I realized how Michael could have been murdered! I was watching the boys who went before me load and fire. They would bite off the cartridge paper to pour the powder and ball down the muzzle for each shot."

"That ain't nothin' new," Davey interrupted. "We saw that there thing at the Patent Office. That's how you always load and fire."

"Yeah, but then it was my turn. After a couple of shots, I bit into the paper and realized that was how Michael could have been poisoned! It was the cartridges! Michael's must have been tampered with. That's the only thing that makes sense. It couldn't have been the food or the water because everybody ate and drank from the same bucket. Michael didn't eat anything on the road, so the surgeon's guess that he might have picked up what killed him there can't be right. I'm telling you, I think it was the cartridges."

"Wow," said Davey, "that is really some smart thinking. I don't know how you done figured it out, but that sure is something." Patrick was nodding his head and looking impressed.

"The thing is, if the cartridges were poisoned, then one of his tent mates must have done it. Remember, we each got sixty rounds in the late afternoon before we moved out. We kept them in our tents with us so they wouldn't get wet. Everyone was alert. A stranger couldn't have gone into Michael's tent to tamper with the cartridges. It had to be someone who belonged there.

"We have to be absolutely sure that Michael was killed that way before I can go around accusing anyone. I'm pretty sure, but we need proof. Do you fellows have any ideas about how we can get it?"

It was Patrick who answered the question. "Didn't yourself say that you kept Michael's cartridge box?

"Right."

"And would there be any cartridges left in that box?"

"I think so, but I'm not sure."

"Well, then," he continued, "easy it is. If there be any cartridges left in the box, we try them and see if they're tainted, don't we now?" This didn't sound right to me but Patrick proudly continued. "We just catch some animal, have itself nibble on some of them cartridges, and see for ourselves what happens."

"But the gunpowder in the cartridges would probably kill an animal, anyway."

Patrick replied in a 'you must be stupid' tone. "Don't we dump the gunpowder out first? That way the animal nibbles only the paper. Don't you bite into nothing but the paper when you're loading? If it ain't poisoned, the cartridge ain't neither."

"What do we do with the animal afterwards?" I asked. "If the animal is tainted we don't want anybody eating it."

Patrick brushed aside this concern with ease. "If it dies, we'll just bury it, won't we?"

Patrick's idea seemed sound and he had quickly answered my questions. I couldn't wait to get started. "Let's get passes to leave camp and try out your idea."

We walked back to our tent being careful not to let people overhear any talk about Michael's killing. I was in a hurry to get back to the tent to see whether there were any cartridges left in Michael's case. Patrick and Davey seemed to be in as much of a hurry as me. We ran into a couple of people who seemed to have nothing to do. When it looked like they wanted to talk, I told them that we were going to get some paper and a pencil to write letters. The fellows understood that we had to go. At our tent, I found the case and looked inside.

"Okay, boys, take a look! There are five cartridges left in Michael's case. I'm going to take three of them out and put them in my pocket so I'll have them whenever we can get passes to leave camp. I'll leave two in there. That way if the cartridges we test are deadly, and we need to show anyone what was in Michael's case, we can show them the remaining two."

Davey was excited. "I'm mighty glad there are cartridges we can try. Figuring out how Michael was killed was a real brain tickler. I can't rightly believe how you did it. If we didn't have the cartridges, I don't know how we would've proved it."

"Sure, it'll work," Patrick, the man of few words, said with a pleased tone since it was his idea. I could see his eyes sparkling because he had figured out the puzzle. Patrick was smart. All he needed was someone to pay attention to what he had to say. I was ready to do that.

CHAPTER TWENTY

August 12, 1861

It was days before all three of us could get passes to leave camp at the same time. A lot of the boys wanted to leave camp to have some privacy, or to wash up in the creek instead of just a bucket, so we had to wait our turn. And it was even harder to get three passes so all of us could leave together.

Finally, we had our passes and started walking out of camp. That's when Davey raised a question we should have thought about beforehand. "How do you catch a critter? When you hunt, you kill it and that won't do us no good."

"Never have I trapped an animal before." Patrick added.

"Me neither," I said. "We used to go down by the ferry to kill rats, but I never tried to trap anything."

Davey added, "I used to kill rats, too. Tho' we had a cat who was a whole lot better'n me at it."

"That's all fine, but we can't kill this animal, can we?" Patrick reminded him. "We gotta take it alive to see if it dies from the cartridge paper, don't we now? How do you s'pose we do that?"

I had an idea. "Why don't we head for the creek? Animals like water. Maybe we'll think of something on the way."

As we walked, we tossed around ideas about how we could trap the animal. Davey suggested a box with a stick holding it up, and a rope attached to the stick so that when the animal went under the box to get some food, we'd pull the stick out and trap the animal in the box.

Unfortunately, we didn't have a box or food or a stick or a rope to attach to the stick. So that idea wasn't too good.

Then Davey suggested, "If you fellas don't like that idea, why don't we chase some critter down? There's three of us and only one of it."

We walked down to the creek and sat around waiting for some animals to show up. None did. We were wondering why we hadn't seen any animals, and then it dawned on me. "We've been in camp here for weeks. Fellows who want fresh meat instead of the boiled stew the army serves have been killing every animal that walks on four legs. We've all seen the boys cooking up what they shot. All you need is a spit and an open fire. This area may be all hunted out."

Davey asked, "So what do we do now?"

"Isn't there a farm about a half mile from here?" Patrick replied. "If we had some money, we could buy some old chicken what's not laying anymore. We could try stealing one, but sure there'll be hell to pay if we're caught."

I thought that idea had possibilities. "I have about three dollars saved up. I keep the money on me because I don't want to leave it in the tent. I don't know if that would buy a whole chicken." It was a lot of money for me to spend, but if it helped in finding out who murdered Michael, I was more than willing to do it. So I told Patrick and Davey, "Good idea. Let's walk over there."

It was a bright sunny day, not as hot as it had been, even though it was August. The sunlight sparkling in the woods looked beautiful, and you could smell the grass and trees and wildflowers. It all made me feel glad to be alive. But that made me think about the battle and all the fellows who ended up dead. The woods didn't look as beautiful then, and suddenly there was no sweet smell in the air. I shook off those memories as quickly as I could, and started to feel good again.

We all enjoyed the walk. We talked about our families, and wondered how they were doing. "Camp life is pretty good, but I do miss home." I said. "I miss my parents. I hope they're doing ok. They wouldn't tell me if they weren't. Before the war, I gave my parents the money I earned. If we needed more money, I would work more hours. Now I send home money, but I can't earn extra and send more if they need it. That worries me. And I remember the nights we would just sit around with me reading out loud to please my father. At the time I didn't much like it.

But now I realize my folks didn't much like it either. They were putting up with it for me, and making it seem like they were enjoying it. We would break up the reading with just talking. We talked about my work, my father's work, the neighborhood and the neighbors. There were a lot of folks from Germany around, so it was kind of a close group. I just miss home."

Patrick took his turn with few words. "That's nice. My home was not so good."

Patrick stopped as if that was all he had to say. I didn't want to pry, but I did want to know him better. So I pressed on gently. "What do you mean?"

"It was rough, our life in shanty town in Manhattan, wasn't it? I couldn't find regular work, and most of the talk was about what I done to find work, and how hard it was. My missus and me, we fought a lot. Worse it was with three kids screaming around us. Now I eat good and get to send money home. I like it here."

"Me, too," Davey piped in. "Our small farm in Flatbush didn't make much, and I was hungry lots of times. Now, I'm with Patrick, the army gives me plenty of food, and I have money to send home. I miss my sisters and brothers, but I don't miss scrambling around for food."

"Have you heard anything from home?" I asked.

"No," replied Patrick and Davey almost together. Patrick added, "The wife and children can't read or write. Themselves would have to pay someone to write a letter, and sure they have better use for the money. Sometimes the wife will go to the priest to read my letters or to write one to me. The priest is very busy with writing letters for all those what can't, so she doesn't like to ask him for help that much. I understand."

"Yeah, me and my brothers and sisters can't read or write neither. My folks can, but the farm keeps them pretty busy. No time to write. I don't mind it none."

My parents wrote often, but now I felt bad telling them about the letters I'd received. It sounded too much like bragging. "Well, I get a letter sometimes. The latest one talked about how busy the Navy Yard was.

The war has created a lot of work for people in Brooklyn. Did you know, there are now Negroes working in the Navy Yard? You fellows ever hear of the Underground Railroad? That's what they call the escape route for runaway slaves. That's how they would get to the north and freedom. A lot of them ended up in Brooklyn, working at the Navy Yard."

Patrick immediately got angry. "Are you telling me that I couldn't get work, but the Negroes we're fighting for can jus' walk into the Navy Yard and get a job? Sure, that ain't right."

I'd hit on a touchy subject. "Well, maybe there aren't so many of them. Besides, with the war on, there's a lot more work at the Navy Yard now. Those Negroes probably couldn't have gotten work there before the war, either. Let's just focus on finding Michael's killer." I could tell that Patrick was still angry, but he kept silent.

When we got to the farmer's house, we knocked on the door. The old farmer inside opened the door, and he was carrying a gun. "Don't shoot us!" I said. "We just came by to see if we could buy a chicken."

The farmer, a sturdy old man with a face lined from thousands of hours out in the sun, grunted, "You soldier boys been stealing me blind. If anybody makes a move to the chicken coop he's gonna get shot."

I pulled out my money and said, "Hold on, hold on. We're not here to steal from you. We came here to buy something. If you're not willing to sell it, just say so. Besides, if we were here to steal a chicken, do you think we'd knock on your door? Have any of the soldiers who've stolen from you come to your door before they did it?"

The farmer thought a moment and relaxed. "I guess you're right, "he said, lowering the gun slightly. "But I can't sell you no chicken for three dollars. I need the eggs from those chickens what I got left. I could use the money, but I just can't give up a chicken. If it's food you're interested in, my grandson's been taking care of a rabbit. He's mighty fond of the critter, but I'll buy him some candy with some of the money. I'll sell you the rabbit for two dollars."

I said, "I'll give you fifty cents for the rabbit. You know some soldier is gonna steal it anyway. And if some soldier doesn't steal it, you'll still just end up eating it, and making your grandson sad either way."

"A dollar and a half," the farmer said. "One dollar," I replied.

"Sold," said the farmer. "Okay, you boys wait here, and I'll bring along the rabbit. I want to get it so my grandson don't notice."

The farmer went around to the back of the house, where he must have kept the rabbit. Patrick, Davey, and I waited at the front door. The farmer's grandson was nowhere to be seen, which was a good thing. I didn't want the boy crying in front of us when his grandfather turned over the rabbit to us.

"That was some bargainin', Jack. Where'd you learn to do that?" Davey asked, obviously impressed.

"I learned it from my father. He said that more than half of what a lawyer does is negotiate. Whether it's dealing with the lawyer on the other side to get what your client wants, or dealing with your client about the fee, there's a whole lot of it involved in being an attorney. So my father would practice with me. When there were chores to do, my father and I would negotiate about who was to do what. I would never let my father do too much, but the back and forth itself became fun. Pretty soon that sort of thing was second nature to me."

"Your father, sure he sounds like a good teacher--and a good father," Patrick said wistfully. I could tell Patrick was thinking about what kind of father he was to his children. Unable to find a job, fighting with his wife, and probably screaming at his children did not make for a happy home.

Fortunately, just then the old man showed up at the front door with the rabbit. I handed over the dollar and he gave me the rabbit. I let Davey carry it. The three of us walked back toward camp with a spring in our steps. It was Davey who brought us back to reality when he said, "Now that we got the animal, what do we do with it?"

Since it was Patrick's idea to begin with, he felt obliged to speak. "We'll have itself nibble on some cartridge paper, and see what happens. It might take a while for the animal to decide to nibble, or for anything to happen to itself. We have to be back in camp soon, so's we don't have the time for that, do we now? Sure we can't leave the cartridge paper here. If the rabbit gets itself poisoned somebody may himself get killed if he finds the rabbit and eats it."

"So what should we do?" Davey asked.

"That's a fine question," replied Patrick, who was speaking more than I ever remembered him talking. I could see that he was proud that he had come up with the idea to use an animal to test my theory about how Michael was murdered, and he was not going to let some minor details spoil his idea. He continued, "We can't keep no live animal in camp, can we? And sure we can't kill it. Don't we have to find a place to hide it 'til we can test for the poison; some cave, or a hole in the ground, to keep the rabbit overnight, or maybe longer if we can't get passes tomorrow? We've no need to worry about other animals eating the rabbit 'cause there maybe aren't any other animals left in these parts. If we can get passes, sure we'll be out right after drill in the morning. "

So we left the road to look for some place to hide the rabbit.

After a while we came across a hole in the ground about three feet across, and a foot deep. We made it deeper by digging it out with our hands. When it was about three feet deep we decided that the rabbit couldn't get out if we covered it over with sticks and leaves. So that's what we did, leaving a little grass at the bottom of the hole for the rabbit to eat, so it wouldn't starve.

We hurried back to camp in time for evening roll call. I was really tempted to sneak out and go back to the rabbit, but I decided I'd better wait. Morning came soon enough. After company drill and breakfast we had some time before regimental drill. I found Davey and Patrick. We figured at least one of us could get a pass at this slow time of day. We were in luck, and were able to get passes for all of us right away. We headed out for the rabbit. I was still carrying the three cartridges from Michael's box.

We found the trail we had left and followed it right to the hole with the rabbit still in it. I wasted no time in carefully emptying out the contents of each of the cartridges so that just the paper was left. I dropped the three papers in the hole, and we all waited. The rabbit sniffed around the papers but wouldn't nibble.

"What's the matter with that rabbit?" I complained, worried that our experiment wasn't going to work.

"It knows it ain't food, don't it" Patrick replied. "Put some grass on the paper. When it eats the grass, sure it'll have to chew on the papers, too." I pulled some grass and laid it on the papers. Thank goodness, that turned the trick. Patrick was right. The rabbit immediately went over and started nibbling on the grass, and since the grass was right on the paper, the rabbit began chewing the paper, too. We watched about half an hour before the rabbit started to show the same signs that Michael had shown the day he died. The rabbit staggered and bumped into the sides of the hole like it was stiff and dizzy at the same time.

About 20 minutes later, the rabbit just froze up and laid down. I picked it up carefully. It was dead. Its eyes were wide open and its pupils were really big just like Michael's eyes had been.

"Well, boys," I said, both sad and excited, "That does it for me. Michael was killed because someone tainted his cartridges. There's no doubt about it now. It worked an awful lot faster on a little rabbit than it would on a man, but I'm sure that the same thing that killed Michael killed this rabbit."

"So who done it?" Davey asked.

"Yeah," added Patrick. "Who was it?"

"I don't know," I sighed. "But this narrows down the possibilities a whole lot. They gave us the cartridges in the late afternoon before we moved out to the fight. And we all kept our cartridge boxes in our tents so they wouldn't get wet if it rained. So it's not like Michael's cartridge belt was laying around for anyone to get to."

"That's right!" Patrick agreed. "After they gave ourselves the cartridges, you couldn't really move around much in camp. There were guards all over because we were in enemy territory, wasn't we. Everyone stayed in their tents. If a boy came into the tent who didn't belong there, them in the tent would have noticed. So the only ones what could've poisoned the cartridges are them that shared Michael's tent."

Davey was excited. "I know who they were. It was Steve Cooper, George Hudson, Bill Shannon, Peter Glasson and Robert Lewis. I remember because I had to walk by them every time I went to drill. It was the shortest way, and I was always in a hurry. I was just scared to death of being late. Even though I was hurrying by, the six of them were always still around seeming not to be in any hurry at all. That's why I remember it so good."

"Murder Michael? Sure, I can't believe any of them would." observed Patrick thoughtfully.

"Me neither," added Davey.

"Look," I said, "none of us can believe it, but Michael was killed. We know he was murdered, and we know how it was done. And now we also know that there are only five fellows who could have pulled it off.

Obviously one of them must have had a reason - that's what we have to find out. I can tell you that there was something going on with Steve, Bill, and Robert. I heard them saying some really bad things to Michael after a couple of the base ball games. I asked Michael about it, and he wouldn't tell me anything except that there had been some troubles before they were in the army Another thing is, I wonder which one of those five knows anything about poisons. If we get the answers to those questions, we should know who killed Michael."

"What is it you want us to do?" asked Patrick. Davey was nodding his head beside him.

"The first thing we have to do is fill in this hole and bury the rabbit in it so that no one will find it and eat it. After that, I want you to ask around at all the drugstores and sutlers in the area to find out if they have poison, and if anybody bought some before the battle. Don't tell them the real reason you're asking. Make up something. Tell him you got some animal that keeps coming into your tent, and you want to get rid of it. You wonder if anybody else has bought some so you could ask them how it worked."

"But this area's all hunted out, ain't it?" Davey objected. "There ain't no critters left to come into a tent."

"Just because there are no animals you would hunt for food, doesn't mean there are no rats, or some other kind of vermin. That's it. Just say you have a rat problem in your tent, so you need something to get rid of them. I also want you fellows to see if any of those five received packages before the fight. You can check with Sergeant Manderville. He works in the camp post office, and I think he probably knows everything anybody's gotten.

"I'm going to write to Mr. Gault and ask him to find out information on the five of them. I want to let him know that we figured out how Michael was done in, and the names of the five suspects.

"I'm also going to talk with the five of them. I'm not sure what I'm going to ask that wouldn't tip my hand. I guess I'll try to find out what they thought of Michael and what kind of experience they have with chemicals and medicines and things.

"Let's get back to camp now. Remember, don't let on that anything's wrong. Especially don't tell anyone what we're doing, or what we found out."

CHAPTER TWENTY-ONE

August 13, 1861

When I got back to my tent, I took out my pencil and paper and wrote a letter to Mr. Gault.

August 13, 1861

Camp Porter

Dear Mr. Gault,

I received your telegram confirming that Michael was poisoned, and I write to let you know that I have found out how it was done. The killer tainted Michael's paper cartridges, so every time he loaded his rifle and bit the cartridge, he took in more of the toxic matter (as the doctor called it).

In case something happens to me, you can get information from my two best friends in the regiment (now that Michael's gone), who are working with me to try and find out who murdered Michael: Patrick Murphy and Davey O'Connor. We have kept what we are doing secret from everybody else.

The way we figure it, the killer has to be someone who shared the tent with Michael. Since the army issued our ammunition late in the afternoon the day before the battle, and everyone stayed by his tent, no one else could've gotten to Michael's cartridge case.

The five boys who were in the tent with Michael were Bill Shannon, Steve Cooper, George Hudson, Peter Glasson, and Robert Lewis. I would appreciate it if you could find out information on each of them. What I'm looking for is any reason any of them hated Michael enough to want him dead, and whether any of them knows anything about toxic substances.

I and my two friends will continue our efforts here to the best of our ability. Thank you in advance for your help. Again, please accept my condolences for the loss of Michael, and pass on my deepest sympathies to Elizabeth.

With my appreciation and respect, I remain

Jack Muller

I re-read the letter to make sure it sounded right and asked for all the information I needed. I was once again grateful to my father who insisted that I practice writing along with reading. He told me over and over that those were two skills I needed if I ever wanted to be a lawyer.

When I was satisfied with the letter I sealed it in an envelope that I bought earlier from one of the camp sutlers. You could get most anything you wanted from the sutlers, who ran a sort of a general store out of their wagons. They would follow the regiment and offer things for sale that you might need. They had everything from food, like dried beef or apples, to shaving items like razors and soap. Since our camp sutler was selected by the regiment's officers, I thought I could trust them to be fair. Another nice thing about the sutlers was that they sold you what you needed on credit. All you had to do was sign an IOU, which let the sutler collect the amount owed at the next pay day.

I addressed the envelope and dropped it into the sack for outgoing mail, remembering my visit to the massive post office when we were in Washington. Here's another letter for you folks to deal with, I thought. It was still unbelievable to me that the post office could actually take a letter from me in camp, and get it to a specific address in Brooklyn (even if it could take weeks), along with the thousands of other letters they had going to different places. This thought caused me to worry that my letter to Mr. Gault might not reach him. But there was nothing I could do about that, so I wiped the thought from my mind and hoped for the best.

CHAPTER TWENTY-TWO

—

August 16, 1861

I needed to talk to each of the five soldiers who might have killed Michael. They usually all stayed close together, so if I went to see one, I would probably run into the others. But I didn't want any of them to get suspicious about what I was doing, because the real killer might decide to cut short my questions by doing to me what he did to Michael. Since I wanted to talk to each one separately, I couldn't go to their tent. Also, I didn't want it to seem like I was making a special trip to ask questions about Michael, because that too would make the guilty one suspicious.

I needed to find some excuse for talking to each of them in a private place. I decided to speak to Steve Cooper first. Steve was a gambler. I knew this because I overheard Michael talking to Steve about not betting on our company's base ball games. Michael told Steve, "Everyone knows you gamble a lot. That's your own business, but not if it involves our base ball games. If you bet on the games, you're off the team."

There were plenty of other opportunities to gamble. You could play dice or cards. Boys would race and people would bet on the winner. Boxing matches were set up, and again there was plenty of betting on who would win. I asked around, and found out that poker was Steve's favorite game. There was a good chance that Steve would be wherever there was a poker game going on.

I was not a gambler, and everyone knew I couldn't be one because I sent most of my money home to my parents. But I figured I could pretend that I wanted to learn about cards so I could win more money to send home. I heard that Steve frequented a game run by Arthur Fitzpatrick of Company A. Because officers did not like the fellows gambling, the games were held inside the tents. I headed over to the Company A area. If Steve was in the game, he would have to take a break some time and I would talk to him then. I knew where Fitzpatrick's tent was, so I started walking that way.

Before too long, I saw George Hudson heading my way. I figured that it wouldn't make much difference which suspect I spoke to first. Since George was right there, I might as well question him now.

"Hi, George, how are you?"

"Not bad, Jack. How about you?"

"I'm still pretty low about Michael's death in the fight we had. You know, he was my best friend in the regiment."

"Yeah, I know that. He thought very highly of you." George's comment only made me feel worse. "I feel kind of bad that I missed the fight. I was in the hospital until after the battle. I had the trots really bad, and my stomach hurt like hell. They didn't know what it was, but I think I just ate some bad berries from the woods. The doctors put me in the hospital, but after the battle they had to throw me out to make room for the wounded. I didn't mind, a stomach ache doesn't compare to a boy with his leg shot off. I'm alright now, but I do feel guilty about missing the fight. From what I heard, it was pretty bad."

"Yeah, it was. Going in, we all thought that a battle was a lot of heroics and glory. It turns out that it's really a lot of fear and blood. You were lucky to have missed it."

"Well, I'm sorry about Michael, and all the other boys who were killed or wounded."

If George was in the hospital from before the fight until after it, then he couldn't have poisoned Michael's cartridges, which weren't given out until the day before the fight. I would have to check his story, but there was no reason not to believe him. I started to think that if the innocent suspects were this easy to eliminate, maybe finding the killer wouldn't be as hard as I thought.

I decided to put off my talk with Steve Cooper and immediately check George's story with the regimental hospital. I went over to the infirmary to speak with a surgeon to see if I could confirm that George was in the hospital before and during the battle. As I was approaching the tent I saw Dr. Joseph Homiston, the regimental surgeon, sitting outside on a rocking chair smoking a pipe. When he saw me approaching the tent, he greeted me with, "Hello there, my lad. You missed sick call, but I'm not doing anything now. So what ails you?"

It was hard to believe that this friendly, jovial man sitting in such a relaxed way had been sawing off the arms and legs of wounded soldiers only weeks before. I would have thought someone like that would be permanently saddened. I guess he felt he was saving them, not maiming them, and that made it all right. Maybe it was, but I could not lose the image I had seen of the surgeon in a bloody apron with boys all around him screaming and moaning, and arms and legs on the floor in the middle of more blood than I had ever imagined. But that was weeks ago, and it seemed to be all but forgotten by many.

"Nothing ails me, sir, but I have a problem you may be able to help me with. My friend George Hudson has not been looking well. I don't know if you remember him, but he was in the hospital before the battle. He's such a good soldier, he won't go back to the infirmary to get checked. My question is, how do I get him to come to see you to get examined?"

"Oh, sure, I remember Hudson because we had to kick him out of the hospital after the battle to make way for the wounded. He came in with stomach cramps and diarrhea a few days before the fight. Probably some bad water. We gave him medicine for the stomach cramps, and he seemed to be improving. But when the wounded started to arrive, we had to discharge him because we needed his bed. Just tell him I said to stop by if he's still having problems."

"Thanks sir, I will."

I walked away, thinking that George was in the clear. That was easy. One down, and only four to go.

I went back to my tent to try to find Patrick and Davey to let them know what I found out about George Hudson. I saw them outside the tent just sitting around, talking with some other men. When they looked up, I signaled for them to join me. That way we could walk around camp and no one would overhear what we were saying. They came right away.

"Did you find out anything?" Davey asked eagerly.

"I sure did. George Hudson couldn't have killed Michael."

"Why not?" asked Patrick.

"Because he was in the hospital tent. George had the quick step, and the surgeon put him in the hospital a couple of days before the battle, until they threw him out right after the battle so they could have his bed. Since the cartridges weren't handed out until the day before the battle, no way he did it."

"Well then, we don't have to worry none about him." Patrick summed it up in his usual way, using few words, but getting his point across. "What now?"

"Hold on," said Davey. "If George was in the hospital he could get poisons easy, I bet. And if he went in his own tent, no one would say nothin'. Seems to me, he ain't saved yet."

I was impressed with Davey's thinking. "But there's a problem with that," I argued. "Even if he could sneak out of the hospital, he would still have to walk across camp at night. Remember, no one was walking around camp after they gave out the ammunition the afternoon before the fight. The guards were jumpy and no one wanted to get shot."

"Well," Davey replied, not giving up, "it couldn't hurt none to check with George's tent mates to see if he came back that night."

"Okay, I'll do that. But for now, we carry on just as we discussed. Besides George, we have four suspects. The questions still are who hated Michael, and who had access to whatever did him in? When we answer those, we should find our killer. Let's keep going."

CHAPTER TWENTY-THREE

August 26, 1861

Between drilling, picket duty, and target practice, it was some time until I had another chance to try to get Steve Cooper alone. Even then it was more difficult because it was getting harder to find a poker game. Little Mac had cracked down on gambling, so the games were not as frequent. Of course, he couldn't stamp out games of chance completely, but Little Mac made an example of some of the boys they caught playing cards. He had them hung by their thumbs for hours with their toes just touching the ground, so they could repent their evil ways and act more professionally. That really took the wind out of everyone but the most incurable gamblers.

I figured that Fitzpatrick's card game was still my best bet to find Steve and talk to him alone. I meandered past Fitzpatrick's place for days after my meeting with George Hudson, but there was nothing going on.

Finally, one day I saw a lookout standing around in front of the tent. That meant that there was likely a game going on because the players would always pay someone to watch for officers. The lookout would shout some prearranged phrase and the fellows would hide the cards and money by sticking them in their pockets. It took no time to do that, so I guess the men felt pretty safe.

There was smoke coming out of the tent flap which meant a bunch of boys were in there sucking on their pipes. Since they usually would have been smoking outside, this confirmed to me that I had found what I was looking for. I just hoped that Steve would be there.

I passed the lookout and he didn't even blink. I'm not an officer, so the sentry probably figured I was going to join the game. I went inside and, through the heavy smoke, saw a bunch of men playing cards. Some had tin cups of what I figured was coffee, but no one was eating. They were concentrating on the game, and not bothered by the pipe fumes. The fellows looked like the way I felt going into battle, wondering if I was going to survive. It seemed strange to me that the men were going through this voluntarily. I wouldn't choose to have that feeling.

Steve was in the game. He was also winning, which put him in a good mood. The problem was that he was not going to get up -- no matter what the reason -- while his run of good luck was continuing. So I waited around, pretending to be interested. One of the men in the game asked me if I wanted to sit in. "Not now," I told him. "I'm just seeing how the game is played. Once I figure it out, I'll try my luck. If I want to win your money, I should know what I'm doing." The men around the game laughed at that.

Finally, Steve's luck seemed to change for the worse, and he got up to stretch his legs, promising, "I'll be right back."

Steve left the tent and started to walk around. It didn't look like he was going anywhere in particular. I followed him for a bit, and then decided to speak with him.

"Hey, Steve. How are you doing?" "Pretty well, how about you?"

"I'm doing fine, too. Say, weren't you in that poker game I just watched? You seemed to be doing well there."

"Yeah, I was doing real good, then my luck changed. So I thought I'd take a little walk to get my luck back." He sighed and whined, "I finally had a nice run. It's about time. I'm a good poker player but it's been too long since fortune smiled on me. You can be the best poker player in the world, and still lose if your luck is bad. Say, I haven't seen you in the game before. Are you going to join?

"Like I told the boys, I'm just seeing how it's played before I do anything."

"I thought you sent most of your money home, so I figured you didn't want to risk losing it. Change your mind?"

"Sort of. I figure that if I know what I'm doing, I can win more money to send home. So what's the game you're playing?"

"It's called draw poker. You're dealt five cards, and people bet on how good their hands are. When that round is over, you can get rid of up to three cards for new ones. Then you bet again. When the betting is over, the best hand wins."

"That sounds simple enough. How do you know who has the best hand?" I asked.

"Wow, you really don't know anything," Steve laughed. "There are rules. Two pair beats one pair, and three of a kind beats two pair. That sort of thing. You know what?"

"What?"

"You shouldn't be playing in a big group. After I explain the rules, you and me can play." I saw the corners of his mouth turn up like he was holding back a grin. "That way you can get prepared to play with a bunch of boys. It's much harder, you know." Steve's eyes looked all around, like he usually did. I didn't trust someone who wouldn't look at you when he was talking to you.

"Most likely you would lose all your money in a game with a number of boys. Knowing the rules, which you don't, is only a part of it. You have to know how good your hand is, and what the chances are of making it better by exchanging one, two, or three cards after the first round of betting. Then you have to know how good the other hands are. That's where playing against a whole gang of people is harder than playing against one."

"How do you tell how good the other hands are? You don't see their cards, do you?"

"No, you certainly don't. So you have to know how to read the other players. For example, are any of them bluffing--betting a lot when they don't have the cards to back it up?" Now Steve's grin was getting bigger but he was still trying to hide it.

"Why would they bluff? Isn't it stupid?"

"It could be. The idea is to scare the other players into giving up and dropping out of the round. Then you would win, even with bad cards."

"Oh, that makes sense." Suddenly I was a big fan of bluffing. "You could do that all the time, and win."

"No, you can't," Steve replied impatiently. "If the other folks in the game think you're bluffing, they will stay in the round of betting. Then your bad hand would lose once the betting is over. It's even harder to read everyone in a bunch of fellows than just one player. Do yourself a favor and just play with me until you're ready."

"But I can't win a lot of money if it's just one other person in the game."

"Maybe so, but you're also less likely to lose your money than you would against a gang of men." That made some sense to me, and I saw Steve's "trust me" smile. My father had warned me never to trust the "trust me" smile. But I wanted to ask Steve questions about Michael so I didn't want to insult him.

"Let me think about it," I replied. "Sure."

This seemed like a good time to change the topic to what I was really after. "I wish I could get Michael's advice about playing poker. You know, I really miss him a lot," I said.

"You and him got to be pretty close, didn't you?" Steve asked.

"Yes, we did. I wasn't in the unit nearly as long as you and Michael. He helped me out a lot, and I appreciated it."

"Yeah, Michael was that way. He was a real goody goody. He didn't do anything that wasn't 'right'." The words were kind but Steve's tone was bitter and sarcastic.

I could feel my anger rising at his criticism of Michael, but I managed to control myself. At the moment, I was more interested in finding out information than in punching Steve in the nose.

"What do you mean?" I asked, innocently. "I thought you two were close. Didn't you grow up together, and didn't you play ball with Michael?"

"Yes, that's all true. It's just that what might be right and wrong seemed to be more important to Michael than friendship."

"I don't understand," I said.

"You don't have to," he answered curtly.

It was clear from his voice that he wasn't going to talk about Michael any more. I didn't know what he meant by putting right and wrong over friendship, but it sure seemed to bother him. I remembered how he acted after the base ball games, whenever anyone suggested that Steve wasn't as valuable to the team as Michael. Steve had a real temper, and if he didn't like Michael, he was capable of doing anything. I wanted to ask a lot more questions about his relationship with Michael, but that wasn't going to happen now.

At least I didn't have to ask him any questions about what he knew about poisons. His family owned a drug store and I knew that Steve had worked in it. Since he didn't seem sorry to see Michael gone, I couldn't help thinking that Steve may very well have been the one who killed him.

But I needed to find out about all five of Michael's tentmates, so I changed the subject again. "Hey, Steve, how's George Hudson feeling? I heard he was in the hospital a few weeks ago."

"Yeah, but it turns out it was the luckiest case of the quick step ever. He missed the fight."

"They didn't let him out to go with the company?"

"No, They didn't let him out at all. We didn't see him until after the fight, when they tossed him out of the hospital because the doctors needed room for the wounded boys."

"Well, I hope he's feeling better,"

"He is. And Jack, remember what I told you about our card game."

"I will. Thanks." I walked away thinking that I would never ever play cards with him. At least I confirmed George Hudson's story and eliminated him as the murderer.

It was still early in the day. I decided to walk around and think. Most of the boys were talking, or writing letters home. I kept mulling over Steve's nasty comment about Michael. What had Michael done to Steve? I knew they were friends so Michael must have done something or refused to do something that Michael thought was wrong, and that Steve thought a friend should've done. I couldn't figure it out. In the time I had known

Michael, I came to believe that he would do anything for a friend, including die for him. Michael took me under his wing and taught me how to survive in the army, and the war. He was understanding, patient, and kind. We talked for hours. He taught me base ball and put me on the company team. His strength kept me from running away during the battle. What could have been so bad that Michael would have refused his friend's request?

More days passed, and I couldn't seem to get the other suspects alone so that I could talk to them one at a time. Also, I couldn't stop myself from thinking that Steve killed Michael. One day, I was so wrapped up in my thoughts that I barely noticed Patrick and Davey coming toward me. "Hey, Jack," Davey called, "What're you doing? You look like you was walkin' in your sleep!"

"No, nothing like that. I was just thinking."

"Did yourself find out anything more?" asked Patrick.

"No. It's not that." I had already told them about my talk with Steve, and that I had confirmed George Hudson's story. "It's just that the more I think about it, the more it seems to me that Steve must have killed Michael. Things just seem to fit. Steve pretended to be Michael's friend, but he really disliked Michael. He didn't seem upset that Michael had died, and he knew about poisons."

Ever practical, Patrick didn't hesitate to rein me in. "Sure you're goin' a mite too fast."

"What do you mean?"

"There's still a lot to do. You got to talk to the other boys who could've done it. We ain't finished checking all the drug stores and sutlers what might have sold the poison to see who it was they sold it to. And we ain't heard back from Mr. Gault with the answers to all them questions you asked himself. I know you want to find Michael's killer. I do, too. But it's too early to say that Steve did it, isn't it now? Everything might seem like Steve done it, but one of them other boys might have done it, too."

Patrick must have thought this was important because he usually didn't talk that much. I saw Davey with his mouth hanging open, surprised that Patrick would speak so much at one time, and make such good sense. Patrick must have felt strongly about me not jumping to conclusions, and I had to admit that he was right. "Okay, Patrick, I see your point. We'll keep going on like we talked about until we have proof of who did it. And that reminds me, I have to write to Mr. Gault to let him know that George Hudson can't be the killer."

Just then we saw Bernard Carney walking nearby, looking upset. "Hello, Bernard," I shouted. "Are you alright?"

"Hello, fellas, and no I am not."

"What's the matter?" Davey asked.

"I can't decide if I'm sad or angry or both. I just heard that the Postmaster General, a fellow named Montgomery Blair, ordered the post office to stop carrying five New York City newspapers, including the Brooklyn Eagle. He claims those newspapers are disloyal and support the Confederacy. Now, I don't know about those other newspapers, but the Brooklyn Eagle is loyal as can be. Before the war, the Eagle may have been

226

pro south because of all the cotton trade with the north. But after Fort Sumter, the Eagle has been pro Union all the way. They published my letters, and I'm certainly not for the secessionists. I'm sad for the Eagle, and angry at the post office."

I wondered how the post office could stop carrying a newspaper. I thought about that huge building in Washington that we had visited, handling all the mail, and wondered how it could pick out certain newspapers not to deliver. Then I guessed that the Government would probably have ordered the newspapers not to mail them in the first place. No, wait, that wouldn't work. My father could buy a newspaper and mail it to me. The Brooklyn Eagle could give newspapers to others and they could mail the papers. This whole problem was giving me a headache, so I just stopped thinking about it. Instead I asked Bernard, "What about you? Are you going to stop your 'reporting' in camp?"

"Hell, no." Bernard responded, angrily. "I'm still going to get news and send it on to the Brooklyn Eagle. They'll publish it. We'll show the government just how pro Union we are."

"Good for you." We all supported Bernard, who turned to walk away. "Excuse me, boys. But now that I said it, I have to get back to work seeing if there's anything new to report."

Patrick, Davey, and I looked after him and chuckled. "No stopping that fella," Patrick laughed.

We split up after that. I decided to head back to my tent so I could write to Mr. Gault and let him know what I'd learned about George Hudson. I didn't know exactly what Mr. Gault was doing to find out the information I asked for on the five boys I originally suspected, but there was no reason for him to be spending his time investigating an innocent man. When I got to my place I found a piece of paper and a pencil, and immediately began to write:

> *August 29, 1861*
>
> *Camp Porter*
>
> *Dear Mr. Gault,*
>
> *I hope you and Elizabeth are bearing up under your grief as well as possible.*
>
> *I write to send you information that I have found out since my August 13 letter to you. George Hudson could not have done what we talked about. He was in the hospital days before the battle, and stayed there until after the battle, when he was discharged to make room for the wounded. You do not need to find out the information I asked for about George, but I still need that information for the other four boys. Thank you for your help.*
>
> *I remain yours sincerely,*
>
> *Jack Muller*

After I finished, I went over to the sutlers tent, purchased a stamped envelope, and mailed the letter.

CHAPTER TWENTY-FOUR

September 1, 1861

A few days later I saw Peter Glasson coming my way from out of the woods. I needed to use this chance to speak with him, since I was having trouble getting the suspects alone.

I approached him and said loud enough to get his attention, "Hello, Peter. How are you?"

He stopped and looked at me. "I'm well, Mr. Muller," he said, "and how are you?"

"To tell you the truth, I can't get over missing Michael."

Peter said, "I know what you mean. Michael was a fine man. But you know, Jack, there were a lot of fine men killed in that battle. I mourn them all."

I said, "I can't help feeling that if I'd gotten him to the surgeon quicker, he might have been able to save Michael."

"Did the doctor say that?"

"No."

"What did he say?"

"Only that Michael was dead."

Peter shrugged and said, "I don't know much about medicine, but I do know that you can't keep blaming yourself.

You did everything you could in getting Michael to the surgeon. Yet poor Michael died. All of us miss him, but we have to go on."

I decided to change the topic since I couldn't think of anything else to ask about how Michael was killed without revealing more information than I wanted to. No one in the outfit knew that Michael was poisoned except for me, Patrick, Davey, and the killer. I needed to keep it that way.

"You and Michael went back a long ways, didn't you?"

"Yes, we had been friends since childhood. We played the same games, went to the same parties and even loved the same woman."

"You mean you were in love with Elizabeth, too?" I wasn't shocked, exactly. I had sensed that Peter was overly fond of Elizabeth, but I was surprised that he was willing to share this information with others.

"Yes, I was," Peter sighed. "But she just thought of me as a friend and preferred Michael. I couldn't blame her. He was good looking, he was smart, and he was honorable. Logically, if I were Elizabeth, I'd pick Michael too. I feel terrible for Elizabeth's loss. I've written to her to let her know of my support, and to see if there's anything I could do to help her through this terrible time, even though I'm hundreds of miles away in the army."

"That's very kind of you," I said. "It looks like this war isn't going to be over any time soon. And we signed up for three years so I guess you won't be able to do much for a while."

"That's true," Peter replied. "But I know she finds comfort in my letters, so I'll continue to write to her to give her the help I know she so desperately needs."

Peter excused himself to continue walking, saying he was actually composing a letter in his head. "That was why I was walking around. I find it relaxes me, and removes other thoughts. I can concentrate on one topic. This conversation has interrupted my thoughts. Now I have to start over."

I apologized, and Peter just brushed it off. We parted and I thought about what I had learned. Of the two, Steve was much more likely to have killed Michael than Peter. Michael married Elizabeth who Peter loved, but he seemed sincere when he said he could understand why Elizabeth would pick Michael. It sounded to me like Peter viewed it as a fair fight that he lost, with no hard feelings. Also, I didn't know how much Peter knew about toxins. Although his father was a doctor, Peter was interested in other areas like art and architecture. That made it even more unlikely that Peter had anything to do with Michael's murder, compared to Steve. If I was looking for someone who knew about poisons and bore a grudge against Michael for something, Steve seemed to be a much better candidate. I needed to know what his "something" was, and whether it would be a motive for murder.

The day was clear, which should have helped my thinking. I continued to walk around camp, saying hello to the fellows I knew. The fine day seemed to put everyone in a good mood. The beating we took was in the past, and so were the lives that were lost. I guess you need to think that way, or you would never be able to show up for the next fight. But I couldn't stop thinking about Michael's killing. It quickly reached the point where all I could think was that I had two more suspects to talk to. I continued walking and thinking. Maybe Peter was onto something when he said walking helped him think.

I didn't get much more thinking done because Bernard Carney came running up to me, almost yelling, "Those damn rebs disgust me. Now they're having women fight their war for them."

"Hold on, Bernard. What are you talking about?"

"They arrested this woman named Rose Greenhow in Washington for spying for the enemy."

"Who is she?" I asked.

"Some wealthy widow. You know, one of those society people. They also arrested one of her friends, another woman named Eugenia Phillips, who is married to some big time Washington lawyer, but this Greenhow woman is supposed to be the leader. They say these women and others sent information to rebel General Beauregard before the battle about our troop movement. What do you think about that? Now those secessionist bastards are using females. I say hang the ladies. If a woman wants to take on a man's role, she should be treated like a man."

"What did they do to Greenhow? Did they lock her up?"

"Get this. They put both of them women under what they call house arrest. That means they get to stay in their homes while the ladies await trial. Any of the boys here would volunteer to stay in their houses. That's not arrested. That's a holiday!"

"Well, Bernard, I have to agree with you that they should be treated like men. We lost friends in that battle. If those women were responsible for the death of even one soldier, they should pay the price. But females are entitled to a trial, just like men would be. Until their guilt is proven, we can't punish them."

"Yeah, but house arrest? That's nothing."

"You can't just throw ladies in prison with a bunch of men." "Just put them in separate cells. That's what I say."

"Maybe that's what will happen, Bernard. Let's see how it goes."

That's your opinion, but I don't agree with it. I'm going to talk with the other boys to see what they think. Then I'm going to write the Brooklyn Eagle so it can publish what the soldiers think should be done with those traitors." Bernard walked off in a huff. I went back to walking and thinking about catching the person that did in Michael. I was actually grateful to Bernard for giving me a break from the frustration of trying to figure out how I was going to do it.

CHAPTER TWENTY-FIVE

September 10, 1861

I decided to speak with Bill Shannon next. Bill loved to drink, and I knew from talk around camp that his favorite place around Arlington was Taylor's Tavern in Falls Church. It was about two miles from camp, but Bill must have thought it was worth the walk. I had to watch to see when he requested a pass and then try to get one at the same time. This turned out to take more days than I had expected. Eventually, I got my pass and I went straight away to the tavern.

It didn't take me long to find Bill. Since it was still early, he was not too drunk. It was clear, though, that he was well on his way; he was polishing off drinks at a good clip. I figured I'd better talk to him sooner rather than later. I wanted him to be in a good mood and talkative, but I didn't want him to be so drunk that he wouldn't make sense.

"Hello, Bill, how are you?"

"Well, if it isn't my ol' teammate, Jack." Bill clapped me on the back in a show of friendship. But he was so strong, the pat knocked me forward two steps. "Fancy meeting you here. I didn't know you came here. Now that I think on it, I didn't know you drank at all."

"Well," I said, "I don't drink a lot, but I was feeling kind of bad today."

"What's the matter?" Bill asked, looking sincerely concerned.

"I was thinking about Michael and feeling sad."

"I know what you mean," Bill said. "I think about the boys that died or got wounded, and I feel bad too. Maybe that's why I drink. No...I was drinking before the big fight so I guess that's not it. But I do know there's a lot of boys that I won't be seeing again. And even those I will be seeing again will never be the same." Bill looked like he was about to cry. "None of us was ready for what happened out there. We all thought fighting would be fun, and the war would be over real soon. Well, we were wrong. I never saw so much blood as in that fight."

I interrupted, fearing that his sentimental rambling would go on forever. I wasn't going to get any information that way. "You're so right," I said.

"But Michael was my best friend in the regiment. So I guess I miss him more than most. Didn't you and Michael join up at the same time?"

"Not quite," Bill replied, signaling for another drink. "Michael joined up before me. We had known each other since we were children. Me, Michael, George Hudson, Steve Cooper, Peter Glasson and Robert Lewis grew up playing together. We lived in the same neighborhood in Brooklyn Heights so it was easy for us all to get together. But joining an army regiment didn't seem like the right thing for me. So when Michael joined, I let it pass. Then I ran into a little trouble with a girl from outside the neighborhood. My parents thought it would be a good idea if I enlisted in the regiment. They thought it might improve my discipline. Anyway, Michael and I have known each other for a long time.

"Then you must feel as bad as me about Michael dying."

"Yes and no, Jack." The drinks were loosening his tongue. "Michael disappointed me. I thought we were really good friends, but then I found out that our friendship didn't mean as much to him. He talked to me about us being real good friends, but when it came right down to it, he wouldn't help me out. That's all I'm gonna say on the matter 'cause the man's dead. It wouldn't be right to say any more." I guess the drinks only went so far, and Bill was apparently done talking about Michael.

I decided not to press him directly. Instead I asked, "Your family's in the tavern business, aren't they?"

"That's right," he said, a little bitterly. "We own two taverns in Brooklyn. My family does real well. They do so well, they think they're part of society. So if I do anything they don't think is right for their image, I hear about it. They once even threatened to cut me off."

"When was that?" I asked.

"I don't want to talk about it. You could've asked Michael if he was still alive. He knew about it really well," Bill added angrily.

This seemed like another area that might have ended the conversation, so I shifted topics again.

"The tavern business is kind of rough, I hear. There was all sorts of talk in my neighborhood about tavern owners slipping something in a guy's drink and when the guy woke up, he wouldn't have his money anymore."

"Yeah," replied Bill with a smile. This was something he was ready to talk about. "My folks know all about that from their tavern near the docks." Bill's dislike of his parents seemed to be more powerful than his reluctance to talk. "In fact, my parents showed me how it was done. My father told me it was just so I could make sure it didn't happen to me. He said they certainly don't do it themselves now that they're part of society. Maybe so, but there was a time when my mother and father were making money the easy way. Over the unconscious bodies of unsuspecting young boys."

As we were talking, Bill was still chugging down drink after drink. His words were getting more and more slurred. I figured he was going to pass out before too long, so I asked, "Do you need help getting back to camp?"

"Nah, I haven't missed a roll call yet," and he clapped me on the back again.

"O.K. Bill, take it easy. I'll be seeing you around."

I left the bar thinking about what I'd learned. Bill definitely had a grudge against Michael over something. He also knew how to put something in a drink to make you pass out. So maybe he knew how to put something on cartridge paper to make you die. Bill was definitely a suspect, although Steve was still my prime candidate. Steve knew more about poisons and had a clear grudge. I walked on, considering the possibilities.

CHAPTER TWENTY-SIX

September 24, 1861

Robert Lewis was the last of the four I wanted to talk to. Just like Bill Shannon, I knew where Robert could usually be found. It was common knowledge that he liked prostitutes. He especially liked one named Lynda who could be found in a brothel on County Road about a mile from camp. The house had been doing a booming business "helping" the soldiers. All of us around the camp knew about it, and that Lynda worked there. She was very popular.

Again, just as with Bill Shannon, I had to get a pass the same day as Robert so I could "accidentally" run into him outside of camp. I watched Robert every day to see when he went to the sergeant's tent for a pass. After a number of days, I finally succeeded at getting a pass at the same time as Robert. I saw him get his pass, and quickly received my own.

Robert headed directly to the brothel on County Road, so that's where I went at a very brisk pace in order to beat Robert there.

My plan worked, because I saw him approaching the house, obviously looking for Lynda. I pretended that I just happened to be there and tried to look a little surprised at seeing Robert.

"Hello, Robert. How are you?"

"I'm fine, Jack." He must have been so excited to see Lynda that he didn't even inquire about what I was doing there. Instead, he asked,"Have you seen a buxom young lady with black hair?" Robert had a big smile on his face.

"Sorry, I haven't. But I'll be happy to help you look for her."

"That's mighty nice of you, but don't you have anything else to do?"

"Not really," I said. "I've just been kind of walking around. Lately I've been feeling really bad about Michael dying."

"Oh, yeah, that was a shame," Robert said, almost as if he had forgotten all about it.

"I thought Michael was one of your best friends, so you would be feeling as bad as me?"

"Michael was an old friend," Robert answered carefully. "But friendship didn't rank high enough with Michael for him to be anybody's best friend."

I asked Robert what he meant.

"Nothing," he answered. "Except that if Michael had a choice between friendship and something else, friendship didn't always come first."

"I don't understand," I said. "Michael was my best friend in the regiment. He was always generous. I can't imagine anything he wouldn't do for a real pal."

"Well, I don't care if you can imagine it or not, but it's the truth and I don't need to explain myself to you."

I changed the topic quickly. "How's your family?" Everyone in Brooklyn knew about the Lewis family because they controlled Brooklyn politics. This question, however, didn't lighten Robert's mood at all.

"Still running Brooklyn, I guess. They'll do anything to keep control of that city. And come to think of it," he added bitterly, "they have done everything."

"Come on, Robert." I fished for details. "They wouldn't murder somebody for politics."

"Don't bet on that," Robert said. Just like Bill, Robert's dislike of his parents somehow got him talking even when he didn't seem to want to talk. "Of course they wouldn't shoot a man down in the middle of the street in broad daylight, but they would remove a threat in some quiet way where afterwards people would say he died of an accident or a medical condition."

"Really?" I asked, stunned. I may have been in the middle of a murder investigation but I was shocked at someone casually talking about his family being involved in killing someone.

"Really," Robert replied bitterly.

At that moment Robert's eyes left mine to look down the street. He spotted Lynda and his face lit up. He called out, "Hey, Lynda. Don't you look beautiful today! Jack, you'll have to excuse me, but I have a friend who I must talk to." He winked and strode away.

I headed back to camp, thinking as I went. Robert was certainly in the running of people who might have murdered Michael. He too had some grudge, although he wouldn't give me the details. And Robert's family seemed to have some knowledge of how to get rid of people-- and maybe by the use of a toxic substance. If they had used poison, Robert was smart enough to have picked up how to do it.

It was hard to believe, but there you have it. Before this started, I couldn't imagine Michael having any enemies. Now, the people who I thought were his best friends actually didn't like him all that much. Steve, Bill, and Robert all admitted to ill will against Michael for some unknown reasons. And Peter may have hated Michael for having wed the woman Peter loved, but I found that difficult to believe. All of them except Peter apparently knew a lot about poisons, and since Peter's father was a doctor, he had to know something too. I wanted to get back to camp and speak with Patrick and Davey. They had been checking the sutlers and drug stores to see if anyone had bought any toxins before the battle. That was a big job, but they had been working on it for weeks. I wondered what, if anything, they had found out, and what they would think about my discoveries.

I had narrowed down the five possible murderers to four. I had thought that after I had eliminated George Hudson so quickly, I would be able to continue eliminating others just as quickly. But I was wrong. I still didn't know who among the four left was the killer. I hoped Davey and Patrick would help me think of some way to cut down the list.

When I got back to camp I hurried to find Patrick and Davey. Before I could locate them, I saw Bernard Carney heading my way. "Jack, I'm glad I saw you so I could tell you all about what's been going on in this war. We're not the only ones fighting the Confederates. There's action all over."

I really wanted to see Patrick and Davey, but Bernard's news sounded too interesting to walk away from. Bernard continued, "There's fighting going on at the Kansas and Missouri border. Our General Fremont had declared martial law in Missouri, and freed the slaves of anyone fighting for the rebels or helping them. Then old Abe Lincoln asked General Fremont to change the order so that only slaves used to make war against the United States would be freed, which is what an act of Congress already says. In the meantime Kansas Jayhawkers are fighting the traitors in Missouri.

"And there's more. The enemy invaded Kentucky, which has been trying to stay neutral. Looks like that's not going to last. After the rebels seized Columbus, Kentucky, our General Grant organized a force to take Paducah, Kentucky. Well, sure enough Grant steamed upriver and took the city. I guess 'took' is too strong a word since the enemy ran away before he got there. That General Grant is mighty impressive. As soon as he heard about the rebels taking Columbus, he knew that if they took Paducah too on the Ohio River, they could isolate our base in Cairo, Illinois. So he put together a force of soldiers and made it his business to make sure Paducah was safe from the enemy. I hear that the secesh are sending in more soldiers, and so are we. The Kentucky Senate has passed resolutions blaming the Confederates and asking citizens to repel them, but the governor has called on both sides to withdraw all their soldiers and let Kentucky be neutral. I don't think Kentucky is going to continue that way for long."

"Thanks for the news, Bernard. It's good to hear what others are doing."

I said as I turned to leave. I still wanted to find Patrick and Davey "Wait, there's more. Remember when we took the train from New Jersey and you asked me about all the soldiers patrolling in Maryland, and I told you about the large number of reb sympathizers there?"

"Sure, I remember that."

"Well, they finally arrested a bunch of people in Maryland, including the Mayor of Baltimore, other government officials, businessmen, and newspapermen. How's that for action?"

"Things are surely happening. You can lose sight of the fact that the war is a whole lot bigger than just us. So I appreciate you letting me know all this news." Bernard hurried off to let others know what he learned, and I went on my way to see Patrick and Davey to find out if they had learned anything helpful to our investigation.

I found them with a group of the other fellows from the regiment outside of our tent. I heard one of the men talking about the battle we'd fought in late July. "We may have lost the fight, but it wasn't through any fault of the 14th. We kept at 'em, charging up Henry House Hill over and over. And that was after those Zouaves had run away. That rebel General Jackson was heard yelling to his soldiers, 'Hold on boys! Here come those red legged devils again!' That was us, the red legged devils. We'd have taken that hill if they hadn't called off the fight!" The other soldiers in the group nodded their heads in agreement.

Part of me was glad to hear the men talk this way. We felt so defeated right after the encounter that I didn't know if we could ever go into combat again. Now our spirits were coming back. We would be able to fight. This war was not over. We would still win it. But hearing about that battle, another part of me was reminded of Michael's murder. We did fight well, and so did Michael. Instead of being able to join this talk today, Michael was dead – and at the hands of one of his own so-called friends. I just had to find out who did it.

When I saw them, I motioned for Patrick and Davey to come over, so they left the group to walk with me. "I didn't find out much," I confessed. "All four of the fellows that we suspect had a reason to dislike Michael, or at least thought they had a reason to dislike him. Michael married Peter's girl, although Peter says he lost a fair fight to a better man. Bill, Steve and Robert all said that Michael didn't do right by them, but I couldn't get any details. But they sure made it clear that there was something each of them hadn't forgotten. I think they all knew how to poison a man, too. Steve's family owns a drugstore. Peter's father is a doctor. Bill's family got their start in some seedy bars where slipping the customers something harmful in the drink was part of the business. And Robert's family did some mighty nasty things in politics, which could include eliminating people using poison. So I didn't have much luck in trimming down the list of four. What have you boys found out?"

Patrick answered first. "Not much. We spoke with all the sutlers, and none of themselves sells poisons. And into town we went a few times to check all the drugstores. We told the man in each store that we needed something to get rid of rats and wanted to know if any fella from the regiment had bought himself anything what could do that so we could ask how it worked. Near as we could tell, no one from the regiment bought any poison from in town."

Davey added, "The storekeepers all said that they'd remember a boy in a soldier's uniform buying somethin like that. Also Sergeant Manderville, the fella in charge of sorting all the mail what comes into camp, done told us that he couldn't remember no one gettin' any packages before the battle. He said with all the soldiers movin' around, it was real disorganized and fellas'd be lucky if letters got through."

Patrick was nodding his head. "Where we go from here, I don't know."

Davey scratched his arm and said, "I've been thinking on it, and it seems to me the fella coulda brought the stuff with him from Brooklyn when we moved out. Then we got no chance of finding out who it is."

"I don't think someone would carry the toxin with him," I argued. "There'd be too much of a chance of it being found. There isn't much privacy in camp. I figure that the person would want to keep it on him as little time as possible. So I don't think he brought anything like that from Brooklyn.

"You know, the fellow who did this was smart. He didn't want Michael living through the battle. By tainting the cartridges he knew that either Michael would get shot, or he'd die from the poison. His only mistake was figuring the time it took for it to work. And that must be hard to judge. If that crap he put on the cartridges had worked faster, and Michael had died during the battle, no one would have suspected that he was murdered. What's one more dead soldier in the middle of a battle? No, this killer is really smart. He's not going to take the chance of carrying poison around with him for any length of time.

"Here's what I think we should do: let's talk to people who know the four to see if they know anything. Now, Robert has a strumpet who he sees regularly. Her name is Lynda. I'll go talk to her and see what I can find out. Bill drinks at the same tavern whenever he's in town. Any of you boys know someone who drinks with Bill?"

"Sure, I do," said Patrick. "Don't you know Sam Talbert's a regular in that tavern, too. I'll talk to himself and find out if Bill ever did tell Sam anything we want to know."

"That's good," I said. "Now Steve plays cards all the time. Either of you two know anybody that plays cards with Steve? There might have been some talk over a game that might tell us something."

Davey, still scratching his arm, replied, "Yeah, Jesse Harkin gambles a whole lot. Says he wins all the time, tryin' to get me into the game. I don't set much store by him. He just likes to act tough, thinkin' it's easy to be tough around a kid like me. I think he's just an ass! Anyways, I'll talk to him and find out what he knows about Steve."

"All right. We know what we have to do. I want to tell you again, you should be careful to not let on why you're asking about Bill or Steve. Say, Davey, what's wrong with your arm? You keep scratching it."

"Yeah, Doc says I got poison ivy. Must've got it from the woods around here, lots of boys are gettin' it."

"I'm sorry to hear that," I told Davey. "But you talking about the doctor makes me think I should find out if the fellow we're after could have gotten the poison from the hospital tent. We haven't checked that. All four of our possible murderers knew enough about toxic substances to know what to ask for. I'll look into that when we're done. Anyway, take care of yourself, Davey."

"I surely will."

"Getting back to the investigation, we still have to find out more about Peter. He's a loner, so it's going to be tough to find anyone who knows him. But I just had an idea. I'll set up a base ball game! Everyone knows that I kept Michael's bat and ball to continue the company team. During the game, Peter may have his guard down, and talk more freely. The other boys may be more talkative too."

"That's a plum good idea!" Davey said, while Patrick nodded his head. "You can talk to them when they're not in the field. And boys watching the game stand so close to the players, we can try talkin' to them too."

"Let's get back before we're missed." I suggested. "We all know what to do. Let's hope we find out more than we have so far.

CHAPTER TWENTY-SEVEN

October 1, 1861

About a week later, Bernard Carney told me that I'd gotten a letter he brought to the tent. I looked down to where he was pointing. It was from Mr. Gault. The envelope was thick, indicating this letter had several sheets of paper and my hopes soared that it contained useful information. My fingers shook as I tore open the envelope and began to read:

September 13, 1861

Dear Jack:

I received your letters of August 13 and August 29 with mixed feelings. I was not prepared for the names of the possible murderers you sent to me. It is infuriating to think that Michael survived the enemy's bullets only to die at the hands of one of the men he thought was his friend.

I was glad to hear that you eliminated George Hudson as a suspect. It should make your job a bit easier.

I know the families of each of the remaining boys you named. It pains me to think that one of them did it.

Please keep the information I give you confidential because I do not want to hurt the families of the boys who are innocent.

Steven Cooper gambles to excess. About three years ago he had run up substantial gambling debts. Some of the debts were to rather unsavory types who threatened Cooper with bodily harm. He approached Michael about having the bank make Steven a loan to pay off the debts. This would obviate the necessity of having to go to his family for the money, since they disapproved heartily of Cooper's gambling. Michael refused the loan. He was not going to allow the bank to make a bad loan just to help one of his friends.

I understand that Steven was very angry at Michael because Cooper was beaten up by some thugs "collecting" the debt.

Somehow he managed to pay off the obligation. Many suspect he stole the money to do it. This episode took place about three years ago. I do not know if he ever got over his anger at Michael. Cooper is, of course, familiar with toxins since he has worked in his family's drugstore.

Robert Lewis also had money problems. As you know, Robert comes from a family that has become very successful by controlling Brooklyn politics. To his credit, Lewis did not want to use his family connections to make his fortune. Unfortunately, Robert has always been too trusting. This may be a reaction to his family, who have managed to stay in Brooklyn politics by not trusting anyone. Thus, he has often been the victim of fast-talking men and women. Lewis lost money in a number of get-rich-quick schemes, including one to build a bridge between the City of Brooklyn and the City of New York. About two years ago, Robert, like Steven, went to Michael to request a loan from the bank to pay off the debts he had accumulated from these bad investments. Lewis counted on his friendship with Michael to secure the loan, even though he had no assets of his own. Michael would have none of it, and refused the loan. Lewis was very angry, and was unable to pay what he owed. Because of his powerful political family, Robert's creditors chose not to take him to court to collect. However, they spread the word that no one should do business with him. This deeply embarrassed Lewis, who turned into a ne'er-do-well, socializing with disreputable types of both sexes.

The only information that I have been able to obtain about Robert's familiarity with poison is rumors that his family made use of such things to eliminate threats to their power. I do not know how much Robert himself knows, but he is reputed to be a fast learner. He could have picked up the information watching his family members.

Peter Glasson was in love with Elizabeth, although Elizabeth was never in love with Peter. Since Elizabeth spoke to me about her relationship with Peter, I know that she told Glasson her true feelings. My family and his are, and have been, very close, so they were constantly together since childhood. Peter introduced Elizabeth to Michael and she immediately fell in love. Peter and Michael were friends before this introduction, but afterward any hope Peter may have had for a life with Elizabeth ended. As you know, Michael and Elizabeth were extremely happy and devoted to each other. Peter appeared to take it well. He was Michael's best man at the wedding. He seemed to be resigned to the situation and has maintained a friendship with the couple.

My only information about Peter's familiarity with toxic substances is that his father is a doctor. Although Glasson has shunned his father's profession, he may have been exposed to information about poisons while growing up. He has attended numerous schools. As a result, he was not living at home for an extended period of time. I do not know what he may have been exposed to during that time, but I have confirmed that he never studied medicine or chemistry.

William Shannon is an embarrassment to his family. He drinks to excess and then gets himself in trouble. His family, as you know, is in the tavern business. They have worked hard to upgrade their social standing, and William's activities while drinking are a constant source of embarrassment. The incident involving Michael took place about three years ago. I had to talk to a number of people before I was able to obtain the details. Shannon got drunk and raped a girl. She did not have the same social standing as William's family, but she threatened to go to the authorities. At the least, the publicity would have severely damaged his family's reputation. Michael refused William's request to provide him with an alibi for the time of the violation, and Shannon viewed it as disloyal.

Michael and William had known each other for years, and Shannon apparently believed that gentlemen friends should provide alibis for one another. Michael disagreed and told William that he should do the right thing and admit to what he did.

Shannon was forced to go to his family who settled with the girl's family. There was no publicity, but his family threatened to disown him if he did not change his ways. Shannon could easily know about poisons. The first tavern that his family owned was located near the docks with a very rough trade. There were rumors that certain of the patrons' drinks were drugged, and the customers robbed. My sources say these rumors are reliable. Although Shannon was not directly involved in any of the incidents, he may very well have learned about drugs or toxins through these activities.

I sincerely hope this information is helpful in finding out who killed Michael. When we spoke, I told you that if you were not able to find out by the end of November who caused Michael's death, there would be an official investigation of the entire incident. That deadline still holds.

While I appreciate your concern for the honor of your regiment, the reputation of the innocent suspects, and, of course, the feelings of Elizabeth, the responsible party must be found. It is simply wrong for a man in the service of his country to die, not in battle, but at the hands of his fellow soldier.

Continuing in my sincere hopes that your work concludes soon, I remain

Daniel Gault

I re-read the entire letter, which confirmed much of what I already knew, but gave details I did not have. All four boys had a reason to kill Michael, and all four apparently knew enough about how to do it.

Although Mr. Gault's letter revealed each boy's grudge against Michael, I couldn't see how that would help me identify the killer. Refusing to use the bank's money improperly to get Steve or Robert out of trouble; refusing to give a false alibi for Bill; or marrying the woman Peter loved, each provided enough motive to seek revenge. But none of them stood out as so much greater than the others.

When Patrick and Davey got back to the tent, I suggested that we take another walk around camp. I wanted to read Mr. Gault's letter to them, and we had agreed not to speak of our investigation inside the tent where anyone could walk in on us. As we walked, I read them the letter. To anyone seeing us, it looked like I was sharing my sweetheart's latest letter with two friends. Of course they wouldn't know that I didn't have a sweetheart, or that the only reason I was reading the letter to them, rather than just giving it to them to read, was that Davey couldn't read and I wanted to avoid embarrassing him.

"Well, I guess you was right about all four of them having a grudge against Michael." Davey said after I finished reading. "The reasons are kinda interestin'. I wouldn't have guessed that those four high falutin types would have done those things-- tryin' to cheat a bank, tryin' to get Michael to lie, and being mad cause a woman loved another man. But does any of that stuff help us?"

"I don't think so," I replied thoughtfully. "We can't get rid of any of the suspects from what the letter says, but it does confirm what we found out about all of them. And remember what Mr. Gault said about keeping this information secret. Don't tell anyone."

Ever practical Patrick added, "Sure, no better or worse off are we than before. We just keep looking till we find the bastard who done Michael in."

"You're right." I agreed. " Did you get a chance to talk to the boys that know Steve or Bill?"

"Not yet." Davey and Patrick answered at the same time.

"All right. Let me know how that goes. I'll be talking with people in the hospital to see if the murderer could have gotten the poison there."

CHAPTER TWENTY-EIGHT

October 8, 1861

ecause of picket duty, drilling, and other activities in camp, it was a few days before I could get over to the hospital tent to find out about the toxic substances they kept there. As I approached the tent, I saw a man sitting on a rocking chair in front of the tent. I recognized him as Doc Homiston, the surgeon I spoke to about George Hudson. I was worried that it would look suspicious for me to keep showing up at the hospital when I wasn't sick. That might lead to him asking me what I was up to. But I quickly realized that I didn't have to worry. The doctor didn't seem to remember me. I guessed that he sees a lot of fellows, and only remembers the unusual cases. He remembered George Hudson when I asked about him only because the doctors had to throw George out of the hospital to make room for the wounded. Homiston greeted me casually. "Hello, son. Is something ailing you? Why don't you step inside and I'll have a look at you."

"No, sir. I'm not sick, but I have a problem that you may be able to help with."

"I'll do what I can. What's your problem?"

"Well, sir, rodents keep coming into my tent and chewing things up. I was wondering if you had something I could leave around the tent to kill them."

The surgeon stood up and stretched. He was a fleshy man, about thirty years old, not tall and not heavily muscled. He was bordering on fat, but not there yet. Maybe because of his body build, his full beard gave him a jovial look rather than a sad one. He probably grew the beard to look more serious, but it had the opposite effect. "Lad, we don't give out toxins here, we heal people. It's true that some of the medicines we have here could cause death if taken improperly. That's exactly why we don't give them out. If someone is really sick, they stay in the hospital where we can control the dosage they receive. If someone isn't that sick but needs drugs regularly, they report back here to get them. There's no way we'll give out the dangerous medications you're talking about."

"I guess I understand," I said, "but there are some other boys who have put stuff in their tent to get rid of rodents. I thought they got it from the hospital."

"They didn't," the surgeon replied authoritatively. "They may have gotten it from a sutler or a drugstore in town, but they didn't get it here. The medicines are kept locked up. We're very careful about handing them out. Also, you have to remember that there are mascots in camp. Captain Baldwin has a dog that is Company D's mascot. If that dog died from something that was given out here, there'd be hell to pay. No, those lads did not get whatever they used from the infirmary. If you've really got a problem, you can try a drugstore in town or the sutlers. But you better be careful. Like I said, if one of the officer's dogs gets sick or worse from something you left around, they'll be calling out a firing squad to deal with you."

"Thank you, sir. I'll keep that in mind." I walked away thinking to myself, "How on earth did the killer get the poison?" Patrick and Davey had checked the drugstores and sutlers in the area. Before the fight, no one had bought toxins and there were no packages delivered here from Brooklyn. All four of the boys we were investigating had a reason to kill Michael, and all four had the know-how to do it. But now it appeared that none of them had any way of getting what he needed. So how were Michael's cartridges tainted? I just couldn't see an answer to the question. I figured that if I just kept looking into it, maybe something would turn up.

CHAPTER TWENTY-NINE

October 14, 1861

Next, I wanted to go see Lynda, Robert Lewis' "girlfriend." Maybe I could find out something more about Robert from her. She saw him regularly, so he might have told her something he hadn't told anyone else.

I'd never been with a woman before, so I wasn't sure how to go about approaching Lynda. I knew she sold herself to men for money because that's what prostitutes do. I didn't know how you make the arrangement with her, or once you make the arrangement, what you do next.

It took a while for me to be able to get a pass to leave camp. As soon as I did, I went to the house where Robert had met Lynda before, figuring that was the easiest way to get to speak with her. It was a plain looking white two-story building set back a little from the road. There was nothing to show that it was a place where women like that worked. I guess that wasn't necessary since the boys talked with each other.

Anyone could find the location by asking around. I already knew where it was, so there was no need for me to ask anyone. I was glad about that. I would have been ashamed if the fellows found out where I was going.

I got a pass, walked to the place, and went in. Expecting to see bright red walls and gaudy furniture, I was surprised at how tastefully the parlor was decorated. The walls were white, with paintings of landscapes hanging on them. There was a light colored sofa, and opposite the sofa three equally light colored arm chairs. The furniture formed a kind of circle as if the people sitting in them could have a nice visit.

There were no other soldiers in the parlor, and I was glad about that. The fewer who knew what I was doing, the better. The whole thing was kind of embarrassing, but it needed to be done to find Michael's killer. So I just stood in the parlor waiting for someone to join me. I wasn't in there long before Lynda herself came in. She was beautiful; black hair, pale white blemish-free skin, blue eyes, and large breasts mostly showing in the dress she was wearing. She couldn't have been more than eighteen years old.

Lynda had walked into the room purposefully, so I tried to act confident, too. I walked towards her. She was the first to speak as I got near. "Hi, soldier, wanna have some fun?" Her tone didn't match her words. The words were like an invitation to a party, but her tone was bored and business-like.

"Yes ma'am, if you're Lynda," I said. "That's Lynda with a 'Y,'" she emphasized. "Robert Lewis told me to look you up."

"Bobby?" she said, perking up, "He's such a sweetheart! You want something special like Bobby?"

I had no idea what special meant. I wasn't even sure I knew what regular was.

"No, ma'am," I said. "I think I'll just have the regular."
"That'll cost you a dollar," she said.

I tried to hide my surprise at the price. It seemed like an awful lot to pay, but I couldn't tell her that. First, I didn't know if it was a lot or not. And second, if she went off in a huff, I couldn't ask her about Robert. "All right, ma'am," I said.

"Stop calling me ma'am," she said. "My name is Lynda. Ain't you never done this before?"

"Actually, ma'am, er, Lynda, I guess I haven't."

"Well, I usually charge more for beginners, but since you're a friend of Bobby's, I'll still only charge you a dollar."

I said that sounded fair. She grabbed my hand and started pulling me along to the stairs. "A bunch of us girls stay here," Lynda said. "Ma Bennett rents us rooms. It's kind of expensive, but Ma doesn't give us any problems. What with us bringing in strange men, that means a lot."

I followed Lynda up the stairs into her room. It wasn't much considering how nice the first floor was. There was a plain bed, a chest of drawers with a wash basin on top and one big chair for sitting.

"Let's get to it," Lynda said.

"Robert speaks really highly of you," I said, trying to get her to talk about him.

"Bobby's a steady customer. He's a real nice boy." I almost laughed. Here was Lynda, no older than eighteen, calling Robert a boy. "He comes to see me at least once a week." There was nothing in her manner to show that she liked me or Robert. All I saw in her eyes was impatience.

"Robert says you and him talk a lot."

"Then Robert's puttin' you on," Lynda said. She already had her dress off and was lifting up her petticoats getting ready to lay on the bed.

"What's taking you so long? Time is money. I'm only charging you a dollar so you better get to it."

Then she seemed to realize something. "My goodness," she said. "This is not only your first time paying for it, you ain't never done it before, have you?" She walked over to me and started to unbutton my pants.

"Don't you and Robert talk at all?"

"You're cute," she said. "I do believe you're trying to stall." She continued to unbutton my pants. "Of course Bobby and I talk a little bit."

"Does he talk about the other boys in the regiment?" I asked.

"What's your name, honey?"

"Jack Muller," I replied.

"Oh, yeah, Bobby says you're a great soldier," she said, continuing to work on my pants.

"What about Michael Gorman?" I asked.

"Oh, Bobby said he's a great soldier, too."

"Robert said that? Did Robert say that Michael died?"

"What are you trying to do, hon, trick me? Oh, so Michael isn't a great soldier because he's dead. But maybe Bobby said he was a great soldier. Enough of this foolishness. Bobby doesn't talk much at all. He comes here to take care of business. I know what he likes, and I do it for him. Now it's time for you and me to take care of business."

She came over to me, took my hand, and started to lead me towards the bed. It was funny. She had her bloomers down to her ankles and my pants and underwear were also down at my ankles. So we were both taking little hopping steps towards the bed, her leading me by the hand. I realized I wasn't going to learn any good information from Lynda, but I didn't know how to get out of our deal. We tiny-stepped over to the bed, and she laid down still holding my hand. She yanked me to her.

All I could remember was that it was over pretty quickly. I got out of bed, pulled up my underwear and my pants, and saw Lynda's hand out.

"You want to do it again?" I asked, a little anxious.

"That's up to you. But you owe me a dollar for what we already done. If you wanna go again, it will be another dollar and a half. Takes longer the second time, 'ya know."

"No, thanks," I said. "Here's your dollar." I was in a hurry to get out of there. This was a big moment in my life. Lynda would forget about this in a day if she hadn't already, but I would remember it for the rest of my life. I'd been with a woman for the first time, even though I still wasn't sure what had happened. I didn't get any information about Robert, I was disappointed about that, but at the same time I thought I should feel pretty proud about what I had done. I left the house in a great state of confusion.

My next stop was to try and find Peter. I already had a pass, so I decided to look for him in the woods outside of camp where he walked regularly. After that, I would talk with Patrick and Davey to see what they found out. I couldn't forget that Mr. Gault had only given me until the end of November to find Michael's murderer, and it was the middle of October already. If I couldn't figure out how the murderer got the poison, then I needed something else. I wasn't sure what that 'something else' was, so I had to keep going blind.

I quick-marched back from Lynda's place, and headed straight for the woods looking for Peter. I hoped that he might reveal something if I could just strike up a conversation. It didn't take me long to see him. As usual, when we didn't have some specific duty, Peter was walking along the paths in the woods. I didn't know how he was able to get all those passes to leave camp. He must have had some arrangement with the sergeant giving out the passes.

"Hello, Peter," I said. "I've been looking for you."

"Hello, Jack. Why were you looking for me?"

"I wanted to talk to you about the law," I answered. "After this war is over I hope to become a lawyer. I was wondering if your studies included the law?"

"As a matter of fact, I did dabble in the study of law. But I found it too confining. You end up arguing over trifles.

Creativity is stifled, since you are always looking for precedent. It's a perfect field for a narrow mind. My interests are much more far-ranging. I want to learn about history, music, architecture, and a host of other subjects. I find medieval studies affords me the opportunity to expand my horizons into all areas to become a well-rounded scholar -- a Renaissance man, if you will."

"What about medicine?" I asked.

"Not really. It too lacks creativity. You examine the symptoms and administer the medicine. Same symptoms, same medicine. If the patient is wounded, amputate the wounded limb. Nothing creative about it. No, the sciences hold little interest for me." Peter spoke disdainfully. "My focus is on the arts."

"Why do you walk in the woods so much?" I asked. "There isn't any art or music or architecture here."

"Aside from the beauty of nature, I enjoy the solitude of walking in the woods," Peter's use of the word 'solitude' and his tone suggested I was an unwelcome intrusion.

I gave it one last try. "Did you ever walk in the woods with Michael?"

Peter became suspicious. "Why do you ask?"

"Michael was interested in music, art and architecture as well," I guessed. "It seems like the two of you might have talked about those subjects."

"First of all, Jack," Peter said, clearly running out of patience. "Michael had no such interests as far as I knew. He was a banker. Like anyone in that profession, his interest was money, and how to make money. He would not get involved in what money can buy except to the extent that it acts as collateral to repay a loan. Secondly, I said I enjoy the solitude of walking in the woods. Solitude means alone."

Any question about whether Peter was dismissing me was cleared up. This was the end of our conversation, and Peter proved the point by walking away from me.

"Good-bye, Peter," I yelled after him. He raised his hand in a kind of backward wave, but it struck me more like a king dismissing a servant.

It was time to meet up with Patrick and Davey. I had learned nothing, but maybe they had found out something. I went back to our tent, and sure enough Patrick and Davey were both there. I asked them to walk with me. They appeared anxious to talk with me and readily agreed. I hoped that their anxiety was because they found out something, and not because they hoped I did.

"Well, I didn't learn much new," I said. "How about you?"

"About the same," Davey and Patrick both responded.

"Let's see what we got." I told them about my talk with the doctor who said no one could have gotten poison from the medical tent. "They guard it carefully. There may be a bunch of reasons for that, but the doctor said that if one of the officer's dogs got accidentally poisoned, there would be hell to pay."

I then told them about my conversation with Lynda, leaving out certain parts of the meeting. "Anyways, she said Robert was a nice fellow who didn't tell her much. After I informed her that Robert was the one who recommended her to me, she said he told her I was a great soldier.

When I asked if he said anything about Michael, she replied that he said Michael was a great soldier too. But Robert didn't tell her that Michael was dead. I think if I asked her if Robert said anything about you two, Lynda would've told me that he said you were great soldiers as well!"

"Why, I ain't even met her," Davey said. "She can't know that."

"That's the idea, Davey." I laughed. "I can't be sure Robert told her anything, but it sure seems like Robert's interest in Lynda is not for conversation."

While I was speaking, I noticed that Davey was still scratching his arm. "Still itching, Davey?" I asked.

"Yeah," Davey said. "but I think it's getting better with the medicine the doc gave me."

"Good." I went on. "I found Peter walking in the woods again, and tried to start a conversation with him. He cut me off pretty good, and I didn't get anything from him. According to Peter, he's not interested in the sciences but rather in the arts. He told me he walks in the woods because he likes the solitude of it." I tried to mimic Peter's sarcastic tone. "In case I didn't know it, Peter told me solitude means alone. Like I said, we didn't have much of a conversation, and I didn't learn any new information."

Patrick spoke next. "I spoke with Sam Talbert and a couple of the other boys what drink with Bill. Sam told me that mostly Bill talks about his family, and sure he don't like them. His family treated himself unfairly, Bill thinks. Like a priest talkin' about sin, he will go on and on about it to anyone what will listen. According to Sam, Bill mentioned that Michael made everything worse when he wouldn't help him out. The boys I spoke to, they all remembered how angry Bill got when Michael's name came up. From Mr. Gault's letter, we already know the why of it. By my way of thinking, Bill himself had a reason to kill Michael, didn't he?

Trouble is, we know that the other three did too."

Davey chimed in. "I done spoke with Jesse Harkin and some of the boys that play cards with Steve. They say he don't talk much about the boys in the regiment neither. Mostly he talks about his family, how rich they are and how much richer they would be if they done listened to him. He figures that when he gets back to Brooklyn he's going to take over their business and be rich. The boys Steve plays cards with don't like him none. They keep playing though 'cause Steve mostly loses. So they'll let him go on about being rich so long as he goes on giving them money.

But there wasn't nothing to learn about Michael."

"It looks like we haven't made any progress," I said. "The four fellows we've been looking at all had a reason to kill Michael, and all knew enough about how to do it. We still don't have the answer to how the killer got the poison." Davey's scratching was starting to bother me because it was so distracting. "We know Michael was killed by someone tainting Michael's cartridges. It had to be done the night before we moved out for the fight by one of the five boys who shared his tent. We know it wasn't George Hudson because he was in the hospital. I think if we knew how the killer got the poison, we'd know who he is."

"I'm thinkin' you're right," Patrick said. "But sure I don't know what we do from here. We spoke to everyone we can think of, and checked all the possible places the killer could have gotten the stuff, didn't we now? And we're no nearer to finding him. Maybe it's time to let Mr. Gault bring on that official investigation. I think we're done."

"Me too," agreed Davey.

"I don't want to give up." I replied stubbornly. I did not want to admit to Patrick, Davey, or myself that we had failed. I remembered that we talked about using a base ball game to question the suspects, hoping their guard would be down. I knew this was unlikely to result in anything, but I was desperate not to end our investigation. If I telegraphed Mr. Gault to tell him I failed to find Michael's killer, he would start an official investigation right away. That would ruin the reputation of the 14th. So in an effort to buy time I said, "I know that talking to all the people we have spoken to has not revealed the bastard who did Michael in. But we already said that we could use a base ball game to try to get the one who did it to say something incriminating at a time when his guard is down. I still want to try that. If you boys want to stop, I understand. You're still my best friends in the regiment. Thank you for everything you've done, but I'm going to continue trying to find Michael's killer."

"Hold on," Patrick and Davey exploded at the same time. "Sure, I agreed to help you because it was the right thing to do. And you're my friend. None of that has changed, has it now?"

"That's right," Davey said excitedly. "If you're still in, Jack, so am I."

"Me, too," agreed Patrick. "I said what I said cause it needed to be said. But sure we did talk about trying to learn something new at a base ball game, so let's do that. How long will it take yourself to set up the game, Jack?"

"I could probably arrange it for a couple of weeks from now. The teams in the regiment lost some boys in the battle. Whichever team I can get to play us will need some time to find replacements. I have Michael's bat and ball, so that won't be a problem. I'll arrange the game."

CHAPTER THIRTY

October 18, 1861

I asked around, and found out that Company A was anxious to play us in base ball. They wanted to avenge their 17-16 loss. We won that game on our last at bat, and Company A hadn't forgotten it.

The captain of Company A's team was Nathan Teasdale. I needed to talk with him to arrange the game, so I walked through camp toward his tent. I saw him standing outside talking to a couple of other fellows who I recognized from his company. Nathan was tall, over six feet, and clean shaven. He was broad shouldered, which gave him a lot of power when he hit the ball. Nathan was a nice fellow until he got on a base ball field. Then he turned into a fierce competitor who would do most anything to win.

Once, during a game when Nathan was on first base and he knew the umpire wasn't looking, I saw Nathan punch a fielder who was trying to catch a short fly ball between first and second base. The umpire, Lieutenant Jeptha Jones of Company D, didn't see it, but he did hear the spectators yelling about it. The Lieutenant went over to Nathan, and everyone within one hundred feet could hear what he said. "Listen here, Private Teasdale, I didn't see what happened so I can't punish you. But

I have no doubt you did something against the rules. So this is your warning. If I catch you doing anything improper I will throw you out of the game, and have you hung by your thumbs for four hours. Am I clear, Private Teasdale?"

"Yes sir," replied Nathan without hesitation. After that, Nathan played hard, but clean, for the rest of the game. The umpire's threat must have left an impression on him because when we faced Company A a few days after the warning, Nathan had again played a clean game.

"Hello, Nathan," I said as I approached him, "how are you?"

"I'm fine. I think I can guess why you're here. You want to arrange a base ball game between Company A and Company B, right?"

"That's right. We haven't played in a long time, and I thought that all the fellows would enjoy a game."

"I agree. You know we're still angry about that 17 to 16 loss you gave us. I'm not saying you boys played dirty or anything, but we think we had the better team, and should've beat you."

"Well, this will be your chance to prove it. When can your team be ready to play?"

"We lost some boys in the battle and I'll have to find replacements. And then we'll need some time to practice with the new fellows. I think two or three weeks should do it."

"That's fine. We lost Michael Gorman, our center fielder, so I'll have to find a replacement for him, too. Two or three weeks works for us, too. I have Michael's bat and ball, so we don't have to worry about getting equipment."

"That's great. I'll arrange for an umpire. Any officer, as long as he's not from Company A or Company B, all right with you?"

"That will be fine. We'll pick a day for the game after we both have a chance to talk with the players on our teams."

"Great. I'll be seeing you soon."

I was glad that I had arranged the game, but I knew it was not likely to tell me who Michael's killer was. Patrick, Davey and I would try to find out what we could during the game by talking to all of the players who might have done it. Although it was a long shot, I needed the time. And who knows; if we could get the suspects by themselves, the atmosphere of the base ball game might cause them to let their guard down.

I decided to take a walk around camp to try to think about how I might approach the suspects during the game. What would I say to them to start the conversation about Michael? How could I possibly get the guilty one to say anything revealing? I had no answers to these questions, but I kept walking. I was by the parade ground, a corner of which was used for target practice. Beyond the target was the woods.

Company E was shooting when I approached. This meant that the woods would have been checked to make sure that no one was there who could be hit by a stray minie ball.

Lieutenant Middleton was in charge. Just like when Company B practiced, Company E lined up in columns with six abreast. Then, in groups of six, they would march up to the firing line. Each group would fire off four rounds at will aiming for the stacked logs set up about two hundred yards away from them. After firing their four shots, the group would march to the back of the line, and the next group of six would take their turn.

I heard Bill Nutman of Company E say, "This is a waste of time. Them stacked logs ain't no battle line of rebs. Problem is, them logs don't shoot back and I sure don't see no smoke coming from them. Being able to hit those logs ain't no sign of how you'd do in a battle."

Jim McAuliff agreed, "Yeah, it ain't a battle, but it's better than nothin."

Just to watch, I went off to the rear and right side of the soldiers firing. Shortly after the second group of six began to discharge their weapons, I heard a low thud at my feet as if something hit the dirt in front of me. I looked down and saw a little furrow in the ground that started at my feet. Following the groove to the end, I bent down, wiped away some dirt and saw a minie ball in the ground. I picked it up and felt that it was warm. I could barely believe it, but someone had taken a shot at me!

This must be Michael's killer. It looked like he found me before I could find him.

From the angle of the furrow, I guessed that the shot had come from the woods outside of camp, about three hundred yards away. No wonder he missed, I thought. That would have been a hell of a shot.

The group of six had just finished firing their four rounds and were marching back to their company. The next group of six was ready to go forward and take their turn. I had another thought. The shooter had timed his attack to take place when the group of six fired. I was safe only until the next group began. I turned around and high tailed it away from the woods. If anyone wondered why a soldier was running alone by the parade ground, I didn't care. Let him think I realized that I was late for something, and was hurrying to it.

I needed to get back to my tent to speak with Patrick and Davey. They had to be told that Michael's killer was on to me, and maybe them.

Neither of them was in our tent when I arrived. But on leaving the tent, I saw them both about twenty yards away talking to some other fellows in the company. I ran up to them, and signaled excitedly that I needed to talk. They separated from their group and came up to me.

"What's going on?" Davey asked. "Why are you runnin' around camp, lookin' like you seen a ghost? Did you figure out who done in Michael?"

"Yes and no." I replied while gasping for breath. "The killer is the fellow who just took a shot at me, but I don't know who it is."

"What!" Patrick was shocked. "Someone shot at you, did he?"

"Keep your voice down, and yes. I was standing behind the men from Company E who were taking target practice, and a minie ball landed right at my feet! From the angle of the trench the ball made, I figure that damn assassin must have been in the woods about three hundred yards away."

"That's some shot," noted Patrick. "It's tough to hit anything at that distance, ain't it now?"

I agreed. "I guess it may have been a warning shot, but…"

Davey interrupted, "Ain't those woods cleared before the shootin' starts? We're always bein' told to stay away from there."

"Yes, that's true," I replied, "but I guess someone could've snuck back after they were checked. They're not guarded or anything."

Patrick stated firmly, "You got to report it."

"I can't report it. First, I wasn't hit. Officers wouldn't trouble themselves with what they'll see as an accident. They'll say a musket discharged accidentally during practice, and it's lucky no one got hurt. Tomorrow we'll just get an order to be more careful during target practice. Second, the officers are bound to ask why I think anyone would try to kill me.

How do I answer that? 'Well sir, I've been looking for the killer of Michael Gorman. He must have found out I was on his trail and tried to shoot me.' That will lead to exactly the kind of investigation we're trying to avoid. No, I can't report it, but I'm worried that you two might be in danger as well. I don't know what to do."

Ever practical, Patrick had an answer. " Davey and me are in no danger. You're the one what's talked with the boys we think might be the killer. He knows you, don't he? He don't know us. We talked to sutlers, drug store owners, and boys in the regiment. Innocent enough were all our talks. You're the one what's in danger, and needs to be kept safe.

"But first, there's an idea in me. Let's find out where the four boys are right now. If one of them boys was doing something somewhere else, like if Robert was with his 'friend' Lynda, sure he ain't the killer."

"Great idea," I replied, impressed with this thinking. "Let's go over to their tent and see who's there. When we get there, you boys hang back. I have a reason to talk to them. You don't. I can tell them about my conversation with Nathan Teasdale, and ask them when they are able to play base ball against Company A." We walked over to their tent, and I went inside.

The only fellow there was George Hudson. He was writing a letter. I wondered why he was writing it inside when the weather and light were better outside. Maybe the letter was something he wanted to keep private, like a letter to a girl. I decided not to ask.

"Hello, George, how are you feeling?"

"Very well, Jack. The stomach problems I had seem to have all gone away. Thanks for asking. What brings you here?"

"I was looking for Steve, Robert, Bill, and Peter. I'm trying to schedule a base ball game with Company A, and I wanted to know when they would be able to play. Do you know where they went?"

"A base ball game sounds like a great idea. I enjoy watching them. But no, I don't know where they are."

"Thanks, I guess I'll try to find them." Leaving the tent, I saw Patrick and Davey waiting for me. Davey asked, "So, any of them boys in there?"

"No, not a one. We have to try to find them. We know where each usually goes. Bill will be at his favorite tavern; Robert will be with Lynda; Steve will be playing cards; and Peter will be walking in the woods. I'll get a pass and look for Bill and Peter. Since Lynda's place is far from the tavern. Patrick, you can look there. And Davey, you can see if Steve is in the card game where he goes."

Davey was the first to respond. "No way. You ain't leaving camp. Someone just shot at you! Might be it was only a warning, but if you go traipsing after any of the boys we think's a killer, the next one might get you."

"Sure Davey's right." Patrick said authoritatively. "You got to stay near the tents. Whoever is trying to kill you, or scare you, won't try again in the middle of camp, will he now? Davey and me will get the passes. I'll go to Lynda's place. Davey is a might young for that job." He smiled and winked. "Davey, you get to the tavern and the woods. Jack, you look for Steve at the card game. This way, you don't leave camp."

"All right, all right, I guess you're correct. Let's get going. I'll see you boys when you get back." Davey and Patrick headed off to get their passes, and I went looking for the card game. I went straight to Fitzpatrick's tent. It was clear the game wasn't going on there because I didn't see a lookout. When I checked inside the tent I did see John Cronan, one of Fitzpatrick's tent mates from Company A.

"Hello, John. I was just looking for Steve Cooper. I'm trying to arrange a day for a base ball game between our Company B team and your Company A team."

"I don't know where he is. Did you try his tent?"

"Yes, and he wasn't there. I figured he usually comes here for the card game, so I would give your place a try."

"He is a regular here. But I haven't seen him today."

"Is there another game in camp where he might be playing?"

"No," chuckled John. "He wouldn't go to another game. Word is out that he owes so much money here, no one else would welcome him. We let him play here only because we know he'll pay some day when his family gives him the money. In the meantime, we can afford to wait since we have all the money he's already lost. The funny thing is that he thinks he's going to win it back, which is as likely as reb president Jeff Davis sitting in for a couple of hands."

"Thanks, anyway. I'll look around for him. See you."

"See you too, and good luck, even though you're playing my company's team. I just enjoy watching base ball games, and I hope you can get one set up."

I left Fitzpatrick's tent thinking that Steve must have left camp. Where he went I had no idea. He could have been the one in the woods so I couldn't eliminate him as one of our suspects. If anything he looked guiltier. All his losses here may have reminded him about how Michael didn't help him when he needed to pay off other earlier losses. That very well may have made him mad enough to kill. All I could do now was wait for Patrick and Davey to get back to find out if we could eliminate any of our other suspects.

Patrick was the first to get back to camp. I saw him approaching the tent, and went out to greet him. "Hello, Patrick. Let's walk around a bit." As we started to walk, I couldn't hold back any longer. "What did you find out?"

"Nothin'. I went to Lynda's house, and saw herself. Robert wasn't with her. I even asked if she saw Robert--which she didn't. She must've thought I was there to do business because she asked if I wanted to go upstairs and have some fun. I told herself I didn't have any money. Don't you think she started yelling at me that she doesn't give credit, and that I should know better. 'You soldier boys always thinkin' you can get somethin for nothin.' Well, her yelling then was nothing compared to when I asked herself if Robert sees other girls. Sure, she screamed at me, 'You gol dang fool. Robert loves me. I'm the only one he goes with. You get the hell outta here, and never come back.'

"'Yes ma'am,' was all I could say before I ran out of there. After that, I walked around some looking for Robert, but I didn't see him."

"Thanks, Patrick. I'm sure sorry you had that run in with Lynda. She can be pretty scary."

"That's all right. Kind of funny it was now that I'm lookin back on it."

"So we can't drop Robert as a possible murderer." I concluded. "I wonder where he did go."

"Makes no never mind. We can't say he wasn't in the woods shooting at you, can we?"

As we were walking, I saw Davey, and motioned for him to join us. "Hello, Davey. Did you learn anything? Patrick and I couldn't find out where Robert or Steve was when someone shot at me. Hope you had better luck."

"Nope," Davey replied. "Bill weren't in the tavern, or anywheres else I looked. But while I was walking to the tavern through the woods, I done seen Peter. He was just strolling around, looked to be thinking hard about something. I didn't go up to him, or call out. He didn't even notice me."

"Peter always walks in the woods." I noted. "He says it helps him think. So that doesn't prove he was the shooter. Did he have a musket with him?"

"It also don't prove he weren't the shooter. And no, he didn't have no gun with him, but he very well might have hidden it before I saw him."

"Well, this hasn't gotten us very far. Any of the four boys we suspect could have taken the shot at me. We don't know where Steve, Robert or Bill were at the time of the shot. All we know is that Peter was in the woods, and that's where the shot came from--but that's where he always is when he gets a pass. We can't drop any of the four boys from our list of suspects."

"Why don't we just ask 'em where they were at the time of the shot?" Davey asked. "Then we'd know."

"Because it's too dangerous." I said. "One of the men we would be asking is the killer. I can't ask you two to speak with them because then the murderer would know you're involved in the investigation, and he would go after you. I can't ask myself because then he'd know I was continuing the investigation, and that his shot didn't scare me off. Next time he might not miss. I think we have to play it out, and see what we can learn at the base ball game. I'll talk with the four boys and the rest of the team and get the game set up. I told the people I spoke to today that the reason I wanted to find the boys was to do just that. If the killer hears about me trying to find him, he won't think I'm continuing the investigation. All I'm doing is arranging for the base ball game."

"I guess so." Patrick responded doubtfully. "But we got another problem, don't we? What if the shot at yourself was no warning? What if he was trying to kill you, and took a chance even at that distance? Sure, if he killed you, people would think that it was just bad luck, and everyone should be more careful. The minie ball came mighty close to hitting yourself, didn't it?"

"I guess it did."

"That means you're in danger. What are we goin' to do about that now?"

"I don't know." These questions were making me nervous.

Then Patrick answered his own question. "You stay close to the tents. The bastard won't try to shoot you there, would he? Sure you can leave the tent area only for drill, shootin' practice, or picket duty. Drill and practice should be safe enough because all four of them suspects will be with you, plain to see. Picket duty is harder. Ourselves may not be able to keep track of all four of them."

I knew what Patrick meant. In picket duty, the whole company forms up and marches out to man picket posts a ways outside of camp. The posts form a ring around the camp. Each one is manned by six fellows. Out in front are sentries or lookouts who are on the alert, and ready to sound the alarm. The six soldiers in the picket post rotate sentry duty. The idea is that the watchmen will be the first to hear or see any trouble. If they do, they fire a shot and the boys in the post can run up to support the sentries until they all get back to camp. Meanwhile, the camp has been alerted and has time to get ready for whatever the trouble is.

"Since the whole company has picket duty at the same time, sure the murderer will be out there with you." Patrick continued. "But alone he won't be, unless he has lookout duty in front of the post. Even then, you'll always be with a group of boys at the picket post."

"But I have to do sentry duty, too," I objected.

"No, you don't!" Patrick was emphatic. "Me and Davey will be in the post with you, and won't one of us take your watchman duty. No one's going to object to trading places with us so's we can be in the same picket post as you. And no one's going to care a lick if we take on extra sentry duty. Sure, if you have to leave the tent area for anything else, me or Davey will be with you. Alright with you, Davey?"

"Sure is. We agreed to help find the murderer, and that looks like it includes keeping you alive, Jack. Golly, Patrick, I don't think I ever heard you talk so much!"

I laughed at that, but then said, "That's mighty nice of you boys. How long do we have to keep that up?"

Again Patrick had the answer. "Until we get the one what done in Michael."

"Might be we'll find him at the base ball game," Davey suggested.

"Hope so," I answered. "If we don't, I'm at a loss about where we go from there.

CHAPTER THIRTY-ONE

November 9, 1861

The three weeks leading up to the base ball game were pure hell with me looking over my shoulder all the time. I mostly stayed around my tent, and kept to Patrick's plan when I had to leave the area. Patrick and Davey were as nice as could be.

My goal was to make it seem as though I stopped looking into Michael's murder. I didn't speak to anyone about Michael. I restricted my conversations with Steven, Robert, Peter, and Bill to base ball only. They were excited about finally playing base ball again, and wanted to know if we had a bat and ball, as well as a new center fielder. I told them that we had a bat and ball, and promised to find a new center fielder before the game.

I spent a lot of time thinking about Michael's killer. How that bastard got the poison was the key question. I believed that I should know the answer. The information was in the back of my brain, and I just couldn't move it to the front. It was unlikely that I could get information at the game that would let me know his identity, but saying that I needed to talk with the suspects at the base ball game bought me time before I had to admit that I failed.

With all that thinking about the murder, I forgot to get a replacement for Michael in center field until the day before the game. John McNamee and Hugh Doharty were with me in our tent when I finally remembered . "Hey, fellas, have you two ever played base ball before?"

"No, I haven't." Hugh replied.

A rush of relief came over me when John said, "I have." John looked fast enough, but I had no idea if he could catch, throw, or hit.

"That's great, John. Did you play for a team?"

"I sure did. The Star Club of Brooklyn. It wasn't the Atlantics or the Excelsiors, but we were pretty good."

"What position did you play?"

"I played all the outfield positions at one time or another." A second rush of relief came over me.

"Why don't we go outside and throw the ball around?" I suggested.

"Sure, let's go." I pulled Michael's ball from my things, and headed out with John.

When we got outside we found an open stretch of space and started throwing the ball back and forth. I gradually increased the distance between us until we were about sixty feet apart. John was throwing the ball easily enough, and catching it well. I liked what I saw, even though I still didn't know if he could hit.

There was no time to check his hitting, since I needed him for the game tomorrow. The only place where he could hit the ball was an open field like the parade ground, and we couldn't do that because of my promise to Patrick and Davey that I wouldn't go there without them. My safety came before a tryout. There just wasn't time to find Patrick or Davey and go to the parade ground to let John hit the ball. I remembered that Michael put me on the team without seeing my hitting, trusting his instincts, and decided to offer John a spot on the Company B team right then.

"John, are you interested in playing on the Company B base ball team?"

"I sure would love to play, but don't you boys have a game tomorrow?"

"Yes, we do."

"Well, I'm kind of rusty. I don't want to let you fellows down by playing poorly. Maybe I should wait to join the team, and get in a little practice."

I started to worry. While being so relieved to find someone with base ball experience, it never occurred to me that he might not want to play. "That's all right, John. I've seen you throw and catch just fine. I figure you can hit the ball, or you wouldn't have been playing on the Stars. We need a replacement in centerfield. Michael Gorman was killed in the battle. If you don't play, I'm going to have to find someone else for tomorrow. If he does well, I may have to keep him on the team, and he would take the spot I'd like you to have. So, come on, say you'll do it."

I could see in his eyes that he was torn. He didn't want to embarrass himself by playing poorly because he had no chance to practice. But he also didn't want to lose the opportunity to play on the company team. I think John finally decided that being on the team was worth the risk of not playing so well. He must have figured that there would be more games, and if he were on the team he could practice with us, and make up for any bad showing tomorrow. "Alright, I'll play."

"That's great. I'm sure you'll do fine." John returned to the tent while I continued thinking about how to get more information from the suspects during the game. After all, the base ball game was just an excuse to speak with them.

I didn't have much of a chance to think about anything because Bernard Carney came running up to me with his "I have news" look on his face. "Hey, Jack. I have news!" Uh huh, I knew it.

"What is it? It seems like a long time since we've heard anything."

"Yeah, it has been a while." Bernard stroked the few hairs on his upper lip, which he liked to pretend was a mustache. "My main source of outside information was the Brooklyn Eagle, and when the Post Office stopped allowing it in the mail, I had to scramble for news. So some of what I have is pretty old. They're still battling in Missouri and Kentucky, and fighting has heated up in western Virginia. Looks like that area of western Virginia may break off and join the Union. That news is weeks old, unfortunately, and you probably knew it already. Did you hear about the battle at Ball's Bluff?"

I was sorry to disappoint him. "Yeah, I already know about Ball's Bluff, in northern Virginia. The battle there was a disaster. Our men were driven back over the bluff and into the Potomac. The rebs could just shoot down at them like ducks in a barrel. A lot of good men were shot, drowned, or just surrendered. It was horrible."

"Yes, all that's true. But I bet you don't know the worst of it. The officer who scouted the position said it was an abandoned rebel camp.

However, it was night and he was looking at a line of trees. Next day, when they moved in to attack, they ran into a company of Mississippi infantry."

"That's terrible! All those men killed or captured because some officer didn't know what he was doing."

"I agree, but that's the army for you. I just hope our officers do better, or we're not going to make it through this war. I feel pretty good about our chances, though. General McClellan was just made general-in-chief of the whole army after General Scott resigned. Little Mac is a good man, and he'll do a good job.

"And let me give you some good news. A couple of weeks ago they finished the transcontinental telegraph by hooking up two lines in Salt Lake City, Utah. Now you can send information from Washington and New York to San Francisco in an instant. Isn't that something?"

"It sure is," I replied. All I could think of at that moment was the trip I had made with Patrick, Davey, and Michael to the Patent Office building, and how we'd seen models of inventions, including the telegraph. Then I thought about Patrick saying those things didn't matter to him, and Michael explaining to Patrick about how inventions like the telegraph could affect him. The memory of Michael made me sad again.

I woke from my daydream to hear Bernard saying goodbye, and I just waved back to him. Thoughts about Michael also reminded me about the base ball game tomorrow. Given the news from Bernard, a base ball game didn't seem all that important, compared to men fighting and dying. But this game was different. It might be my last chance to figure out which of the four suspects was guilty. If I didn't identify the killer by the time the game ended, I was afraid that I would have to admit I was done, and let Mr. Gault start the investigation. With that idea in mind, I continued to think about the murder.

CHAPTER THIRTY-TWO

November 10, 1861

The next day was a beautiful day for a base ball game. We were lucky with the weather, cool but not cold. At that time of the year it could have been a lot colder, although I realized that I didn't know much about the climate in the south. The sun was out and the air smelled fresh, and that seemed to put everyone in a good mood.

The Company A and Company B teams were at the parade ground, along with hundreds of spectators. Just one look at the players showed that they were eager to begin, shifting their weight from one leg to the other, or pacing up and down the field. Their eyes burned with an intensity you would have thought was reserved for battle.

The game was about to start. I had laid out the bases with Company A's Nathan Teasdale. They consisted of some rags held down with a rock, and a barrel top for home base. All the players from the two companies were ready to play. Our umpire, First Lieutenant David Myers of Company C, was standing in the middle of the field set to go. There were hundreds of boys from all the companies standing by shouting as if the game had already started.

I did not share everyone's good mood. I kept thinking that I was playing ball with a killer on my team. Someone who had taken a shot at me.

My job today was a real long shot: to identify that person. The problem was that if I didn't, I was at a loss for what more I could do. That made me tense. I knew that if I kept thinking like this, it would hurt my game. But I couldn't help it. I had to find a way to get each of the four suspects separated from the crowd and the other ball players, so I could talk to him and try to get some information. I could see Patrick and Davey in the front of the crowd trying to get in a good position to be able to speak with the ball players. They too would try to get one of the quartet to say something that would help to identify him as the one.

I heard Lieutenant Myers yell, "Play ball!" The players from Company A ran onto the field. We had agreed before the game that Company A was the home team, so we batted first. We scored two runs in our first at bat. There were five one base hits. Peter Glasson drove in Steve Cooper for our first run, and Bill Shannon drove in Robert Lewis for our second run. When it was my turn, I hit a weak ground ball to second base for an out.

Company A scored five runs in their first at bat, partly due to how badly we played. With one out, Manus Geary, Company A's second baseman, hit a fly ball to me in right field. I saw it clear as day, but started to think about catching the killer instead of the ball. Next thing I knew the ball was bouncing in front of me. Because the drill field where we were playing was full of ruts, the ball took a strange bounce and got by me. By the time I ran it down, the runner was on third base. He scored when Dan Teasdale, Company A's shortstop, hit a one base hit to left field.

That was followed by two more one base hits that left boys on all the bases. Nathan Teasdale, Company A's first baseman, then came up to bat. He hit a shot to deep center field that went over the head of John McNamee and just kept rolling. By the time John ran down the ball, everyone had scored. John was just not as fast as Michael, who would have caught that ball.

The game continued in that way with Company B scoring in every inning, but Company A scoring the same or more runs when they came to bat. By the fourth inning, we were losing twelve to seven. I really didn't care too much about the score. I wanted to speak with Steve, Bill, Robert and Peter alone. This was proving difficult because the players bunched up when they weren't on the field, or talked with other soldiers who were there to watch the game. Then, while we were batting in the fifth inning, I saw Steve standing alone behind first base and went up to him.

"Steve, we're getting beaten pretty bad. It's a shame Michael isn't alive to be here. We could sure use his help in center field."

"You play the hand you're dealt, Jack. I'll just have to play harder and pick up the slack."

"Too bad Michael died in that battle. I keep thinking he didn't have to die. You saw him after the battle. He wasn't even shot!"

I looked into Steve's eyes to see if there was any reaction to what I said. There wasn't. "It's a shame anyone died in the battle,

Michael no more than any of the other boys who did get shot. When your time's up, it's up. I don't know what killed Michael, but his time was up." Then Steve ended the conversation. "Now let's get back to the game."

I hoped that we would have had a longer and more useful conversation. I knew no more about Steve as a suspect than I did before the game. I kind of knew deep down that hoping someone would confess during a base ball game was foolish. But at least the game was buying me time to continue my search for Michael's killer.

The fifth inning proceeded like the ones before it. We scored two runs, but Company A scored three. They would have scored even more runs, but John McNamee made a great catch and throw from center field to end the inning: Dan Teasdale had come to bat with runners at first base and second base with one out. He hit a long ball to center that John ran down and caught on one bounce for the out, then he made a terrific throw to third base to get the runner out who was trying to advance from second to third. If the ball is caught without hitting the ground, the runner has to return to the base he was on. But if, like here, the ball is caught on a bounce, the runner doesn't have to go back to the base and can try to advance to the next base.

John had made an exceptional play and the team loved it. I hoped that might lift our spirits and turn around the game.

When we came to bat in the sixth inning, I saw an opportunity to speak with Peter, who was standing alone between home base and first. I approached him and asked, "What do you think about the game so far?"

"Well, we started the game down some runs and have not succeeded in reducing their lead. I think we should endeavor to play better."

Although that was hardly helpful, I decided not to comment on it. Instead I tried to bring the conversation to the subject that really interested me. "I sure wish Michael was out there. John is playing pretty well, but Michael was a better hitter, and faster in center field."

"Yes he was, but Michael is unavailable, so we have to make do with who we have. John made a very fine play in center field. I remain confident that we can overtake the Company A team."

"I hope you're right, but I still wish Michael were out there."

"Look, Jack, the loss of Michael was a tragedy, but we must make do. Wishing will not win this game. So I suggest we get back to playing as best we can." Peter walked away, and I was left thinking that again I had learned nothing new, and that this idea never stood a chance.

The game went on and by the end of the eighth inning we had managed to reduce Company A's lead to two runs. The score was Company A eighteen and Company B sixteen. Between the sixth and eighth innings our bats had come alive. Hanford Hovey, our left fielder, and Tom Abbott, our third baseman, struck four base hits with men already on base. Bill Shannon and Peter also struck four base hits. Meanwhile Company A had scored only three runs in that span. Everyone on our team was excited and really believed we could win this game.

We came to bat in the ninth inning knowing that we had to score at least two runs to tie the game or it would be over. If Company A was winning after our at bat in the ninth, there was no need for Company A to hit at all.

While we were getting ready to hit, I saw Bill alone and approached him. I wanted to try one more time to find out something from at least one of our suspects.

"Well, Bill, this game has gotten a lot more exciting. I thought for a while we were in real trouble. Now the game is very winnable."

"It sure is. After we came back from so far down in runs, I would hate to lose."

"I think we'd be winning now if Michael had been here to play," I said.

"You might be right, but he isn't here. That's a darn shame. War is terrible. But right now we have to play ball with the boys we have."

"It just seems so unfair. You saw him on our retreat from the battle. He wasn't even shot. He just got sick and died."

"I know, but there are a lot of things in battle that we don't understand. They just happen. Look, we have a tight game, and I don't want to spend time talking about something that's over when I have to think about what's happening now. I may get to bat this inning." Bill walked away. Again, I had learned nothing.

I turned my attention back to the game. Our first striker, Steve Cooper, grounded weakly to Nathan Teasdale at first base.

One out. The next striker, our pitcher George McIntyre, hit a ground ball to Dan Teasdale at shortstop, who threw to his brother Nathan for the out. Two outs, and things were not looking good.

The next two batters, Robert Lewis and John McNamee, both got one base hits. Two out, and two on base, with the tying run at first base. As he thought might happen, Bill Shannon came to bat. He didn't even swing at a number of pitches, seemingly waiting for his pitch. The umpire warned Bill that he would be calling strikes because Bill had not swung at pitches that were within his reach. The next pitch was a strike, then another. One more strike and Bill would be out and the game would be over. Luckily, Bill swung at the next pitch and hit a very hard ground ball to Aaron Schwebel, Company A's third baseman. Aaron knocked the ball down, and in the time it took him to find it, Robert had reached third base from second. Meanwhile Bill was running so hard to first base that he didn't see the difficulty Aaron was having in fielding the ball.

All Bill knew was that he had to get to first base before the third baseman's throw. Bill ran as fast as I have ever seen him run.

Unfortunately, Bill was going so fast that he couldn't stop, and over ran first base. He struggled to get back. Aaron had thrown the ball to first base after Bill had already touched and passed it, perhaps hoping this exact situation would occur. Bill arrived back at first base at what appeared to be the exact same moment that Nathan Teasdale tagged him. Company A called Bill out, and Company B said he was safe. Both teams argued loudly, shouting back and forth at each other. Finally, the teams asked the umpire, Lieutenant Myers, to make the determination whether Bill was safe or not. Michael had told me that the rule in base ball is that the teams decide the outcome of plays. However, if the teams cannot agree, then the umpire makes the final decision. Everyone turned to Lieutenant Myers. "The runner is out!" Myers yelled. "The game is over!"

There were a lot of angry Company B players and their fans, but no one could say anything. You are not allowed to argue with the umpire. Here he was an officer, so even without the rule, no one was going to challenge him.

I didn't have time to stay and join in the griping about how we really should have won the game. I wanted to catch up with Patrick and Davey to see if they found out anything. It didn't take long to find them, but I couldn't tell from their faces if they had news or not.

"Hey, boys!" I shouted from about twenty feet away. "Let's walk around and talk about the game." They came over to me and we started to walk so no one could overhear us.

"I didn't learn anything." I complained. "I did get to speak with Steve, Bill, and Peter, but they said nothing of interest."

"We didn't even get to speak to any of them suspects," Davey replied. "None of them was ever alone when we were near them. It just didn't work no how."

I concurred. "Whoever the killer is, we know he is smart and cunning. The way he committed the murder and then managed to take a shot at me with no one the wiser should have told me that he wasn't just going to tell us he did it. I wanted more time to figure out how the killer got the poison, so I used the base ball game as an excuse to keep the investigation going. The problem now is that I don't know what else we can do."

CHAPTER THIRTY-THREE

November 10, 1861

It seemed hopeless. We still didn't know how the killer got the poison and we didn't know how to find out. I was about to suggest that we go back to our tents and think about it some more when I saw Davey scratch his arm again. The blood rushed to my head. I felt dizzy and nearly stumbled. Suddenly it all made sense. The idea in the back of my brain finally moved to the front. I realized what I had been missing all along, and how the puzzle came together.

"Are you alright, Jack? Sure, you look sick!" Patrick asked.

"I think I know who killed Michael," I blurted. Patrick and Davey were stunned.

Davey was as excited as I had ever seen him. "Did one of them say somethin'? Did you see somethin'? Who is it?" His eyes were wide open.

"I'm not sure yet, " I said. "I have a couple of things to check before I tell you."

Now Patrick and Davey looked angry, rather than excited. "That ain't fair," said Davey. "We've been in this with you from the beginning and we oughta know what you're thinking."

Patrick, generally the more patient of the two, voiced the same opinion.

"All right," I conceded. "I'll tell you what I'm thinking. But I'm not sure yet, and until I am no one can do anything. Fair?" They quickly agreed.

"I think it came from the woods." Davey and Patrick looked at me like I didn't know what I was talking about. "Just like Davey got poison ivy from the woods, the killer must have gotten the toxin from there too -- from some kind of plant. I remember reading how some plants could be medicines, but different plants or different parts of the same plant could be deadly.

"So now the question is who would know what plants to look for. The killer must have pretty good knowledge of seeds and the like, but if he knew everything about them he would've known that Michael wasn't going to die right away. So I figure Bill and Robert didn't do it because they didn't know enough, and Steve didn't do it because he knew too much. Bill's family is in the bar business, and if they slipped any customers any drugged drinks, I don't think they got them from the woods. Same thing applies to Robert, and any of the political murders his family might have gotten involved in. I suspect they buy their poisons ready-made. On the other hand, Steve worked in his folks' drugstore. Steve would know how fast toxic substances work, or don't work. If Steve had been doing the killing, Michael wouldn't have lasted so many hours after the fight. That leaves Peter. I have no proof he's the killer, but it sure seems likely. I'm going to go over to the surgeon's tent and ask the doctor what kind of poison you can get from the plants in the woods around here. Then I'm going to telegraph Mr. Gault, and ask him to find out if Peter studied plants in any of the subjects he's taken up."

"We're goin' with you," said Patrick. "We've been in this too far to be cut out now, haven't we?" Davey was even more emphatic about going along.

"All right," I said. "You two have been in it from the beginning, and you deserve to be in it at the end. So come on along."

We walked as fast as we could to the surgeon's tent, and found the same Doctor Homiston I'd spoken to earlier sitting in the same chair outside of the same tent.

"Hello, son," he said to me. "Back again? And this time I see you brought a couple of friends."

"Yes, Doctor. These are tent mates of mine. Remember I was asking about poisons for some rodents that keep getting in my tent? Well, they're just as interested as me. You told me that no one could take out any poison from the hospital tent. We were wondering if we could get what we need in the woods. Are there poisonous plants out there?"

"Sure are," said Dr. Homiston. "But you have to know what to look for. Plants have been studied for hundreds of years. Many plants form the basis for the most helpful medicines, but those same plants could be deadly if they are prepared differently or given in a different dosage. For example, Night Shade or Belladonna can be very useful in minute amounts in liniments because each of them paralyzes nerve endings. In fact, ladies in Venice applied the juices from Belladonna to their eyes to dilate them and make them sparkle. On the other hand, Belladonna can also be a deadly toxin. The paralysis that makes it a good lineament can make it deadly if it's swallowed.

"Same thing with Monkshood and Foxglove. Monkshood has been used in tiny doses for heart problems because it is a heart depressant. But that same feature makes it a deadly poison even if you take just a few nibbles. Foxglove has been used since the 1600's for heart problems, yet any part of the plant can be a deadly toxin. The list just goes on and on -- from herbane to Lily of the Valley. Some of them don't kill, and some of them taste so bad an animal won't even eat them. So you better know what you're looking for before you start bringing plants into your tent. You might all end up with poison ivy like your buddy there. I remember him from the sick call."

I tried to chuckle and said, "Thank you very much. I guess we better not use the plants in the woods since we don't know anything about them."

"That's a good idea, son."

"Thank you, sir," I said. Patrick and Davey made their good-byes too. The surgeon gave us a good-natured grin.

As we were walking away, I exclaimed, "So that's it! The killer got what he needed from the woods! But the murderer had to know what to look for. If Mr. Gault tells me that Peter studied plants, I think he's our man.

Patrick said, "But we can't prove nothing, can we?"

Davey said, "Yeah, we can't just bring him up on no charges. We ain't got no proof, and darn if it wouldn't ruin the regiment."

I had thought of that before when I spoke with Mr. Gault, but I hadn't wanted to deal with it then. The scandal of one soldier in the regiment murdering another would be truly harmful to the reputation of the 14th Brooklyn. I didn't want that, but I didn't know what to do about it. "At least we'll know the answer," I said.

We all were lucky enough to get passes, and raced into town. We headed directly to the telegraph office, where I used the last of my money to send a message to Mr. Gault. The telegram was short and to the point: "**URGENT. DID PETER STUDY PLANTS?**"

We weren't sure the telegram would be sent right away because the military had priority. Fortunately, there seemed to be a lull in military use of the telegraph, so my message went right through.

The three of us had no trouble convincing each other to wait around to see if we got a response. We figured it would be delivered right away because Mr. Gault is such an important person. And I knew that Mr. Gault was so interested in this that he would respond right away if he knew the answer. Since we had the passes anyway, we decided to stay in town, walk around, and check back later at the telegraph office to see if my question had been answered.

We walked down Pearce Street and Chestnut Street, just looking at buildings and into store windows. It was a beautiful day. Hard to believe that we were in the middle of a war. The homes were nice looking two- storied buildings, painted white. Most had wide porches, and there were a few people sitting out and enjoying the day. Looking in the store windows, we could see womens' dresses and mens' work clothes, as well as tools, shaving materials, and other things that caught our interest. We went into a picture store and talked about getting our photograph taken, but we couldn't afford it. We stopped in a number of other stores, but the result was always the same. I didn't have any money left, and Patrick and Davey didn't want to spend their money on the things we saw, even when we liked them. We figured that we didn't want to have to carry any more things with us on the march, which we knew was coming eventually. So after walking around for a couple of hours we headed back to the telegraph office.

Sure enough, there was a reply waiting for me. It was as to the point as you would expect from Mr. Gault: "**P.G. STUDIED BOTANY AT HARVARD. WHY DO YOU WANT TO KNOW? ANY PROGRESS?**"

I read the response to Patrick and Davey outside the telegraph office. I should have answered Mr. Gault's questions. I hadn't been keeping him informed, but I decided to ignore that for now. Anyway, I didn't have any money to send another telegram.

"What the heck is botany?" Davey asked.

"That's the study of plants," I replied.

"That about wraps it up!" said Davey excitedly.

"Everything seems to point to Peter, don't it now?" Patrick echoed.

"It all makes sense. I was looking at the motive the wrong way. For Steve, Bill and Robert, their motives for killing Michael were all connected to events that happened years ago. They may have been really angry, but why wait years to kill him? On the other hand, Peter's motive was the future. Michael married the girl Peter loved, and Peter never stopped hoping he could get her back. Remember Peter telling me that he wrote to Elizabeth to tell her he was there for her? That bastard figured he could come back from the army with Michael out of the way and marry Elizabeth.

"And how does he know that himself will be comin' back?" asked the always pragmatic Patrick."

"Yeah, none of us knows for sure that we'll make it through the war," added Davey.

"I bet Peter has it figured out. He will wait enough time after Michael's death so his leaving won't look suspicious. Then he can fake some medical condition, and fool the doctors into discharging him from the army. There's been no real fighting since the battle back in July. So it's been safe enough to stick around."

Davey was really angry at that thought. "Son of a bitch. I bet you're right. That man is a rat!" Patrick nodded his head in agreement.

"Peter also didn't tell us the whole truth. He said he wasn't interested in the sciences, but now we know that he studied botany. His specialty is the middle ages. I remember from some of the books my father had me read that around that time they didn't have medicines. All they had were plants and roots they used for healing. And from what we learned from the surgeon, the same stuff that could heal you could also kill you.

"Peter's a cold one. This killing was ruthless, and had to be planned out carefully. By tainting Michael's cartridges, Peter was planning that Michael would never make it out alive from the fight. If Michael got shot and killed, that would be fine with Peter. If Michael didn't get shot, Michael would shoot more bullets, use more cartridges, and die from the poisoned cartridges. Peter obviously figured that Michael would either get shot in the fight, or shoot off a high number of rounds. Either way, Michael was going to die.

"Peter took a big chance. Tampering with Michael's cartridges had to be done the night before we moved out for the fight because they only gave them out that day. So Peter had to get the material from the woods, probably that same day, since he wouldn't want to take the chance of having it lie around the tent. Then, at night, Peter had to contaminate Michael's cartridges without anyone waking up. I suppose, if someone did notice, Peter could say that he just wanted to check his own ammunition, and took Michael's case by mistake. It was still risky, because someone may have noticed the toxin Peter would have tried so hard to hide."

"Sure, Peter is so full of hisself, he must have felt no one could catch him," Patrick interrupted. "And right he almost was. If not for you, my boy, Peter would've gotten away with the murder. Most would've figured Michael's death was just another death in battle. Even if someone thought somethin' weren't right, there was just too many puzzles for anyone but you to sort out. I ain't never seen such stubbornness. You never gave up. Sure, Michael was lucky to have a friend like you, wasn't he now."

"Wait a minute," I cautioned Patrick. "We're all talking as if this is over, but it isn't. You said it, we don't have any proof. And Davey, you said an investigation and court martial would bring scandal down on the 14th Brooklyn. Well, you're both right."

I sighed deeply. "I'm not sure what to do now. We all know it was Peter, but we can't prove it and if the regiment tries to show it, it would just mean a scandal the likes of which this regiment has never seen. The 14th Brooklyn is a proud and honorable outfit. I don't want to be the one to ruin that reputation. Especially over something we may never be able to prove."

"So what are we gonna do?" Davey asked. "I'm not sure," I replied. "Any ideas?"

"Ask Peter if he done it, why don't we?" Ever practical Patrick said.

My first impulse was to laugh at his suggestion. I could see Davey trying to hide his smile behind his hand. But as I thought about Patrick's idea, I realized it might work. Peter was so arrogant that we might be able to get him to admit he did it. Anyway, it was worth a try.

"You know what, Patrick?" I said. "I think you may have something there. Let's wait until tomorrow and see if I can get Peter alone in the woods. I think I should be the one to talk to him, since there's no reason to get you two involved."

Patrick immediately objected. "I won't let you do it alone. Peter's already done in Michael and shot at you, hasn't he now? Sure, if he gets that you figured out he killed Michael, he has to do you too. That's a fact, whether or not you get himself to say he murdered Michael. I'm goin' with you."

"Me too," added Davey. "Patrick's right. If that high falutin son of a bitch figures he can end this by killin' just one more boy, you'd be dead in no time. If Peter gets that at least three of us knows he's a murderer, he'll know by God that he can't kill us all. He may be able to kill one of us, but he won't be able to kill all three."

It was decided.

CHAPTER THIRTY-FOUR

November 17, 1861

W e watched Peter to see when he went to get a pass. For whatever reason, it was a week before Peter tried to leave camp. Maybe he wasn't so much in need of "alone time" with his plan going so well. Eventually, we saw him going into the sergeant's tent for a pass. After he left, we were lucky enough to be able to get our own passes immediately. As the weather got cooler, soldiers were staying closer to the campfires. We headed into the woods around camp where we knew he would be.

While we were walking, Patrick made a suggestion. "You know, Jack, I think it's a fine idea to go at Peter. I want himself to know that the three of us stand together, but Peter ain't going to admit anything in front of the three of us, is he now?"

"What are you saying, Patrick?" Davey asked.

"I'm saying we should change our plan a bit. Sure I think Jack should talk to Peter, but Peter, he should think Jack is alone. That bastard may be full of hisself, but stupid he ain't. If it were just the two of them, Peter may say things he wouldn't say in front of the three of us, because then it would be just Jack's word against Peter's, wouldn't it? Peter thinks he's a gentleman, whose word counts more'n yours. So I'm sayin', Peter may blab to Jack what he wouldn't blab to the three of us. I'm thinkin that we find a place where Peter is likely to pass, and Jack approaches himself there, while Davey and me hide in the woods. There's plenty of cover here."

"Sounds good to me," Davey said.

"I guess that makes sense," I replied. "My first idea was to speak to him alone anyway so there's no difference in that. Having you and Davey backing me up, in case Peter tries anything, could be really helpful."

We knew from our prior walks in the woods that there was a small clearing where a number of the paths come together. We decided that instead of looking for Peter we would wait there -- me in the clearing and Patrick and Davey hiding among the trees. If Peter didn't show up, we'd just have to come back and try again.

Luckily, we didn't have to wait that long. About twenty minutes after we reached the clearing and took our positions, I saw Peter heading my way. Peter spoke first.

"Well, hello, Jack. What are you doing, following me?"

"I guess I am, Peter." There was a flicker of curiosity in his eyes. "Why? This might be amusing."

"I don't think you're going to find it amusing," I decided to get right to the point, hoping that it would throw Peter off. I knew Peter thought I was beneath him, so I figured if I talked to him like I knew more than he did, that would set him off.

"I know you killed Michael, and I know how you did it. I have to tell you, Peter, it was not real smart, and you didn't handle it well."

At first Peter looked shocked. Gradually, that look faded, and he started to look offended. I was watching him real closely, and I never saw guilt. His eyes showed anger mixed with curiosity. "You poisoned Michael by tainting his cartridges. You wanted Michael to die in the fight, and you weren't taking any chances. You figured that either he'd get shot, and then maybe you'd finish him off later if he was only wounded, or he'd die of the poison.

"You got what you needed right here in the woods. Your walks in the forest aren't just because of the solitude, but because of your interest in botany. I know you studied plants, and I know you helped your father in his medical practice." I guessed at the part about helping his father, but he didn't deny it. "You knew what to look for, and you knew how to get it."

Peter's eyes narrowed. Now there was a tinge of fear mixed with the anger and curiosity in his eyes. There was no longer any surprise showing, and he didn't look offended anymore.

"You pretended all along not to mind that Michael married Elizabeth. You even told me that if you were in her shoes you would've done the same. That just wasn't true. You always thought that you were the better man, and that she should have married you. You figured the only way to win her was to get rid of your competition. Since Michael was a soldier going into a fight, him dying in battle wouldn't surprise anyone.

"Elizabeth would mourn him, but once that was over, you thought you could move in."

I decided to repeat what I had said earlier about how he killed Michael. My comments were getting to him. I could see it. Peter couldn't stand that an inferior had figured out his plan and was talking to him as if Peter were the inferior. "The only thing was, you had to make sure that Michael didn't survive the fight. He could've gotten shot in the fight, but that wasn't sure enough for you. You realized that if he didn't get shot, he would be doing a whole lot of shooting. The more he did, the more cartridges he would be biting into, and the more poison he would be getting. He was going to die in battle somehow, and you were going to make sure of it. If he was shot but only wounded, you would have found a way to finish the job. That wasn't necessary, lucky for you, because I was with him the whole time. It would have been difficult for you to finish off Michael with me watching.

"Michael shot off a number of rounds and took in a tiny bit of toxin each time. For a while I thought, 'How could Michael not taste the coating on the cartridges?' But then I thought back to the fight. I remembered how dry my mouth was because of all the smoke from the gunpowder. I kept having to lick my lips and swallow to raise some spit. I couldn't taste anything but gun powder. I figure Michael probably didn't notice the poison because all he could taste was gunpowder too.

"It must have seemed like a brilliant idea to you, Peter. But you didn't count on a lot of things. First, you didn't count on Michael walking away from the fight, and not dying until hours later. That was mighty poor planning. You also didn't count on the questions that would be raised when a perfectly healthy soldier died even though he hadn't been shot. And you didn't figure on me sticking so close to Michael that I could see all the things Michael went through before he died. All those things added up to only one possible cause of death - poisoning. Yeah, Peter, it may have looked like a good idea to you, but it sure wasn't. Matter of fact, I'm surprised that someone who claims to be as smart as you would do something so stupid."

"You twit! You don't know what you're talking about. Even if Michael were given a toxicant during the battle, which I doubt, how can you possibly know who did it?"

"Peter, I'm glad you asked me that, because it shows how stupid your idea really was," I said mockingly. "First, the surgeon confirmed that all the symptoms Michael had before he died could only have been caused by him ingesting some toxic substance. Second, no one else was poisoned in the fight. Third, there was only one thing that Michael alone took into his mouth and that was his cartridges. Everything else Michael bit into or swallowed, other soldiers ate or drank as well. You remember breakfast that morning where groups of fellows shared their food? And Michael was really careful about not drinking all his water, so other boys ran out first and drank from Michael's canteen. And, finally, I tested Michael's cartridges." At this, Peter's look of shock returned. "That's right, I saved Michael's cartridge case. He had five cartridges left. I got a rabbit and made it nibble at some of those cartridges. Wouldn't you know it, that rabbit went through the same symptoms that Michael had, and then the rabbit died -- just like Michael."

"Maybe it died from eating the gunpowder in the cartridges, you idiot." Peter yelled, as if saying it louder would disprove everything I was saying.

"Of course, I poured the gunpowder out first. The rabbit chewed on the paper only. You don't think I'm as stupid as you, do you?" Now Peter was fuming. Calling his plan stupid and talking down to him was working. His eyebrows were raised and his eyes showed pure rage. I decided to press home my advantage.

"After I figured out how Michael was killed, I had to work out who could've done it. I'll explain it to you in simple terms, so you can understand it." If it was possible, Peter got even angrier. "See, it had to be one of his tent mates. They didn't give out the cartridges until the afternoon before the fight, and everybody had to carry their cartridge case around with them in case we had to move out quickly. The only time Michael didn't have his case on him was when he went to sleep. He had to have kept it in his tent, because, like all of us, he would have been afraid that if it rained that night, the cartridges would have gotten wet. You may also remember that everyone was kind of edgy that night, and the guards were especially alert. So none of the boys were walking around camp. No one could have taken the chance of sneaking into Michael's tent with all his tent mates sleeping there as well. You were in his tent, and could have coated his cartridges then. If someone woke up and asked you what you were doing, you could've said you couldn't sleep and were just checking the equipment."

Peter interrupted defensively. "There were four other soldiers in that tent. Why couldn't it have been one of them? George Hudson, Steve Cooper, Bill Shannon and Robert Lewis all slept there. I happen to know they all have reasons to hate Michael. And I believe they all know about toxins. Steve worked in his parents' drugstore. George spent a year in medical school before he dropped out. Bill knows something about poisons from the nefarious reputation his parents' bar business had before they tried to climb the social ladder. And the rumors about Robert Lewis' family disposing of their political foes suggest that Robert has the necessary knowledge too."

I didn't know that George didn't like Michael, or that he spent some time in medical school, but it didn't matter. I replied in my most superior tone. "Well, you're right on all counts but you're missing a couple of crucial facts. First, George was in the hospital from days before the battle until after it, when he got discharged to make room for the wounded. So he couldn't be the murderer. Second, the killer had to get the toxic substance from the woods. I know that it wasn't bought in town, the hospital tent wouldn't give it out, and nobody got any packages. So the only place left is the woods. Bill, Steve and Robert may have known something about poisons, but they don't know anything about the plants that produce them. They're city boys who would only know about the finished product. You, on the other hand, studied plants at Harvard, and studied the middle ages when plants were used both to heal and to kill.

"And third, your motive is the only one that makes sense. Bill, Steve and Robert may have reasons to dislike Michael, but those events took place years ago. If any of them wanted to kill

Michael, he would have done it long before now. While their motives were real old, yours was continuing. You secretly loved Elizabeth and even though she didn't return your feelings, you thought of her as your girl. The way you saw it, Michael stole her from you. He was the better man. You were reminded of that every day. The only way for you to get your girl back was to get rid of Michael. That made your motive current while theirs were stale. No, Peter, you're the one."

He started laughing. His eyes were no longer curious. They showed only fury. "You little insect," he said. I thought about Davey and Patrick hiding in the woods and how right they were in figuring out Peter. He truly believed that no one would take the word of a "flea" over that of a gentleman. Peter continued. "My plan was perfect and it's still perfect. You can't prove anything. You think Michael was such a great man. He stole my life. I introduced him to Elizabeth. A gentleman never would have married a friend's girlfriend. He said they'd fallen in love, as if that would make it right. I pretended that I understood. After all, what good would it have done to make a scene? I knew even then that the only way to restore my life was to remove Michael."

He's been thinking about this for more than two years, I realized. He's insane.

Once Peter started talking, he had no problem admitting what he did. In fact, he sounded like he was bragging about it. "The setting had to be right," Peter continued. "No one could suspect that Michael met with foul play, or that I had anything to do with it. When war was declared, I knew he would be going to fight, and I knew that was the perfect opportunity."

"Is that why you stayed with the regiment, to kill Michael? You don't care about the Union or anything else, except yourself?"

"So what? Everyone has his own reason for fighting in this war. Some men want to get away from their families. From what I have seen and heard, I suspect they need the money and the three meals a day the army offers. I wanted to get rid of Michael and the war gave me the chance I was looking for. I didn't expect the war to last as long as it now seems it's going to last, but I can take care of that."

"What do you mean?"

"That's easy. All I have to do is wait a respectable amount of time, so no one suspects my actions have anything to do with Michael's death. Then I'll come down with some ailment that will lead to my discharge from the army. I know enough about medicine to fake the right symptoms. There are doctors I can call on to verify my condition. After my discharge, I'll go back to Brooklyn and comfort Elizabeth."

Peter seemed to enjoy talking about how he so carefully planned the murder of my best friend. I wanted to kill him on the spot, but something stopped me. Despite the demands of war, I knew I was not a killer. I wanted to become a lawyer to seek justice, not revenge. Doing Peter in might make me feel good for a moment but it was against everything I believed I was and hoped to be. In the end, I decided to just let him talk so that

319

Davey, Patrick and I could hear all the details. They would be helpful in convincing others if there was any doubt that Peter murdered Michael.

"Yes, when the war started, I knew that would give me just the occasion I needed. Michael had to appear to die in battle. However, I couldn't be certain that Michael would be killed, so I had to make sure. You surprise me, Jack. I didn't think you were that smart. I still don't think you're that smart. You just got lucky. There was a possibility that you might have stumbled onto something so I took that warning shot at you. I underestimated your nerve. Your clumsy investigation came to my attention after learning that you had spoken to Bill, Steve, Robert, and George, as well as me, about Michael's death. First, I dismissed you for the fly you are. But then, when you kept at it, I thought that you needed a little discouraging. After all, even a bug might stumble onto something I did not want known. My only regret in this whole affair is that I didn't kill you when I had the chance.

"I did put Monkshood onto Michael's cartridges. If he didn't get shot, he would still die. For your education, people have known about Monkshood since ancient times. You may have heard of it under its English common name, Wolfsbane. It's a pretty plant, with brightly colored flowers. The top sepal blossom of the plant curves up and over to form what some may call a hood. Hence, the name. Even animals know to avoid it."

I didn't understand much of his description but I didn't want to interrupt his confession.

"Although the entire plant is poisonous, its roots and seeds are especially deadly. Indeed, Monkshood is most poisonous just before flowering.

"Rest assured the mixture I made up for Michael's cartridges was deadly. I knew that he might not die for a few hours after ingestion, but that was not a concern. Who would notice another death in a battle? Another body among a sea of bodies should not have caused a stir. You, Jack, and your childish sense of loyalty to Michael were the variables I didn't foresee. If you acted normally, you would have accepted Michael's death as a casualty of war, and simply mourned the loss. Instead, you began a crusade to find out who brought about Michael's demise? Through what I can only believe was bumbling good fortune, you stumbled on the solution.

"By the way, in answer to your question, if Michael was just wounded I planned on being the one to take care of him. I kept him in my sight through the battle to make sure that if the need arose I would be there for him. Your presence made that more complicated, but I'm sure I would have figured something out."

My anger was rising. Peter felt no remorse. In fact, just the opposite. He was still proud of his scheme, and still thought it was the perfect plan. I wanted to put a stop to that right away.

"Your plan wasn't so perfect, Peter. I figured it out. And I'm going to the colonel to make sure that you get what's coming to you. The only thing I don't know right now is whether they execute murderers by firing squad, or by hanging. Whichever one they use won't be terrible enough for you."

Peter started laughing again. He seemed a bit maniacal but I wasn't in the best position to judge. "Jack, you idiot, weren't you listening to me? You have no proof. You have a number of guesses that happen to be correct, but I will deny them with every fiber of my being. And if you try and repeat this conversation, I'll swear that you made the whole thing up. I'll say that you have disliked me from the time you joined the regiment. I think it must be envy. I have everything you want. So if you tell anyone about this, I will sue you for slander. And don't forget what happened to Michael. It could happen to you, too. But don't worry, I know you won't tell because you know as well as I do that the word of a gentleman will be taken over the word of an ant every time."

"How about three ants?" Davey shouted as he and Patrick came out of the bushes into the clearing. This time Peter wasn't laughing. The look of shock on his face was real. His mouth flopped open, and his eyes bulged. He knew he had confessed to murder, and that there were multiple witnesses to his confession.

To his credit, he recovered quickly. "So what are you going to do now, boys?" he said scornfully. "Turn me in? I will just have to swear that you got your two friends to lie for you, Jack." Then Peter played his ace. "But one thing is certain, you will cause a scandal in the 14th Brooklyn, the regiment that Michael loved so much."

"We don't have to tell you what we're going to do," I said, stalling for time. "All you have to know is that three people know that you're Michael's killer. We can go to the colonel any time we want. In the meantime, one of us will be watching

322

you constantly to make sure no harm falls on any of us. Now get out of here, Peter, before we beat the hell out of you."

Incredibly, Peter looked insulted that I could talk to him that way. Here was a murderer being offended that I was talking to him as an equal. I wanted Peter dead, but I didn't want to hurt the regiment that meant so much to Michael. Peter sauntered off down the path, trying to appear confident even though we knew he was not.

After Peter was out of earshot, Patrick said, "What the hell is goin' on? Just go to the colonel and report the whole thing, why don't we? I thought we was trying to find who done in Michael and we did--or you did, Jack my boy. Why ain't we going to the colonel?"

Davey agreed, "Yeah, why are you lookin' so confused, Jack?"

I told them. "That son of a bitch is right. An investigation and court martial would bring down a scandal on the 14th Brooklyn, whether Peter was convicted or not. Peter is also right that Michael loved the regiment. I never would have rested without finding out who killed Michael because I owed it to his memory. But how the hell can I bring on a court martial that could ruin the regiment's reputation? I don't know what I should do."

Patrick, as usual, was practical. "Seems to me we don't have a whole lot of choices, do we? We could do nothing, we could turn him in for a court martial, or we could take care of him ourselves."

I said, "You're right. The way I feel right now I want Peter dead, but I'm not a murderer like he is. I don't like the idea of doing nothing, but I wouldn't want to hurt Michael's memory by making him a part of the 14th Brooklyn's biggest scandal."

Davey finally spoke, "Golly, this is one tough decision for three boys to make. I ain't got no idea what to do."

That gave me an idea. "I think you may have come up with the answer, Davey," who looked mighty confused at my comment. "Why should we be making a decision? We haven't told anyone about what we were doing for fear of hurting our chances of finding Michael's killer. Well, now we found him. When we get back to camp, you can tell all the men what we know. See what they think. We don't have to decide. We shouldn't decide. Whatever we do is going to affect the whole regiment so we should find out from as many as we can what they think should be done."

We went back to camp and split up to talk to as many fellows as we could about Peter, what he had done, and what we should do about it. Everyone would be warned not to tell any officers because if an officer found out what had happened, he might feel obliged to bring a public court martial. I believed that the only way a court martial would be acceptable was if the men in the regiment approved.

Usually, if I wanted to spread a story, all I had to do was to tell Bernard Carney. He would make sure it was all over camp in no time. But in this case I wanted to see the reactions of the fellows to what Peter had done. That meant I had to speak to them myself.

I met with a bunch of the fellows, who all listened intently. After all our time in camp, conversation had become kind of boring. This was the greatest piece of gossip to hit camp since Johnny Mac replaced General McDowell. The men I spoke to were not of one mind. Some thought we should kill Peter, others wanted to have him court martialed, and still others wanted to leave Peter alone because God would punish him. I didn't have the patience to wait for God, but I listened to all of their suggestions.

I was able to talk with a large number of the men in the regiment because my conversations were brief. All the men I spoke to wanted to tell others. You gain some stature among the men if you know something the person you're talking to doesn't. Once they heard my story and voiced their opinions, the men wanted to end our conversation quickly and find someone to tell who didn't already know. That's the way word spreads in camp.

I made it a point to speak with Bill Shannon, Steve Cooper, Robert Lewis, and George Hudson myself. I watched their tent until I saw Peter leave for one of his walks in the woods. I went in and fortunately all four fellows were there. "Men, I don't know if you've already heard, but Michael died because Peter poisoned him." Apparently they hadn't heard because their mouths all hung open like fish. I told them how and why Peter did it.

Robert was the first to speak. "I don't believe you!"

George echoed his response and the other two were nodding their heads in agreement.

I responded quickly, "Look, men, Bill and Steve can tell you that Michael wasn't shot in the battle and died hours later on the road back to camp. When I confronted Peter, he confessed and said no one would believe a gnat like me."

"That does sound like Peter," Robert chuckled.

"The problem for Peter was that Patrick Murphy and Davey O'Connor were hiding in the bushes and also heard Peter confess everything. We planned it that way. Davey, Patrick and I have been investigating this for months, ever since we learned that Michael had died the way he did. Dr. Homiston told me that the symptoms sounded like he ingested toxins, and Michael's father-in-law confirmed it with doctors back in Brooklyn. I still have some of Michael's cartridges that were tainted with the deadly plants Peter found in the woods. Peter murdered Michael. There's no doubt about it.

"I came here for two reasons. First, to apologize to you four for suspecting you of having anything to do with Michael's death. You all had reasons to dislike Michael and you all knew something about poisons."

George, Robert and Bill nodded their heads and seemed to understand. Steve blurted, "How could you think I murdered anyone? That's crazy!" George then shouted, "Shut up, Steve!" and Bill said, "Jack's done something amazing in tracking down Michael's killer. We don't need you giving him a hard time for doing a great job."

"Thank you, Bill. The second reason I came here was to find out what you fellows think we should do about Peter."

Steve jumped in again. "What to do about him? We're sharing a tent with a murderer!"

"You don't have anything to worry about," I told him. "Peter has no reason to want any of you dead, so he's not going to do anything. I'm the one who may be in danger, but I've taken care of that. So what do you fellows think?"

Yet again, Steve was the first to speak. "That son of a bitch should be court martialed! He could have killed me if I took the wrong cartridge case!"

"What about the reputation of the 14th? The scandal would be horrible," I replied. "The reputation of the 14th was really important to Michael."

Steve was not concerned. "I don't care about the reputation of the 14th. That bastard could have killed me and I don't want to sleep in the same tent with a murderer!"

"Hold on," Bill interrupted. "The 14th's reputation is important to me, too. Right now, we're known as the Red-legged Devils for our fighting, and the whole army respects us. I sure don't want to be known as the home of a soldier who murdered one of his own comrades."

"Same here," added Robert.

"Okay," I replied. "We know what Steve would do. What about the rest of you?"

Robert responded that he wouldn't do anything. "I understand what it's like to fall head over heels for a woman and do anything to get her. We all killed people in the battle so we're all murderers."

"That's different," murmured Bill.

Robert continued, "What Peter did was horrible but he will be punished in the afterlife."

George reacted differently. "I'll go along with whatever the rest of the regiment decides to do. I understand punishment now, and I understand punishment in the afterlife, and I can't decide which one I want."

"Well, I can decide," Bill almost shouted. "We should kill him. He murdered someone over a woman. There are lots of other women out there so I don't get that. Anyways, if he felt that strongly about the woman, he should have dealt with it face-to-face with Michael, not poisoned him like a rat. I say we kill him."

"Well, Patrick, Davey and I are speaking to everyone but the officers to find out what people want to do. One of us will let you know how the regiment feels. Again, I'm sorry I suspected you men, I hope you'll forgive me."

All four nodded.

By the time we went to sleep that night, Davey, Patrick and I were pretty sure that every soldier in the regiment, excluding officers, knew the story. Davey and Patrick had the same experience as me. The fellows they spoke to split pretty evenly between killing Peter, having him court martialed, and doing nothing. We still had to make a decision. Little did I know that the situation would resolve itself the next day.

CHAPTER THIRTY-FIVE

November 18, 1861

The 14th had picket duty the next day. Sentries, or pickets, are posted a ways outside of the camp, surrounding the entire camp. Then there are picket posts closer to camp. Each post has a group of soldiers that are held in reserve. The fellas in the picket posts relieve the sentries at regular times. That way the pickets can get some rest during their shift.

The sentries control the people coming into and out of camp. They're about 50 to 100 yards apart. That distance is the soldier's "beat." He walks his beat back and forth, and anyone approaching camp is challenged. During the day, if a soldier comes from inside or outside the camp and has a pass, he is allowed to go about his business. If he has no pass, the fellow is detained until the officer of the day can be called to decide what to do with him. At night, no one can pass into or out of camp without the countersign. Each regiment rotates picket duty. So if there are five regiments in camp, each regiment will have picket duty every fifth day.

There is a ceremony attached to picket duty. The assigned regiment forms up and marches to a selected spot. There they hold out their muskets and appear before an officer who is supposed to inspect the guns and cartridge boxes. After a few more preliminaries, they are divided into two groups and finally ordered "to your posts." The first group marches to the portion on the line it has been assigned for its four hour shift, and the second group waits in reserve at the picket post. After four hours, the reserves will move up to the line, and the group on the line will become the reserve. This process is repeated until the day's assignment is completed.

That was the procedure we used on November 18, when the 14th was covering the portion of the line near Falls Church. Everything was quiet, and it looked like it was going to be another boring day of picket duty. All of a sudden, we were attacked by Confederate cavalry. I ran out of the picket post to support my comrades. This was different from Bull Run, where it was man against man. Here, I was facing an army of rebels on what looked to be huge horses riding at me. They were shooting with pistols and waving sabers like they wanted to cut my head off. Just like my previous battle, I wanted to run away. And just like that fight, I didn't. I had Michael's musket, a new cartridge box, and his bayonet. They inspired me. I couldn't run away and let Michael down.

Besides, we were supposed to engage the enemy to give the camp time to get ready to fight. That was my duty. I was not going to ignore it. I stood there loading and firing as fast as I could.

I wondered how the other boys were reacting. I looked around. They were standing and fighting just the way they should. No one ran. We kept up the fight for what felt like hours, but was probably just a couple of minutes. Then the rest of the reserves showed up, and now the numbers favored us. The rebels withdrew.

When we regrouped before heading back to camp the regiment was buzzing. I found Bernard Carney to ask him what he knew. I have no idea how he got the information so quickly, but he had it.

"Hey, Bernard, what happened out there?"

"Well, Jack, we were attacked by about 500 rebs under Fitzhugh Lee of the First Virginia Cavalry." That number was probably exaggerated, but that often happens when soldiers are talking about battles they've fought. "The 14th fought well against overwhelming numbers to hold the enemy until the reserves showed up. We had three killed, three wounded, and ten taken prisoner. Peter Glasson was one of the ones killed in the action."

"Did you say Peter was killed?"

"Yep, that's what I said. I know what you're thinking, but I couldn't find out how it happened."

"You mean whether it was a Confederate bullet or one of ours?"

"No one I spoke to could or would say if he saw who shot Peter. Since a goodly portion of the boys thought we should kill Peter ourselves, it could easily have been one of the boys in the regiment that shot him. I guess we'll never know."

My first reaction was relief that I wouldn't have to make that terrible decision. Then I felt guilty for being selfish. The point, however, was that Michael's murder was avenged. No matter how it happened, Michael's killer was dead.

"Thanks, Bernard. I appreciate the information."

"You're welcome. I guess we won't have to decide what to do about Peter now. And don't worry. I won't be sending in this story to the Brooklyn Eagle, even though it would be the best story I've had so far. I understand how Michael felt about the regiment. I kind of feel the same way. A scandal would hurt us all. I would much rather have the regiment known as 'The Fighting 14th,' than 'Home of a Murderer.'"

"Thanks, Bernard. I agree with you. It's just as well that we don't have to concern ourselves any more with what to do about Peter."

Patrick and Davey were walking towards me smiling broadly. "I'm guessing you heard the news," Davey said excitedly. "Peter got hisself shot and killed!"

"Yes, I heard," I answered. "Do either of you know any of the details?"

Patrick shook his head. "The stories are different dependin' on who you talk to, aren't they? One has Peter chargin' forward, but another says that he was runnin' away and got shot in the back. Dependin' on the story, Peter was shot with one bullet, two bullets or all the way up to ten bullets."

I sighed deeply. "It sounds like we're never going to know what really happened to him."

"Who cares?" Davey said. He didn't sound sorry at all.

"Right," Patrick added. "We don't have to decide what to do about him, do we?"

"All that's true," I agreed. "I never thought I'd be happy about a person getting killed, but I am. I don't care who did it or how it was done. Peter deserved what he got.

"One thing still bothers me. If Peter was out on sentry duty, why didn't he head back to the picket post right away? And if he was at the picket post, why didn't he stay there? Peter could have avoided being in the fight. We know he was just waiting to fake some medical condition so he could get discharged. Why would he expose himself?"

That was when we saw Bill Shannon approaching us. "Hey, fellas, I wanted to speak with you, Jack." He patted my shoulder. Patrick and Davey started to leave, but Bill told them to stay. "You told me about what Peter did, and that you three were the ones that worked it out. I just wanted to say thank you." To our amazement, Bill shook hands with all three of us. "I hope I have friends as good as you fellas. Michael and I had our problems, but he didn't deserve to be murdered. And Peter wasn't even man enough to face him. The snake poisoned him. He disgusted me. When you asked me what I would do about Peter, you know I said I was in favor of killing him."

"Were you with Peter when he died?" I asked.

"No, but I was with him at the picket post when the shooting started."

"I was wondering about that. Why would Peter expose himself by leaving the picket post? We know he had a plan to fake some illness to get a discharge and get out of the army. Why would he risk his life and head toward the action?"

Bill smiled broadly. "Well, Jack, Peter headed toward the action because I told him that if he didn't, I was going to kill him where he stood. And I told him that I would be watching him to see if he tried to run. If he did, I repeated that I would shoot him. Now I had no intention of watching him during the fight, but I knew that Peter wouldn't know that, and that he was a coward. He would figure that there was a chance that the rebels would do him in if he went forward. But if he didn't attack, he knew that I would make sure he died. As it happened, I didn't see Peter at all after we left the picket post. As far as I'm concerned, though, the story has a happy ending. He got what was coming to him, and we don't have to worry about what to do with him. We should be heading back to camp." Bill walked off leaving me, Patrick, and Davey stunned. We slowly started to walk back to camp.

"Well, that answers your question, don't it?" said Patrick, thoughtfully.

"I kinda like Bill," Davey chimed in. "He sure saved us a pack of trouble by making Peter get into that fight."

"I guess he did," I replied. "I wonder if he was the one that shot Peter."

"Sure, it makes no never mind," Patrick noted. "Peter's dead. Our job is done."

When we got back to camp, Mr. Gault was waiting for me at my tent. He had gone to battalion headquarters, where he had been told that our regiment was out of camp and probably in a fight. Because of who Mr. Gault is, the battalion acceded to his demand to stay in my tent until we returned. I found out later that he had told headquarters that he had some pressing family matters to discuss with me.

Mr. Gault didn't even say hello when he saw me. "Jack, come walk with me. I want to talk to you." As soon as we were out of earshot of everyone, Mr. Gault said, "Jack, you'll be lucky if I don't have you arrested on general principles. For the longest time I didn't hear anything from you about what progress you were making in investigating Michael's murder, and then out of the blue I get a telegram asking a question about Peter Glasson. I answer the question promptly and ask you to let me know why you asked and what's happening, and I hear nothing from you. I made arrangements to come down to your camp because I want answers, and I want them now. If I don't get them, I'm going right over to the colonel's tent and start an immediate investigation. We had a deal, and I don't know that you've lived up to it."

I was tired, hungry, and taken aback by Mr. Gault's verbal assault. On the other hand, we did have a deal, and he was entitled to know what was going on as soon as I knew it. "I'm sorry, Mr. Gault. But things happened real fast. It's over."

"What do you mean 'it's over'?" he asked.

"I found out who Michael's killer is, and he's dead." I told Mr. Gault about the steps leading up to Patrick, Davey and me confronting Peter, and how things seemed to happen very fast toward the end. "Anyway, Peter was right. I didn't have any proof. It would have come down to the word of me, Patrick and Davey against the word of Peter. And Peter was also right, that there would have been a scandal in the 14th Brooklyn which would have hurt Michael's memory. The fight earlier today solved the problem. I've heard all kinds of stories about how Peter was killed, and frankly, Mr. Gault, I don't care whether he was running towards the enemy or away from them or whether he was shot by the Confederates or one of our fellows, or whether he was shot once or ten times. It makes no difference to me. He got what he deserved, and the issue is closed."

"It may be closed for you, but it's not for me," Mr. Gault responded.

"What do you mean?" I asked, fearful that he was still going to have some official investigation that was sure to harm the regiment. My fears were soon laid to rest.

"I mean," Mr. Gault answered, "what do I tell Elizabeth? I've always been completely honest and forthcoming with her. But if I tell her how Michael died and why, she'll blame herself. Peter wanted to marry her, and he killed Michael to get her. Elizabeth will think she killed Michael. Yet if I don't tell her what happened, Elizabeth will mourn for her husband's killer. I don't know what to do."

I wasn't close to Mr. Gault and Elizabeth and I felt able to be more objective. I decided to give him my honest opinion, hoping he wouldn't be offended. "If I may speak frankly, Mr. Gault, this problem seems a whole lot simpler than the one I had to deal with until Peter was killed. First of all, you haven't told Elizabeth about my looking into Michael's death, have you?"

"No, of course not," Mr. Gault said. "But I intended to as soon as we knew anything."

"That doesn't matter," I replied. "You haven't been as forthcoming as you could have been with Elizabeth, and I think that's for the best. With all due respect, Mr. Gault, I think you're being selfish. You know that if you tell Elizabeth who killed Michael and why, it's going to hurt her badly. If you don't tell her, you may not be as forthcoming as you want to be, but you're the only one who's going to know that. Yes, Elizabeth may mourn briefly for her husband's killer, but she won't know that. Her bigger loss is Michael and she still needs your help in coping with his death. I think her need is bigger than your preference to be totally honest."

At first Mr. Gault was taken aback at me talking to him that way. But then his fairness and decisiveness won out. "You know what, you're right. I'll keep this information away from Elizabeth. Jack, you're a smart boy," he continued. "When this war is over, you come see me. I could use a smart boy like you in the bank."

"Excuse me, Mr. Gault," I said, relieved that he was no longer angry with me. "But I still want to be a lawyer. I hope that after the war, if I make it through, I could get a job clerking for a lawyer and then become one."

"Whatever you want to do, I'll help you do it. If you want to read for the law, I'll make sure it happens. I know a number of prominent lawyers. I hope you'll keep in touch with me while you're away, and take me up on my offer when you get back."

"Thank you, Mister Gault, I surely will." We shook hands and parted.

I thought to myself, "I should be feeling pretty happy right now. My dream of becoming a lawyer is going to happen! My future never looked brighter!" But then I remembered, I'm still a soldier in the 14th Brooklyn, and first I have to live through the war.

THE END

AFTERWARD

———

The 14th Brooklyn was real; the murder was made up.

The 14th was recognized as one of the finest regiments in the Union army. It was involved in most of the major engagements in the east, including Fredericksburg, Chancellorsville, Antietam, Gettysburg, and Spotsylvania.

Jack Muller, who solved the murder, sought to avoid an official investigation because of the harm a scandal would do to the fine reputation of the 14th. I did not make up the pride the soldiers of the 14th felt in their regiment. In his Masters of Military Studies thesis on the 14th Brooklyn for the U. S. Marine Corps Command and Staff College, "*'The Red-Legged Devils' Brooklyn's Best Regiment*" (AY 2001- 02), Major Thomas J. Hartshorne wrote:

Five factors, when taken collectively, made the Fourteenth Regiment a superior combat regiment. The Brooklyn communities exerted extraordinary force on the men to fight. As a militia unit, the soldiers had a close relationship to the rest of the community. The support from the citizen[s] created a heightened sense of Espirit d'Corps in the regiment. The existing soldiers and the newer recruits were of the highest caliber facilitating an easy transition from 'citizen' to 'soldier'. As individuals and as a unit the soldiers strove for technical and tactical proficiency. The men fought for the honor of the regiment. The regiment took on a spirit like quality that in return for the men['s] submission to it, returned to the men courage in trying times.

The uniform, activities, and movements of the 14th Brooklyn from Brooklyn to Washington to Virginia are taken from "*The History of the Fighting Fourteenth*," Army of the Potomac Series, vol 4, 1993 ("the History") and numerous letters from members of the regiment printed in the Brooklyn Eagle. I did, however, take liberties with some of the facts from the History. For example, the History notes that the 14th did guard duty at the White House, but I made up the meeting with Lincoln.

Similarly, the History shows that the 14th spent a short time in Washington, but I created their tour of the city.

One of the letters states that some of the 14th stayed at the Washington home of General Dan Sickles when the regiment was in Washington. I found no other reference for that.

I used other resources for a number of the anecdotes in the book such as the one about General Jackson getting the nickname Stonewall because he refused to move to the aid of General Bee (*The Haskell Memoirs, Edited by Gilbert E. Govan and James W. Livingood*, 1960 at 22).

The 14th Brooklyn actually played baseball, but I made up the games. The rules are historically accurate, as is the history of baseball in Brooklyn.

I used many real names from the 14th in the book, but not for the individuals involved in the murder and the investigation. For example, Dr. Homiston was actually the regiment's surgeon. Other officers and many enlisted men named in the book were members of the 14th, but I made up backstories for them. For example, Bernard Carney was 34 when he enlisted with the 14th on April 18, 1861, but I made him a young fledgling reporter.